A BED OF ROSES

The garden was the best place in the world for a rousing game of catch-me-who-can.

Today, she gave her brother to the count of twenty before going to find him. Then she moved down the central path slowly. The gravel crunched softly underfoot. She checked several of his usual places: behind the central fountain, along the trail of sun flowers, in the Grecian grotto. Oh, he'd outdone himself this time. She should at least catch a glimpse of his dark suit among the flowers and bright greens of late spring. She glanced about, searching for some telltale movement, ears tuned for any sound other than the drone of bees and the coo of the dove.

Something dark passed along the far wall.

Celia grinned. She darted back the way she had come. If she cut through the rose garden, she could catch him before he reached the house, where, by the rules they had agreed on, he would win this round. She picked up her skirts and dodged through the thorny bushes. Another flash of black showed her he made faster progress. She picked up speed and hurled herself over the last bit of hedge.

"Got you!"

Her arms caught on something significantly bigger than her brother. Lord Hartley gazed down at her, both brows raised.

"And just what do you intend to do with me," he asked, "now that you've caught me?"

Other Works by Regina Scott

The Unflappable Miss Fairchild

The Twelve Days of Christmas

"Sweeter Than Candy"
in *A Match for Mother*

The Bluestocking on His Knee

"A Place by the Fire"
in *Mistletoe Kittens*

Catch of the Season

A Dangerous Dalliance

The Marquis' Kiss

"The June Bride Conspiracy"
in *His Blushing Bride*

The Incomparable Miss Compton

The Irredeemable Miss Renfield

Lord Borin's Secret Love

Utterly Devoted

Starstruck

PERFECTION

Regina Scott, 1959

ZEBRA BOOKS
Kensington Publishing Corp.
http://www.kensingtonbooks.com

ZEBRA BOOKS are published by

Kensington Publishing Corp.
850 Third Avenue
New York, NY 10022

All Kensington titles, imprints and distributed lines are available at special quantity discounts for bulk purchases for sales promotion, premiums, fund-raising, educational or institutional use.

Special book excerpts or customized printings can also be created to fit specific needs. For details, write or phone the office of the Kensington Special Sales Manager: Kensington Publishing Corp., 850 Third Avenue, New York, NY 10022. Attn. Special Sales Department. Phone: 1-800-221-2647.

Zebra and the Z logo Reg. U.S. Pat. & TM Off.

First Printing: October 2003
10 9 8 7 6 5 4 3 2 1

Printed in the United States of America

To the one and only Myrna Candreia,
a hunter after my own heart,
and to my own beloved hunter,
Larry Linus Lundgren

One

"So that's him?"

The whisper pierced the gloom of the gaming parlor. Brandon Pellidore, Marquess of Hartley, didn't acknowledge the sound. That would ruin the image he'd been cultivating since returning to London six months ago. He laid the ace of hearts down in the precise center of the table and leaned back as much as the elegant Sheraton chair would allow.

His comrades for the evening had less reputation to protect. Chas Prestwick's mouth quirked in a smile, and his tawny head tilted as if to listen more closely; but he did not pause as he tossed the four of hearts onto Brandon's ace.

"No, no," the whisperer was protesting. "I need no introduction, don't you know. I must speak to him directly."

Prestwick's partner, Leslie Petersborough, raised a dark brow and shook his head. The candlelight from the gilded wall sconce behind Brandon made the gold buttons on Petersborough's richly embroidered waistcoat glint in the dusky air.

Across from Brandon, his father's half brother, Lord Edmund Pellidore, threw the seven of hearts into the center and frowned, gray brows drawn over his long nose. Petersborough followed suit, then sighed as Brandon took the trick.

"You shall clean me out if you keep on like this, Hart," he predicted.

"Did I not warn you?" Prestwick reminded his friend, reaching for the glass of Madeira at his elbow.

"You will survive," Brandon predicted. He leaned forward to sweep in the cards, keeping his gaze low and movements slow, as if watching what he did. Under his brows he eyed the gathering crowd.

And he'd thought a gaming parlor would be more conducive to privacy than White's. The corner table at the back of Madam Zala's select establishment had seemed perfect for his intentions. Even Edmund couldn't complain, as he would be allowed to smoke the cigars he so favored. Now, thanks to a country rudesby, the other attendees were alerted to their presence. Already two of the tables in the main salon had emptied, and the dandies who had been playing hazard nearby were trotting over to join them. Someone discompose the infamous Lord Hartley? Now, that would be a rarity worth watching. He could almost see the wagers being laid down.

A tall young man with a weathered complexion obviously made ruddy by drink elbowed his way closer to the table. A short, round dandy intercepted him.

"Easy, Arlington. You're up against the best here."

Arlington shook him off. Brandon squared up the cards, taking the man's measure. Large hands but empty—no immediate threat there. Broad shoulders and long arms—the fellow would have a considerable reach in a fight. No telltale bumps in his simple brown coat and tan chamois breeches, but anything from a dagger to a pistol could be hidden in those out-of-fashion boots. He laid the cards in the growing pile beside him.

"I want a word with you, Hartley, don't you know," Arlington proclaimed.

"I am engaged," Brandon replied. He pushed back his chair as if to stretch his long legs and led with the queen of hearts.

"You can bloody well get unengaged," Arlington declared, stepping up to Prestwick's side. "I want to know what you've done with Celia Rider, don't you know."

Prestwick, green eyes glinting, snapped shut his hand and threw it down. Before he could rise, Petersborough was on his feet and coming around the table.

"Mr. Arlington," he said in a friendly tone that nonetheless had an edge of determination to it, "you are making an ass of yourself. I suggest you leave while you can."

Some in the crowd crowed encouragement to Arlington to stay and fight it out. Others cautioned retreat. Arlington took a step away from Prestwick, but squared his shoulders resolutely. "By your leave, I have no quarrel with anyone save Lord Hartley. I need to know what he's done with my fiancée, don't you know."

Prestwick retrieved his cards as if bored. "Not like you, Hart, to poach on another man's territory."

"Ridiculous," Edmund added, ignoring the cards before him to eye Arlington. His look was nearly as dark as his evening wear. "You obviously have the wrong person, young man."

"Indeed, Mr. Arlington." The silky voice of the establishment's owner was almost a purr as Madam Zala prowled through the crowd. "We have had such a pleasant time that I would be disappointed to have to turn you away."

Arlington blinked at the curvaceous beauty. With her piles of golden hair and black dress dripping jet beads, she exuded sophistication. He did not seem to appreciate the fact, or the strategic positioning of her burly footman beside the door.

"You cannot turn me away," he insisted. "I have a duty."

She raised a hand as if to put it on his arm. He dodged past her and sidestepped Petersborough to close the distance between himself and Brandon. Edmund's dark eyes flashed a warning. Tensing, Brandon shook his head once.

Arlington stared down at him, fists clenched at his sides. "How can you sit there so calmly? Do you think to put me off the scent? I knew whom to seek. Tall fellow, dark hair, dark eyes, dressed in black as if on his way to a funeral. Bit of a legend here in London, don't you know. Lord Heartless."

A murmur rippled through the crowd. Not the most pleasing of epithets, but Brandon could hardly argue with it. He'd worked too hard to give that impression. He thoughtfully thumbed the jack of hearts in his hand and calculated how long it would take him to get to his feet. The position of the table offered protection at his back, at least. Though he did not know them well, he was certain he could count on his comrades to hold off any others. Of course, Madam Zala was unlikely to let things get out of hand. She, too, had a reputation to protect.

Prestwick eyed Brandon. "Do you intend to let him get away with that, Hart?"

"Damme if I would," Petersborough growled, moving up behind Arlington.

The young man paled, but he held his spot as if daring them to attack him. Madam Zala beckoned to her man.

"I cannot swat every fly that annoys me," Brandon replied to Prestwick. "Your card, sir?"

Prestwick threw down a card with an admiring shake of his head. Edmund followed suit more slowly. Brandon nodded to Petersborough, who returned to his seat with obvious reluctance and played a card. Brandon reached out to sweep in the trick.

"Damn you!" Arlington's hand came down hard on the cards, pinning them to the table. "Look at me!"

Brandon slowly raised his gaze. Arlington let go of the cards and stumbled back. Brandon squared the cards, set them aside, and played the ten of hearts. The footman parted the crowd like a hot knife through butter. He put a heavy hand on Arlington's broad shoulder.

"You can't get away with this!" Arlington railed as he shrugged out of the footman's grip. "First you took her fortune, and when she came to confront you, you did away with her, too!"

"Have a care, fellow!" Edmund snapped. "My nephew is known as a gentleman."

"So, now you seduce virgins and take the food from widows and orphans, too," Prestwick said, playing a three of spades.

Brandon watched Edmund play the nine of diamonds. "And if I did, the ton would only admire me the more for it."

"Particularly the virgin part," Petersborough readily agreed, laying down a ten of clubs.

"I'll find someone to believe me," Arlington persisted as the footman grasped his arm and began hauling him toward the door. "I don't care if you're the bloody prince, don't you know. You cannot get away with murder."

"Murder, is it?" Edmund shook his graying head as Brandon pulled in the trick. "I should think murder will be done if that pup keeps yapping."

"Tell me what you've done with her," Arlington cried, digging his heels into the Oriental carpet to keep from being carried off, "or I'll k-k-kill you with my b-b-bare hands!"

This time it was laughter that rippled through the crowd. Arlington sagged with a sob. Brandon surged to his feet.

The room went silent.

He tossed the remaining cards onto the table. "I am finished. Release the fellow."

Prestwick and Petersborough exchanged glances. Edmund rose as well. Brandon shook his head again. The footman obligingly dropped his hold and stepped back, scarred face lighting in a grin at the prospect of violence. The crowd muttered wagers on how many blows Mr. Arlington could stand. Arlington raised his head and brought up his fists. They shook.

Brandon eyed him. "Mr. Arlington, you seem to have a great deal to say to me. I am inclined to be indulgent."

Madam Zala appeared at his elbow. "A private room, my lord? This way."

Arlington stood his ground, though he dropped his fists. "I'm not going anywhere with you, by your leave. How do I know you won't serve me as you did poor Celia?"

Brandon paused in the door to the main salon.

"You wanted a moment of my time. I intend to give it to you. You can join me or go to hell, whichever you like."

"Such a gentleman, my lord," his hostess purred as she led him down a short carpeted corridor. "You should have let me throw him out."

Brandon didn't respond. She was no doubt right, but he could not explain how Arlington's pathetic stammer moved him.

She paused before a polished door, hand on the gilt knob. Dark eyes met his own in speculation. "Or perhaps you have other uses for the fellow?"

His silence must have told her that he had no intention of gratifying her curiosity, for she pushed open the door. Glancing at the tall-backed armchairs surrounding an oak table, Brandon nodded.

"Wine?" she asked Brandon as Arlington slunk in and gazed about himself with obvious suspicion.

"He hardly needs it," Brandon replied.

She did not bother asking whether he wanted any. He had been clear that he wouldn't drink in her establishment.

Brandon walked to the nearest chair and sat, watching as Arlington flung himself onto the chair opposite him. A small chandelier overhead lent a golden glow to the room, but the youth didn't seem to notice. Seeing the fellow up close, Brandon would have guessed that Arlington was in his early twenties. He had thick, curly blond hair, disheveled now; pale green eyes; and a long nose that ended in a round, flat knob, as if God had pressed His thumb print into the clay as He molded him.

"Who," Brandon said, "is Celia Rider?"

"As if you didn't know," Arlington said. It would have been a growl, but his voice cracked on the last word. He crossed both arms over his chest. The gesture seemed more to keep himself from shaking than to look intimidating.

"If I knew," Brandon told him, "I would scarcely ask. I have no time for foolish games."

The youth glared at him, but something in Brandon's face seemed to confuse him. Slowly his dark look faded. "You don't know where she is, do you? My God, what am I going to do?"

Brandon leaned back in the chair. "Calm yourself. Think. I take it your Miss Rider recently left for London?"

Arlington nodded. "Nearly a fortnight ago, by your leave."

"And you think she came to see me."

Another nod. "She must have. It was the only way."

"The only way to do what?"

"To find her fortune. You stole it and—"

"Yes, so I heard. Let us try for reality, Mr. Arlington."

He frowned. "I thought that was reality. Celia said her stepmother took the money, but I knew a woman could never be so devious. You want someone accustomed to working with money to steal an inheritance this size."

Brandon cocked his head. "Ah, *that* Rider."

Arlington's eyes lit.

Brandon held up his hand. "I recall the name. That does not make me a murderer. Let me understand you. You talk of Miss Celia Rider, David Rider's daughter?"

"Damn right! You cannot claim ignorance! She is your own cousin's stepdaughter."

"Second cousin," Brandon replied. "I met her twice, once at my second cousin's marriage to Miss

Rider's father and once at her father's funeral." He remembered no more than a thin-faced child with her father's expressive eyes. Obviously, Miss Rider had grown if she was engaged to this fellow.

"You didn't need to know her to know of her fortune," Arlington insisted. "It was in all the papers, don't you know."

The constant peppering of catch phrases like "don't you know" was beginning to annoy him, but he decided to ignore it for now. Very likely the trait was caused by Arlington's inexperience and insecurity. "David Rider was famous in his day, I agree," Brandon told him. "However, your knowledge of the fortune is just as damning. You could have learned of the girl and come here with false claims, thinking to gull me into agreeing with you."

Arlington sat bolt upright. "Do you doubt me, sir? Where are your seconds? I am a gentleman."

Brandon merely raised a brow.

Arlington deflated just as easily. "Oh, very well. I am the son of a country squire. But Celia is my betrothed. We were to marry as soon as she received her dowry."

And here was another reason for the urgency behind the man's search. "Miss Rider cannot marry without the inheritance?"

He nodded, reddening. "Father insisted on it. *I* would have married her anyway, you understand. But Celia said a bargain was a bargain. She was determined, don't you know."

"She came to London alone?"

He squirmed. "I don't exactly know. She wouldn't tell me all her plans. She's a bit strong-willed, my lord, but I assure you that will change once we are married."

Brandon thought that highly unlikely but decided Mr. Arlington had entirely too many problems already to appreciate having that pointed out to him.

"She's had some queer starts from time to time," he continued, "but she wouldn't just disappear."

"Could she have changed her mind?" Brandon offered. "A fortune that size might give any young lady ideas that excluded returning to the country."

"If it is that size," Arlington muttered darkly. "She was told otherwise. It was supposed to be given on her twenty-first birthday, you see, only the day passed with no word. She did try writing, but they insisted her father left her penniless. My father *would* believe that story." He snorted. "David Rider was wealthy. Stands to reason he left something to Celia."

"So I gather. What made you decide I had taken it?"

"You are the head of the Pellidore family," Arlington pointed out. "The will names you as guardian."

Interesting. He had never been apprised of that duty. Was this another instance of his aunt, Lady Honoria, taking liberties? She was one of the reasons Edmund had insisted on raising Brandon on their Scottish estate, with only occasional trips to their other estates and London. She liked to see herself as head of the family, and his second cousin, Patrice, apparently didn't argue the fact, even when it came to raising her son and stepdaughter.

Brandon eyed him. "Let us assume for a moment that you are correct in that I can control what my family chooses to do. Let us also assume I could miraculously conjure away David Rider's considerable fortune. Why would I do so?"

Arlington licked his lips.

"Oh, come now. You called me a murderer and a thief, Mr. Arlington. Do not turn faint-hearted now."

"Very well. I have it on good authority they won't let you at your own money. Figured you might need some now and again. Look what you do for entertainment."

Brandon did not point out that he had been winning, as usual. "And I am maniacal enough to steal it, even though I returned to the country only six months ago?"

Arlington sighed. "So I thought. From what everyone said, you seemed just that sort of black-hearted bastard."

"Flattery will get you nowhere, my dear sir." He rose. Arlington scrambled to his feet as well. He brought his fists up again. Brandon raised a brow.

Arlington slowly lowered his fists. "You aren't going to call me out?" The tremor in his voice told Brandon how little he relished the idea.

"I would not waste my time, Mr. Arlington. I would rather resolve your difficulty than fight."

Arlington blinked. "You're going to help me? How?"

"It amuses me to look into your story. If you want to hear what I learn, visit my solicitors, Carstairs and Son, in the financial district, on Friday."

"But that's three days!"

"Do you find fault, Mr. Arlington?"

The youth scowled. "It strikes me that three days is a damnably long time. You could have posted to the Continent for all I know by then, don't you know. Why should I trust you?"

"Do you have a choice? I shall see you at three in the afternoon. Until then, make sure we have no more of these incidents. Think how sad Miss Rider would feel if I were forced to kill you."

Two

"Quick!" Martin cried. "Somebody's coming."

Celia Rider crammed her honey-colored hair up under the ribboned cap and flung herself onto the hard-backed chair. Heart hammering, she swung the massive Latin text up in front of her face, taking only a moment to make sure her younger brother, Martin, had squirmed into place at the small table next to her.

"Vox audita perit," she began in the scholarly voice that mimicked Martin's real governess they had left in Somerset. *"Litera scripta manet.* Translation, Mr. Rider?"

Martin cleared his voice importantly. "The loud voice perishes but literature remains?"

Celia peered over the top of the book to find that John, the strapping schoolroom footman, stood in the doorway in his working clothes. With his lower lip out, he looked obviously impressed, though she'd wager he didn't know a word of Latin. Best not to correct her brother. His translation was fairly close to the actual quote, *The word, when spoken, perishes while the written word remains.* She raised her head.

"Did you need something, John?

He nodded. "Begging your pardon, Miss Prim. Miss Lawton says her ladyship wants your help. I'm to watch the lad."

Martin brightened, glancing at Celia hopefully.

And was that gratitude? Here she was, *incognito*, risking reputation and future to find their fortune, and he'd rather play darts with the footman. Still, if Miss Lawton, Lady Honoria's abigail, made a request, it was best she comply.

Setting down the book, she wrinkled her nose. She really couldn't blame Martin. Some days she'd rather play as well. Unfortunately, the men her father had tasked to manage her fortune were obviously untrustworthy, her stepmother was very likely colluding with them, and her fiancé was too countrified to be of any help. What was a young lady to do?

Thank goodness they'd sent John to fetch her. Having never seen Patrice Rider's stepdaughter, he wasn't likely to discover her deception. She felt less comfortable with her stepmother. Patrice hadn't seen her in nearly four years, and then only for the few hours necessary to settle affairs after her father's funeral. She fancied she was taller, curvier, and more confident at nearly twenty-two than the gawky girl she'd been then. Still, she couldn't take chances. Her mission was too important.

"What is it this time, do you know?" she asked John as he moved into the sunny little schoolroom, heavy shoes echoing on the polished wood floor. "Should I bring a book to read to her ladyship?" That sounded submissive enough. With any luck, she could bore the woman to sleep and have a chance to look through the papers she'd seen in her ladyship's suite. It was one of the few places she had yet to search.

The footman shook his sandy head. "You're to report below. Lord Pellidore is visiting her ladyship, and Mrs. Rider needs a chaperone it seems."

Since when? Celia almost said, but she clamped her mouth shut. Her stepmother received an inordinate number of gentleman callers. As a widow living with her grandmother, she didn't seem to think she required the chaperonage Celia knew other women endured for propriety's sake. What was different about this caller that Lady Honoria wanted her granddaughter watched?

"Is there no one else available?" she tried, making no move toward the door.

John frowned. "Perhaps, but Lady Honoria asked for you."

And what Lady Honoria wanted, Lady Honoria got. Even Patrice seemed afraid of her, although Celia wasn't entirely sure why. At nearly seventy, her ladyship seldom ventured from her suite, although she, too, received callers, some gentlemen, some ladies. Lord Edmund Pellidore, her younger half brother, was frequently among them.

Thus far, the so-called Miss Prim had only been required for the occasional reading session or a report on the progress of Lady Honoria's great-grandson's education. Neither type of visit had been particularly pleasant, but she might not have been so nervous if she hadn't kept fearing discovery. That her ladyship would entrust her with this mission must mean she had succeeded in worming her way into Lady Honoria's good graces.

She beckoned to her brother. Martin got up and came around to her side of the table. She was sure John could see the reluctance in the slump of his slender shoulders. With any luck, the footman would think her brother was merely dreading a lecture from the ever-so-serious Miss Prim. She certainly didn't want the man to know that Martin was more concerned that his sister was about to rein in his enthusiasm.

She bent beside her brother. "Why so Friday-faced?" she murmured, resisting an urge to ruffle his straight black hair. "I just wanted to remind you to watch yourself. We cannot be certain whom to trust."

"You should worry for yourself," Martin murmured back, gazing up at her with eyes a mix of blue, green, and gray like her own. "She'll catch you this time for sure."

"Not if I behave to perfection. All I have to do is sit and be as unobtrusive as wallpaper."

Her brother's mouth tightened, and her heart tightened with it. He'd always been such a lively boy; it was as if the joy had leaked out of him since coming to London. "I don't like it," he said. "Mother will be angry when she sees we tried to fool her. What if she sends me back to the country?"

"She will have little power over us soon enough," Celia promised. "I have reached my majority, if anyone chooses to remember. Once I have my inheritance, I can set up my own establishment. You can stay with me."

The look on her brother's face stopped her from straightening. "Do you doubt me, Martin?"

He licked his lips and lowered his gaze. "I know you will take care of me, Celia, even if Father's fortune is gone."

"It isn't gone," Celia insisted, feeling her face set. "It's gone missing. Give me a few more days to learn how."

"Mother didn't do it," he said with the dogged loyalty she had to respect.

"I certainly hope not," she replied. "Now I must go."

Leaving her brother to John's care, she hurried

down the corridor. She sighted her stepmother as she turned the stairs for the second floor. Patrice was waiting outside the doors to the forward salon, foot tapping. Celia's heart began pounding anew as her stepmother's eyes glanced over her, but she apparently was only making sure Celia's demeanor and attire would reflect well on her.

Patrice, on the other hand, always seemed confident in how well she looked. She dressed in gowns with an excess of frills, such as that white muslin day dress with its double rows of flounces at the hem. Her golden hair was swept up in a complicated set of buns and braided loops at the top of her head. Her eyes curved upward at the outer edges, making her look decidedly feline to Celia, even if the irises were a deep shade of violet. Her rose-colored lips seemed perpetually pursed to pout. She had ample curves in all the right places, soft hands that tended to flutter before her when she spoke, and tiny feet. All in all, Celia knew exactly what her father, the consummate merchant, had been about when trading his wealth to marry his beautiful second wife.

Her father had long ago taught her the value of a good bargain and the danger of breaking one. A shame her stepmother hadn't learned that lesson, or Celia wouldn't now be in this awkward position. Martin might insist on his mother's innocence concerning the disappearance of the fortune, but Celia was certain Patrice knew exactly what had happened to the money. If only the woman hadn't spent it all already!

As Celia stepped down beside her stepmother, Patrice thrust a piece of half-finished embroidery at her. "You must keep yourself busy and silent," she instructed. Then she nodded to the footman to throw open the doors.

Celia, entering behind her, took quick stock of the room. Where would an inconspicuous chaperone sit? Not on the camel-backed sofa near the white marble fireplace—that spot would be reserved for family. Not in either of the rosewood chairs flanking it—those would be for guests. Certainly not in the armchair near the multipaned window. A gentleman in black stood next to it, looking out. The only other chair was a Chippendale by the door, next to a small occasional table adorned with a bust of some Greek-looking fellow. She wiggled onto the seat and took up the embroidery.

"My lord," Patrice caroled, moving across the royal blue Aubusson carpet with hands stretched before her. "How delightful to see you!"

The gentleman turned at the sound of her voice. Celia risked a peek and sucked in a breath.

Her stepmother had come up in the world. This gentleman was certainly no merchant. Her father's friends were open and expansive in their gestures, warm of face and kind of voice. This man moved with an economy that spoke of controlled power. His face was a study in contrasts—fair, clear skin and deep-set dark eyes; thick raven hair curling in wild abandon and a generous mouth held tight. His still-ness managed to convey a certain animation, like a calm river where mighty currents swirled just be-neath the surface. It seemed only right for his impressive height and broad shoulders to be dressed in a somber black, even though it was the middle of the day. Even his voice fit the picture—slow, warm, and rich as treacle syrup.

"My dear," he returned, taking Patrice's hands and

bringing one to his lips. Her stepmother simpered. *If that were me,* Celia thought, *I'd pass out straightaway if he so much as looked in my direction.* What would such a paragon want with Patrice Rider?

She kept her head down but watched them from under her lashes. They stood close to each other, but not so close that she would have said they were courting. Patrice, however, was clearly interested in moving in that direction. She could not keep her eyes from the gentleman, gazing up at him with a look that spoke of total absorption. His look was decidedly more cool. His conversation consisted of commonplaces. Her stepmother was hunting, then, and this gentleman was the prey.

Patrice didn't stand a chance.

"And how is your enchanting son?" he asked.

Celia started. He knew Martin? Was this the reason her stepmother had suddenly decided to bring the boy from Somerset? It had been a boon for them, giving Celia the perfect chance to come to London and meet with the solicitors about her inheritance. Unfortunately, Carstairs and Son could only tell her that her father had left her penniless. That made as much sense as Patrice trotting out a son from a previous marriage to impress this gentleman. But why move Martin, then, when she'd never brought him since she'd left the country for London?

"My son is a delight to my heart, of course," her stepmother was answering. "I am very lucky to have someone to comfort me, being widowed so young."

Celia snorted to herself. Comfort indeed. Patrice came to the schoolroom once a day to talk with Martin. Neither appeared particularly warmed by the exchange. If her stepmother could conveniently forget she had a son, she certainly didn't remember she had a stepdaughter, which was just as well. To find the fortune, Celia needed to be considered no more than a servant, a shadow, a cobweb in the corner. The last thing she needed was for Patrice to think of her supposedly absent stepdaughter.

"And how is your daughter, Miss Rider?" he asked.

Celia jumped as the needle pricked her finger and had to stop herself from popping the wounded digit into her mouth. How did he know about her? Why would he ask? Glancing up, she found that he was regarding her stepmother with a slight frown. It could have been from concentration, but she got the odd impression he suspected Patrice of something. She could not see Patrice's face, but the answer set her teeth on edge.

"Doing well at school. We await her come out."

She stabbed the needle into the embroidery. Her stepmother's notorious memory had struck again. Her "come out" had been a discreet affair in the country four years ago. Her father's illness had prevented her from coming to London for her Season, and his death had consigned her to a shadow existence on the Pellidore estate on which they had been living. Her age was also something Patrice chose to ignore.

"I heard she was in London," he persisted.

Celia stared at him. He had leaned forward and was scanning her stepmother's face as if intent on drawing out her secrets. But it was her own secret that was in danger. How had he known? Her mind easily pictured him as some kind of minor deity, capable of reading minds and probing hearts. No, not minor, she corrected herself. This one wouldn't be satisfied unless he was king of the underworld. Very likely she was looking at Oberon.

Or Hades.

Her stepmother looked less fascinated. Patrice
had turned away slightly so that Celia could see her
face. Her stepmother was biting her lower lip and
blinking her eyes. Was she confused or trying to
think of a plausible lie? Somehow, Celia thought this
man would see through anything her stepmother
tried. She found herself leaning forward, awaiting
the answer.

"In London?" Patrice said, returning her gaze to his
and shaking her golden head. "Certainly she is not in
London. I would have called her here, and I did not."
She took his hand once more and led him to the sofa.
"Come, sit by me. We have much to discuss."

He glanced in Celia's direction, and she ducked her
head. She slid the needle along its course so swiftly
that she nearly tangled the thread. Why was he asking
after her? They'd never met; she'd remember him.
Maybe he'd known her father. Still, that didn't explain
why he suspected she might be in London. Had the
solicitors followed her from their office to know that
she had not returned to Somerset?

She hazarded another glance in their direction,
then shook her head. She must remember her role.
A chaperone should be as unfeeling as the ceiling
and as disregarded. She certainly shouldn't be
ogling her stepmother's caller. She had no right to
notice how well the dark jacket emphasized his
physique, how neatly the pantaloons hinted of mus-
cular legs. And when he bent to sit and his coat tail
widened . . .

This time the needle bit her thumb, and she had to
clamp her teeth shut to keep from crying out. Such a
response was no more ladylike than noticing the gentleman's inexpressibles. She counted to ten while

Patrice murmured endearing comments and the gentleman took his seat. He positioned himself to face her stepmother, leaning back against the arm of the settee. That gave him a good view of her as well.

She couldn't help noticing that her stepmother had begun toying with the middle button on his silver-striped waistcoat. She could imagine how Patrice must be peering up at him from under her golden brows. Her voice caressed in a throaty murmur. Her stepmother was awfully good at this sort of flirting. At the Barnsley School, they would have called her sophisticated. The ladies of Somerset had a less kind word for it.

The gentleman did not appear to appreciate her attempts or, if he did, appreciate the danger he was in. His head was cocked as if listening to whatever was pouring from her stepmother's mouth, but Celia thought he looked more bored than intrigued. Sunlight from the windows beyond them glinted on his dark hair and emphasized the planes of his face.

His gaze met hers, touching off an explosion of heat as neatly as a spark to the pan of a primed pistol.

Celia blinked in shock, and the moment passed. His gaze was on her stepmother, and he listened so intently she would have thought Patrice held the secret to eternity.

Celia shook her head. She had obviously been woolgathering. Lord Oberon look at her with something akin to passion? Not very likely. She had done nothing, said nothing, that might give him an admiration for her. The shapeless black bombazine dress all but hid her curves. Between the cap and the bowed head, he shouldn't be able to guess that her hair was a thick, honey-colored blond or her eyes an indeterminate color between green and blue. Sitting as she was he wouldn't even notice that she most likely fit under his chin.

No, she'd taken great pains to make sure no one noticed her, not until she retrieved her fortune. She sighed and took up the needle again. Focusing on the design for the first time, she saw that it was a proverb—*Patience is a virtue.* It was obviously meant for the trousseau for her stepmother's next marriage. The most deliciously wicked thought offered itself to her. She simply could not resist. Tugging out a few stitches was the work of a moment.

She was so intent on the new design that she stitched for several minutes with little notice of the goings-on across the room. Then the rising volume of her stepmother's voice broke through her concentration.

"But I do not wish to talk of Celia," she protested. "Why do you persist in quizzing me?"

Celia bit her lip and glanced up. Patrice's back was straight and head high, the picture of offended womanhood. The gentleman, however, had his arms crossed over his chest and his jaw set, looking just as determined.

"I must insist we discuss Miss Rider," he said to Patrice. "I was informed that I am her guardian and accused of murder. Tell me everything you know of her."

Three

Brandon watched as the maid's head jerked up and color rushed to her cheeks. Patrice might claim ignorance of her stepdaughter's disappearance, but he was willing to wager the maid knew something. Twice she had jumped when Celia Rider's name was mentioned, which meant that either Patrice was lying, or someone else in the household was involved.

Simply having a chaperone was enough to make him suspicious. His cousin had dispensed with such inconveniences every other time he had visited. And the woman across the room hardly seemed the type to be a dour chaperone. She was more likely to give a fellow ideas of how to get closer, to her.

The few times she'd raised her head, he'd caught glimpses of honey gold hair escaping that ridiculous cap she wore, petal pink lips with the lower full and tempting, and soft, creamy skin. The one time their gazes had met, he'd had to suck in a breath at the flash of heat in her wide-spaced, large eyes. She was clearly a beauty, and he could not believe Patrice had knowingly hired competition.

Patrice's offended whine brought him back with a start.

"Murdered?" she said, her face puckered in confusion. "Why would you murder Celia? Have you even been introduced?"

The maid choked and turned the noise into a cough of sorts. Patrice glanced at her, then turned her violet eyes back to Brandon with a flutter of her lashes. "Truly, my lord, you cannot be serious."

"I am quite serious. Did you know I was her guardian?"

She shook her golden head. "No. I leave such matters to Grandmother."

Just as he suspected. "And did you leave her engagement to Lady Honoria as well?"

"She is engaged? How do you know?"

"A country gentleman informed me. He claims he is your stepdaughter's fiancé."

He thought the maid might have apoplexy. Patrice, on the other hand, was obviously doing her all to ignore the gagging sounds from across the room. "What nonsense! My stepdaughter is a child. How could she possibly be betrothed?"

Brandon cocked his head to keep the maid in view. Her lips were working as if she muttered, and the embroidery was taking a savage beating. "I grant you that is odd," he told Patrice. "However, the gentleman assures me that she is of age."

Patrice rolled her eyes. "Then the gentleman is mad. I was a child bride, after all, only nine years older than the girl. If she were twenty-one, that would make me . . ."

"Thirty," Brandon supplied and watched her almond-shaped eyes widen.

"Thirty!" she all but wailed. "I most certainly am not thirty! You see what nonsense this is, Cousin?"

"You may well call it nonsense. However, I agreed to look into the matter. And I shall need your help.

Would you send a note to Hollyoake Lodge to check on the girl? Certainly you would want to know if she were missing."

The maid shook her head and jabbed at the material. She clearly did not want to know whether Miss Rider was missing. What secret was she keeping? He wracked his brain for a way to corner her without alerting Patrice. Surely the maid would say nothing if she thought her employer would retaliate.

"But Celia is at school," his cousin was saying with a frown. "Martin has only recently come up from the country, and he would have told me if his sister had left school for home."

Brandon eyed her. "Your son is in town during the Season? Why is he not at school himself?"

Tears pooled in Patrice's luminous eyes. "Would you deprive me of my one joy in life? He will be grown soon enough. I want to keep him with me as long as I can."

The maid was having apoplexy again, and this time Brandon thought he understood the reason. By all accounts, Patrice had abandoned the boy shortly after he was born, leaving him at the country estate while she returned to the attractions of the city. For a short time she had chosen to rusticate at the lodge, shortly before David Rider died. After his death, she couldn't seem to shake the country soil from her dainty kid slippers fast enough. As far as he knew, she hadn't seen the boy in four years, which meant she likely hadn't seen her stepdaughter for that time either.

"Mayhap we should talk to your son," he told her. "He could shed some light on this story."

She nodded, then turned to eye her maid. "Miss Prim," she said, "will you fetch Martin?"

Miss Prim was it? More than a maid, then, or she'd have likely used only a first or last name. Perhaps a governess, called into duty as chaperone? Whichever she was, the young woman leapt to her feet and fled before he could do more than wonder at her figure in the voluminous black dress.

Patrice edged closer to him, the skirts of her white muslin gown brushing his calves. "Do you know, Cousin," she asked breathlessly, "that we are suddenly alone? Was that your wish?"

"Would that I were so clever," Brandon replied. "However, the thought never entered my mind. Shall I call for a footman to stand guard lest I lose control?"

Her lashes dipped lower. "Oh, no, Cousin. I trust you."

"You are too kind." Brandon rose to put distance between them. He also trusted his intentions toward his cousin. He intended to have as little to do with her as possible.

"You are not close to Miss Rider?" he asked, fingering a crystal globe adorning the white marble mantel.

From the corner of his eye he could see that she watched him with a frown. "Sadly," she said, "we never grew attached to each other. She was away at school, and I had pressing duties." She rose suddenly and came to his side to lay a hand on his arm. "I still have such duties. With my grandmother all but bedridden, I must uphold the duties of her house and yours."

"How delightful for you that I entertain so rarely, then," Brandon countered, relaxing his arm to his side to force her to remove her hand.

"But I still represent the family when I go out," she protested. "My allowance is so pitifully small. I cannot possibly meet my social obligations. Surely you could see your way clear to allow me additional funds."

He made certain she could not see the strain in his smile. "Dearest cousin, you know I would indulge you if I could. Unfortunately, you, Lady Honoria, and your children currently receive a half of the allowance I am granted from the trust. I could not run the rest of the estates if I gave you more."

"Surely the estates pay for themselves," she pressed. "We have some sort of farm produce, do we not? Sheep, cattle?"

"Of course. However, all income from the estates goes to the trust. And all that can come out of the trust is the living allowance." A more than ample portion, he thought, if he had been the only one depending on it.

"Until you reach your majority," Patrice replied.

Legally, he had reached his majority nearly five years ago. His father had set an entirely different date for the receipt of the fortune. "When I reach thirty," Brandon corrected her.

She waved her hand as if that had little import. Easy for her—she hadn't spent her entire life under scrutiny. He felt as if he'd been holding his breath forever. Yet, he noticed, Patrice had an uncanny way of forgetting things that bothered her, like her son and stepdaughter.

Unfortunately, she was equally good at remembering what she wanted. "There must be some way to increase the funds," she persisted. "Surely some economies can be practiced."

His economies, he was certain, not hers. "Doubtless. However, with two households that would not make a difference."

She brightened. "Then perhaps we should all move into Pellidore Place, with you."

Brandon hoped he'd hidden the grimace that tried to escape. "What would your Society friends say? A gentleman and a lady, living together and un-married?"

"Pah!" She waved away that objection, too. "We are related. And you have an excess of rooms. You would hardly notice we were there. And we could grow closer."

Her smile suggested just how close she'd like them to become. Brandon swallowed a sigh of annoyance. He'd seen that his cousin was hunting. She'd been at each of the few balls he had attended in the last month, peering at him coquettishly over her fan and fluttering her lashes as he passed. He had hoped the demonstrations were intended to attract some other more suitable prey by reminding the ton how well connected she was. But it appeared his cousin was after him. A pity he wasn't in the least interested. No woman could distract him until the fortune was his.

"While I would enjoy having my family closer," he said, "there is your grandmother to consider. I doubt Lady Honoria would consent to give up her home, or to move outside London."

Patrice made a face. "But if you were to speak to her, she might relent. Or perhaps you could convince her to increase the amount provided by the trust."

And perhaps he could convince pigs to fly. Lady Honoria was a prudent trustee; she wouldn't let a single penny out of her control sooner than needed. At times, Edmund seemed certain she would never release control. All the more reason for Brandon to behave to perfection. He could leave no doubt that the family curse had ended with his father.

"My father's will was quite detailed," he explained to Patrice. "I fear we can do little to change it."

Patrice let out a puff of frustration. "Then you truly cannot help me? You would leave me alone, destitute?"

Her violet gaze was swimming in unshed tears. How nice to have the ability to change emotions on a whim. He hadn't the luxury of even showing his. Any sign of weakness, and Honoria could declare him ineligible to inherit. He patted Patrice's limpid hand, knowing she would likely read more into the gesture than he read in her tears. "Your courage will see you through. It is less than three months until our fortunes change."

Behind the tears he caught a quick glimpse of calculation before she lowered her gaze demurely. "But three months can be an eternity," she murmured.

Someone cleared a throat. Patrice turned with him, and Brandon saw that the governess had returned. She kept her head bowed, but the stiffness in her shoulders told Brandon she disapproved of Patrice's flirting. Beside her stood a slight, dark-haired boy.

"Martin!" Patrice cried, hurrying forward. She took his hands and led the boy toward him. "Come see who's here, dearest. You remember your cousin, Lord Hartley."

The governess's head came up, giving Brandon his first good look at her. The high forehead spoke of intelligence, the stubborn chin of a will to match. He could not see the color of her eyes from this distance, but they appeared dark against her creamy complexion. They were also compelling, drawing him in, piercing his layer of social polish to see down into his soul. What—was he suddenly a poet? Shak-

ing himself, he broke the gaze to look down at the
boy before him.

Martin bowed. "Lord Hartley, sir."

"Mr. Rider," Brandon acknowledged with an
equally formal bow. "Good to see you again."

Patrice's eyes were misty once more. "Is he not
handsome? He has the Pellidore coloring, but those
are my David's eyes."

The boy reddened, but Brandon could see she was
right. David Rider had been a handsome man, and
except for the dark hair, Patrice's son resembled him
strongly. Few people had that eye coloring—a mixture of gray, blue, and green which changed with the
surroundings.

"You look a great deal like your father, Mr. Rider,"
Brandon said and watched the boy stand a little
taller.

"See how he is grown?" Patrice continued to coo.
"All too soon he will leave me. I do not know
whether I can bear it."

Martin's gaze turned to her. "Did you miss me,
Mother?"

"Miss you?" She bent to gaze back at him, obviously incredulous. "Why, certainly I missed you! I
thought of you night and day. I only wish I could
have called for you sooner."

The boy's look was skeptical, but Brandon was surprised by the sincerity in his cousin's voice. Did
Patrice really consider herself a devoted mother?
Why, then, had she kept the boy from her side all
these years?

"We asked you here now," she continued, "because
Lord Hartley heard a silly rumor that Celia is missing. Please assure his lordship that your sister is safe
in Somerset."

The boy licked his lips, paling. "Celia was quite safe the last time I saw her," he said carefully.

"There, you see!" Patrice proclaimed, straightening with a triumphant look.

"And when was that?" Brandon pressed.

The boy swallowed. "I don't know the exact time."

Patrice glanced up at Brandon. "Is something wrong?"

Something was wrong, but he was beginning to think his cousin knew nothing about it. She claimed ignorance of her stepdaughter's betrothal. Perhaps that was simply Patrice's convenient memory, or perhaps her stepdaughter was in greater trouble than he had thought. Had Arlington pressured the girl into marriage? Had she run to London for help only to find he was hounding her? Perhaps she wasn't sure she could trust her stepmother, seeing how distant they were. Yet surely the governess and the boy were colluding to protect her.

Brandon squatted to look Martin in the face. The boy started, then stood taller, lips compressed.

"Your sister is having difficulties, is she not?"

He blinked rapidly, sucking in breath through his nose. "Maybe," he allowed quietly.

Patrice bent down again as well, frowning. "Difficulties, dearest? Is something wrong with Celia?"

The governess stepped forward to lay a hand on her charge's shoulder. Her fingers were long and supple, pale against the dark jacket the boy wore. "Miss Celia is fine, madam. Master Martin simply misses her, isn't that right, Martin?"

Martin glanced up at the governess and then away. "I do not remember being away from Celia before."

Patrice sniffed. "Oh, my poor dear! I had no idea the two of you were so close." She cocked her head suddenly, so that the heavy braids fell to one side like golden chains. "And how did you manage that? She was away at school. No, wait. We had a ball, yes, right before poor David died. We had a ball for Celia. Did we not?"

"I was four, Mother," Martin pointed out stoically. "I don't remember."

Patrice trilled a laugh, straightening. "Neither do I."

Brandon had watched the interchange with interest. Now he eyed the governess, who stood a little taller. Up close, he could not fail to appreciate her. The tilt to that head challenged him. And those eyes . . . As if she felt him drawing too close, she hastily lowered her head.

Brandon straightened. "And what do you know of Miss Rider?" he asked her.

He knew it was not his imagination that she stiffened. Patrice did not seem to notice, merely frowning as if wondering why he insisted on this questioning. The little governess kept her head down.

"I was never privileged to tutor Miss Rider," she murmured. "However, I believe she has been unhappy alone at the estate except for the boy."

"She is at the estate?" Patrice asked, frown deepening. "Oh, why can I not remember?"

Brandon laid a hand on her arm to calm her. "Was she discontented enough to run away?"

"Perhaps, my lord," the governess allowed. "Although she fills her days well enough, what with helping me with Martin and tending to the tenants. I believe she found a contentment."

"And did you know of her engagement to a Mr. Arlington?"

She nodded. "Stanley Arlington, the son of the

nearest neighbor to the estate. It is considered a very good match."

Her voice held a certain amount of pride. Had she helped arrange the match, then? Was she hiding the girl, or working with Arlington to force her into marriage? Before he could think through the implications, Patrice broke away.

"Why don't I know this?" she wailed. "Celia engaged? Who gave permission for that?"

The governess's voice was almost sarcastic. "She came of age last November. Surely you knew. She wrote to remind you."

Patrice put a hand to her brow. "She wrote? I usually remember if I see something written down. Are you certain?"

The governess clasped her hands. "Completely certain, madam. Miss Rider will marry when she gains her inheritance."

She flashed a quick look up at Patrice, eyes narrowed as if in challenge, but his cousin was blinking in confusion.

"I must speak with Grandmother. Take Martin back up to the nursery, Miss Prim."

"Schoolroom," she muttered under her breath, but she turned away obligingly as if to usher Martin toward the door.

He'd be damned if he'd let her go that easily. She was hiding something, from him and from Patrice. "A moment," he said. She stopped obediently, but the glance back at him showed him how annoyed she was. He turned to Patrice. "Go ahead, my dear. I can see this matter worries you. I shall say my farewells to your son."

Patrice nodded distractedly and hurried from the room. The governess set her shoulders.

Brandon stepped forward. "Mr. Rider, thank you for your time. I hope I have the honor of seeing you again soon." He stuck out his hand.

Martin shook it solemnly. "Thank you, my lord."

Brandon gazed down at the small figure, remembering another boy who had lived such a formal, solemn existence. Glancing up, he was surprised to see the governess regarding him with a gentle smile that eased the memory. Meeting his gaze, she colored and turned as if to flee. Her skirts brushed the chair she had so hastily vacated, knocking her embroidery to the floor. As he moved to pick it up, his gaze fell on the sentiment, and his brow arched. He held out the square to her.

"'Patrice has no virtue'?" Martin read aloud.

She hurried forward, face crimson, and snatched it from Brandon's hand. "Please," she murmured. "I can explain."

Brandon crossed his arms over his chest. She swallowed. Martin stepped between them, raising his head.

"She didn't mean any harm, my lord," he said defensively.

She shook her head and put a hand on his shoulder. "It's all right, Martin. His lordship won't hurt me."

It was a statement of supreme confidence.

"You do not know me well, Lady Governess," he said quietly.

"No, my lord, I do not. However, we cannot speak further here. I often take Martin to the park in the early afternoons. Perhaps you could meet us, tomorrow."

Four

Patrice hurried down the corridor toward her grandmother's suite, her breath coming in gasps. If she kept this up, she would faint, which Grandmother hated. She forced herself to count to five each time she inhaled. She made her steps deliberate and careful. She was a lady. She could do this. She had to be confident when she rapped on that polished door. Anything else would get her eaten alive.

When she did tap lightly on the panel, she had to wait for an answer. Then the door opened, no more than a crack. Sally Lawton regarded her, dark eyes narrowed. "Her ladyship asked not to be disturbed."

Patrice felt her lower lip start to tremble and bit the inside of her mouth to keep it steady. "Nevertheless, I must speak with her. Something has happened to Celia."

The maid cocked her head so that the tight gray curls bounced against her pointed chin. "Is that so? A moment, please." The door snapped shut.

Patrice wrapped her arms about herself. Dealing with Miss Lawton was almost as bad as dealing with her grandmother. Even Martin said he thought Miss Lawton was a witch. She'd seen the woman in the early evening in the still room, brewing potions, her long nose poised over the large crucible. Supposedly she mixed Lady Honoria's cosmetics, but her grandmother was a consummate herbalist in her own right and was still capable of concocting her own cosmetic treatments. Who knew what Miss Lawton was up to? Patrice hid a shudder as the door reopened.

"Her ladyship says you may enter," Sally intoned.

Dropping her arms to her sides, Patrice stepped carefully over the threshold. Her shoulders relaxed as she sighted her grandmother on the chaise lounge. It was so much worse having to speak with her at the great bed in the other room. She always felt as if she were approaching a tomb.

Now the sunlight from the high windows made a halo around her grandmother's thick white hair. Her silver-gray dress was equally bright against the burgundy cushions of the chaise. In fact, with her pale, soft skin and silvery brows, the only dark spots were her deep brown eyes. Patrice hurried to her side and dropped a respectful curtsey.

"Something has happened to Celia, has it?" Her grandmother's long, supple fingers motioned to a nearby chair. "Sit, talk."

Patrice obediently perched on the ornate chair. "Yes, my cousin says that a man claims to be engaged to Celia. How could that be when she is away at school?"

Her grandmother heaved a sigh. "The girl has been living in Somerset for four years, Patrice."

Patrice bit her lip again. "I did not remember."

"Of course not. You are rightfully focused on your duties. We hired a perfectly good staff to watch Martin and the girl."

She nodded. "Like Miss Prim."

Her grandmother smiled. "Yes, exactly like Miss

Prim. Such an obedient girl. But your stepdaughter, it seems, has been quite disobedient. What do you know of the fellow?"

"Nothing!" Patrice protested. "And my cousin says Celia has gone missing!"

Her grandmother sat up, staring at her so fixedly that Patrice shrank back against the chair in alarm.

"Missing?" Her grandmother's voice rose as if she, too, were alarmed. "What do you mean, missing?"

"I suppose I do not know," Patrice admitted, clasping her hands to keep them from shaking. "Her fiancé could not find her. Lord Hartley seemed to think she was in London."

Lady Honoria leaned back, eyes narrowing thoughtfully. "No. She cannot be in London. I would have heard."

Patrice did not question the statement. The servants all spied for her grandmother, inside the house and out. Lady Honoria also had a network of acquaintances and admirers who called on a regular basis. Patrice had been approached by men and women at balls and outings, asking her to relay information, begging her to intercede on their behalves. Usually she forgot their requests by the time she reached home. It was their desperation she remembered.

"Then, if she is not in London and not at school, where could she be?" she asked. "What should I do, Grandmother?"

Lady Honoria pursed her lips. "Leave this to me. I shall find the girl, never fear. We cannot have her wandering about on her own. Who knows what mischief she might get into?"

* * *

Celia took a deep breath as she and Martin climbed the stairs for the schoolroom. Her mind was a jumble, and she was just as glad her brother didn't try conversation until they were safely in the room and John dismissed.

"I heard you," Martin proclaimed then. "You invited Lord Hartley to join us in the park tomorrow. Why?"

Celia shook her head. "Sometimes the best thing to do is surrender, my lad. He knew something was up. I had to fob him off, at least for now. Besides, you missed his conversation with your mother." She went on to tell him about Stanley accusing the marquess of murder.

"But you said Mr. Arlington was too timid to help us," Martin protested when she finished. "How could he come all this way to tell Lord Hartley he was a murderer?"

How indeed? Stanley was a dear—fun loving, good natured—until someone put a bottle of wine in front of him. Even then, she had not known him to pick a fight with someone so much more powerful than himself. Though he was considered the catch of three counties as the heir to his father's sprawling estates, Celia was more likely to stick up for him than to have him rescue her. "I cannot think what came over him," she told Martin. "But I will not risk my future on the chance that he might do it again."

Martin went over to the box beneath the high windows and began to take out the game of nine pins stored there. "If you ask me, he was very brave. Lord Hartley scares me."

He scared her, too, but not for reasons she was willing to explain to her little brother. She didn't want to admit that his look was enough to set her pulse racing or that his voice made her feel as if she were rolling in velvet. She had to focus on her purpose in coming here.

Patrice was clearly hiding something. Her letter to her stepmother couldn't have been misplaced; more likely it had been ignored. Patrice had no intention of releasing control of a fortune she had stolen. But release it she would, as soon as Celia had some proof.

This house held a clue somewhere—bills, banking receipts, cash accounting sheets. She feared the truth would be found in Lady Honoria's suite, which would mean the lady was in on the theft as well. She didn't like the idea of crossing Lady Honoria, but she liked less the idea of continuing to live in limbo. She simply had to search that suite.

In the meantime, she must find a way to appease Lord Hartley. Why had she given in to temptation and changed that embroidery? The piece had been consigned to the trunk in her room until she could fix it. Of course, by the way he had scrutinized her, he had suspected her all along, but of what?

She didn't think he knew who she was, but he was certainly on the trail of Celia Rider. Curse Stanley for accosting him! She had told him she was certain of her stepmother's guilt. Stanley didn't think women smart enough to manage finances. Would she show him a thing or two once they were married!

If they were ever married.

She shook her head. Of course they were going to be married. Stanley's father would relent once she had her fortune. A bargain was a bargain, after all. It didn't matter that Stanley wasn't as commanding as Lord Hartley. It didn't matter that Stanley's voice wasn't as thick and rich as Lord Hartley's. It certainly didn't matter that Stanley's smile made her grin, but one look from Lord Hartley made heat sear from her toes to her top. What mattered was that she had given her hand in a bargain, and she would keep her word.

Of course, she wasn't married yet.

"Why are you smiling like that?" Martin asked. "I haven't even set up the game."

"No?" She blinked, realizing that the pins were sprawled across the board. She shook her head again and set about helping him put them up. She had just swung out the ball when John returned. Her look must have shown her annoyance, for he grimaced.

"Begging your pardon, Miss Prim, but Miss Lawton says her ladyship wants a word with you."

This could be her chance! Celia leapt to her feet, causing John and her brother to raise their brows in surprise. She pasted on a polite smile. "It would not do to keep her ladyship waiting. If you would continue in my place, John?"

"A difficult task," John replied, casting himself down beside Martin with a grin, "but I can sacrifice myself."

A few moments later, Celia tapped respectfully on the door to Lady Honoria's suite. Sally let her in and motioned her toward the adjoining bedroom. Celia swallowed and tiptoed in.

The vast room was in half light, the lamps trimmed to cast a mellow glow over the polished woods and burgundy upholstery Lady Honoria favored. Celia stepped quietly up to the heavily draped bed, the top of which disappeared into the darkness of the high ceiling overhead. "You wanted to see me, ma'am?"

Lady Honoria peered out from the darker recesses, face ghostly pale. Her long nose was wider at the tip, making it appear as if her nostrils were constantly flared to the scent of trouble. "You supervised my granddaughter's visit with Lord Hartley. How did it go?"

That she wanted a spy was a bit ironic, what with Celia wanting to spy on her. "They had a pleasant conversation," she offered.

Lady Honoria clucked her tongue. An elegant hand emerged from the satin bed sheets and motioned to the stiff-backed chair beside the bed. Celia sat.

"Will he have her, do you think?"

Celia blinked. "Have whom, your ladyship?"

"Do not make me dance, child. You must know what I ask."

The voice was quiet, but Celia sat straighter hearing the intensity rise. Sally, standing guard on the other side of the bed, regarded Celia as if certain she was being willful and ready to usher her to hell for it.

"I saw no indication that the Marquess of Hartley intended to offer for Mrs. Rider," Celia said.

Lady Honoria shook her head. "Just as I feared. I do not know whether to be relieved or disappointed. I must care for them both, you see."

Celia put on her most dutiful face. "Yes, Lady Honoria."

"Such an obedient young lady. Stand up."

Sucking in a breath, she did as she was told. "Ma'am?"

"Turn around."

Again she obeyed, but with a sinking feeling. Had she given away the game after all? Had Lady Honoria realized that it was her great-granddaughter by marriage standing beside her and trying not to tremble?

But the old woman merely shook her head, mobile mouth canted in amusement. "You needn't look so frightened, child. I am not trying to determine whether you will be more tender cooked with basil or rosemary."

Miss Lawton chuckled. Celia clamped her mouth shut.

"You are quite lovely," Lady Honoria continued. "How is it that you came to be a governess so young?"

Celia's mouth was dry, but she managed to say the words she had rehearsed. "My mother died shortly after I was born. My father was a soldier who died with Wellington at Waterloo."

"Ah," Lady Honoria put in. "My father died later in life of heart failure, shortly after his third wife, Lord Pellidore's mother. So, you had to find employment, did you?"

"Yes, your ladyship. I had some skill with teaching. Your steward at Hollyoake Lodge thought I would do well with Master Martin, until he went away to school next year."

"Away?" Lady Honoria's feathery brows drew down heavily across her long nose, and Sally scurried forward with a little vinaigrette box. Celia somehow doubted Lady Honoria had ever fainted in her life. Now she merely waved the maid back.

"You are mistaken," she said, and that intensity had returned to her voice. "I insisted that my great-grandson be brought to London so that he could receive the proper tutelage. We will be hiring a male tutor shortly."

Meaning that Miss Prim's days were numbered. "A shame he could not be with boys his own age," Celia tried.

Miss Lawton's look was murderous. Lady Honoria merely narrowed her eyes. "A Pellidore needs no one. He is a law unto himself. Or herself." Her mouth curved upward. "I am satisfied that my methods will result in what is needed for the boy. I will give Martin all that is required to take his proper place in the world. I would turn your attentions toward your future, Miss Prim."

She smiled at Lady Honoria. "I assure you, your ladyship, that is never far from my mind."

Somehow she survived until the following afternoon. At least she knew now why Martin had been brought from Somerset. Lady Honoria wished to see him properly educated. Celia didn't like the idea of her brother alone in this house. All the more reason to find the fortune.

Rumor had it that Lady Honoria would be going out the day after next, giving Celia an opportunity to search. All she need do was keep Lord Hartley off the scent.

Of course, that was easier said than done. Oberon she had named him, and she wouldn't have been surprised could he read her mind. He certainly remained on her mind throughout the evening and day that followed. Funny, but she could not recall thinking more than twice about Stanley since coming to London.

Martin should have been as nervous as she was, given his fear of Lord Hartley, but once they had reached Hyde Park, his enthusiasm began to climb. He loved the greenery and vast open spaces as much as she did. They always chose a time when the fashionable were less likely to crowd the park. Lady Honoria still insisted that they take John, who trailed obligingly behind as they wandered the many paths through the greenery. Other children flew kites or sailed boats on the Serpentine. Martin, however, came for the horses.

"There's a prime bit of blood," he said, pointing to a chestnut that was prancing across the path ahead of them.

"Prime bit of blood?" Celia teased. "Now, where did that come from?" She glanced back at John, who shrugged.

"Henry Mullins," Martin admitted, "the new groom. I like the way it sounds, don't you?"

"It is colorful," Celia allowed. "Just forget the phrase in front of Lady Honoria. She would box your ears for certain."

Martin fingered a lobe thoughtfully. "I suppose she would. I don't think it's that awfully impertinent, do you? Oh, look at that roan, now, would you?"

Celia glanced longingly after the Arabian mare. She'd learned to ride at the Barnsley School but hadn't appreciated the freedom of it until forced to rusticate at the Lodge. There she could fly across the fields, jumping hedgerows and ditches, climbing rises, shooting down valleys. She'd met Stanley for the first time on horseback. He'd challenged her to a race and hadn't been cowed when she'd won. He was nearly as bruising a rider as she was. Even Martin enjoyed the sport.

"What an excellent judge of horseflesh you are, Rider."

Martin paled, but Celia thought her heart would stop at the sound of that voice. Squaring her shoulders and taking a deep breath, she turned to face the Marquess of Hartley.

"And how are you today?" he asked her brother.

Martin stood straighter as well. "Tolerably well, my lord. And you?"

"The same. Out for a walk, were you?"

"Yes, sir. And we will be expected home for tea."
He reached out and took Celia's hand, and it was a
bet which was colder. "Won't we, Miss Prim?"

Lord Hartley was regarding her, and those dark
eyes lured her in. They were a cool brown, liberally
lashed. What would it take to warm them? She
blinked away the temptation to find out. "Yes, Martin, we need to get back. However, I believe we can
stay a while longer."

Her brother squeezed her hand, but in warning or
sympathy, she couldn't tell.

"Excellent," Lord Hartley purred. "I shall join
you."

He didn't ask, merely falling into step beside
them. She cast a look back at John, who shrugged
again. His lordship was a relative and a powerful one
at that. It wasn't as if Lady Honoria would thank him
for chasing the man off.

"Did you ever fly kites when you were younger,
Rider?" Lord Hartley asked.

Her brother glanced at him from the corner of his
eyes. "Perhaps, my lord. Why do you ask?"

To Celia's amazement, the faintest of rose warmed
Lord Hartley's cheeks, and she had to fight a desire
to touch his skin. "Well, you see," he said, "I was
never given the chance to fly a kite. I thought I
might try it today, and I could use some advice."

Martin's eyes were huge. "You want my help?"

Lord Hartley blew out a breath. "You would have
my eternal gratitude. You see"—he bent—"I seem to
have gotten it lodged in a tree."

Martin actually stopped, and Celia knew she was
staring just as pointedly. "Really?" her brother asked.

Lord Hartley nodded, straightening. "Just ahead

there." He waved to a tall tree several dozen yards distant. "Have a look and tell me what you think."

Martin obligingly loped ahead. John gave Celia a quick glance before going after him. She was a servant after all. No need to stay and chaperone. No need to protect her, though she was certain the man beside her had staged the whole act.

"Oh, well done, my lord," she told him.

He shrugged. "You are not the only one who can resort to ruses, Lady Governess. Now, tell me what you have done with Celia Rider."

Five

That stopped her. Brandon halted as well, gazing down at her reddening cheeks. She was so very bad at hiding her emotions. It was delightful to watch, even knowing she was likely part of a plot to harm an innocent girl.

"Well?" he pressed. "You swore to tell me the whole of it if I met you today. Here I am. Where is your story?"

She licked her soft pink lips. It would be a lie, then.

"Miss Rider does not wish to be found," she said. "I assure you she is safe and well. However, she has reached her majority and feels no need to justify herself to anyone."

"Fine. Let me hear that from her directly."

She puffed out a breath of sheer annoyance. "She prefers her anonymity."

"She may have it, once she has told me so herself."

"Why are you so obstinate?" she demanded, raising her head to glare at him. He leaned forward, but she gasped and lowered her head again before he could meet her gaze. "I do beg your pardon, my lord. I have no right to speak to you so."

"No, you do not. And to answer your question, I am the head of the family Miss Rider's father married into. With him gone, it is my duty to see to her needs."

"Your tender sensibilities overwhelm me." Her voice dripped sarcasm. "If you are such a devoted guardian, where were you when she was sentenced to spinsterhood in the country?"

She was the most outspoken woman for a governess. He ought to put her in her place, yet something about her manner intrigued him. "I lived in Scotland until recently. That Miss Rider has vanished without her mother's knowledge is reason enough for me to step in."

"She is not Miss Rider's mother," she said in chilling tones. "And Miss Rider does not require her rescue, or yours."

"Then I will take myself off, once I have met her."

She muttered something. He pushed aside the smile that threatened as she glanced up at him from under her brows.

"If Martin were to tell you she is well, would that suffice?"

"Not in the slightest. How could I know you had not coerced the lad into saying what you wished me to hear?"

She shook her head. "We are at an impasse. I cannot produce Miss Rider, and you will not be satisfied until I do."

He could not stop the smile as he bent closer. "My dear Lady Governess, you seem to think you have a choice in the matter. I came here to learn Miss Rider's location, and I will not leave until you tell me."

Her gaze flickered up at him again, calculating, cool. The minx wasn't the least bit afraid of him. How very refreshing. She licked her lips again, but instead of waiting for the next lie, he found himself wondering just how good she might taste. It was only a little distance to those tempting lips, after all. All he need do was bend a little closer. She raised her head as if anticipating him, lips parting, breath warming his chin.

"My lord, I have it!"

Brandon jerked upright. What on earth was he thinking? He'd come here to expose a plot, not plot a seduction. He had to blink twice before he could focus on Martin's beaming face below him. The boy triumphantly brandished the kite Brandon had borrowed from his coachman's children that morning. Miss Prim stepped out of Brandon's reach, bumping into the footman who was following the boy.

"Your kite, my lord," Martin said, pushing it at him.

Brandon had no choice but to accept it with a bow. "I am in your debt, Rider. It seems your knowledge in these matters far outreaches mine."

Martin colored. "I do know a thing or two, I suppose."

Brandon fingered the thin material. He needed a few more moments with the governess to wring a confession from her. Surely he could ignore her attraction that long.

"Yes, a very nice job," he told the boy. "I wonder if I might request another favor."

Martin's grin faded, and he cocked his head to regard Brandon with obvious suspicion in his changeable eyes. "What?"

Brandon bent low and tugged at the string of the kite so that the tail rippled temptingly along the soft green grass. "Show me how this should work."

Martin's grin reappeared. *Did I ever look that happy as a child?* Brandon wondered. The boy pulled the kite back into his thin arms and headed away from the trees, the footman trotting at his heels like a loyal hound.

"Do you always manipulate people?" she asked at his elbow.

He eyed her, feelings of charity abating. "Easily yet rarely. You have until he is finished amusing himself to tell me where Celia Rider is."

She sighed. "If I tell you, you must swear to reveal the secret to no one else."

"Why? Is she in danger?"

She nodded.

He chilled. "From whom? Why?"

"You will not like the answer."

"You will not give me answers, Lady Governess, so how would you know?"

"Very well. We have reason to believe her stepmother, your cousin, has stolen her inheritance."

"Mr. Arlington said similar nonsense. My cousin is a sweet-natured, ill-focused creature. I sincerely doubt she could manage to steal a coin handed to her, let alone a fortune such as David Rider must have left. Moreover, the fortune is surely kept in trust. My cousin would not have access to it."

He could see her frowning even with her head bowed. "Have you seen the will, then? Is that what it states?"

He hadn't seen the will or he'd have known he was named guardian. Still, he had a fair idea how to remedy that oversight. "Surely Miss Rider would know."

"She was not allowed access to her father's papers. They were sent to London immediately after his death."

"Nevertheless, I cannot see my cousin as a danger."

"Nor did you appear to notice that she was manipulating you yesterday. A family trait, I see. She cannot need money from you, my lord. Even if she did not take her stepdaughter's inheritance, David Rider left her very well off indeed. I am at least certain of that. He made that agreement when he married her, and he always kept a bargain."

Interesting. That was another matter he would look into. As far as he knew, Patrice and her children were the responsibility of the estate. Had they been throwing good money after bad? "Mayhap you are correct. That leaves even less reason for my cousin to steal Miss Rider's share."

"Think what you like, my lord. Someone took the fortune, and Miss Rider will not be satisfied until she has found it."

He frowned. "She intends to do that on her own? A young woman fresh from the country?"

She snorted. "You think little of her all too easily."

"And she takes too much on herself needlessly."

"To whom would you have her turn? Her stepmother, who despite your protests she sees as the enemy? Lady Honoria, who very likely helped in the whole matter? You, a stranger?"

Her fiancé, who appeared to be a well-intentioned idiot? He began to see the problem. "There are the authorities."

"Bow Street? Would they believe the word of a nonentity against the quality? Even a country bumpkin could reason out the answer to that question, my lord."

He nodded. "Very well, I grant you that Miss Rider has a difficult course ahead. I give you my word that I will not divulge her location. However, I must know that she is safe."

She gazed at the toes of her slippers peeping out

from under the skirt of her dark gown. They were an incongruous rose color. Brandon blinked.

"Well, my lord?" Martin bounded to their side, forcing Brandon's gaze and thoughts outward again. "Do you have the hang of it?"

The boy must have made a dozen passes with the kite while they were talking. Slender chest heaving, he held the kite out to Brandon once more.

"You are an excellent teacher, Rider," he said, accepting it. "Thank you."

Martin nodded eagerly. "May I watch while you try it?"

Brandon stared at him.

Miss Prim smiled sweetly. "Yes, my lord, by all means. Give it a try. I would be delighted to instruct you from here."

He felt frozen. The boy had naturally taken him at his word, and the minx beside him was only too happy to see him hoist with his own petard. They had no idea of the repercussions. Lord Heartless, flying a kite in Hyde Park? The gossip would be endless. That he could have handled. It was the speculation that would eat at his soul. The familiar questions would only start again. He could hear Edmund's concerned voice in his mind.

"You do not seem yourself today, Hart. How are you feeling? No headaches? No spots before your eyes?"

"My, how very odd," Lady Honoria would say. "First your grandmother, then your father, and now you. It is almost as if you cannot control yourself."

"You can control yourself, can you not, Hartley?"

"Can you not, Hartley?"

"Can you not, my lord?"

Brandon blinked, refocusing on Miss Prim's face

below him. The challenge in her tone had melted into concern.

"Did you hear me, my lord?" she asked with surprising gentleness. The footman was frowning behind her, and Martin was gazing up at him in obvious confusion.

"No," he replied. "I must ask your forgiveness."

"No need," she said. "It is rather refreshing to know that you are human after all."

He felt a laugh bubbling up from deep inside him. It surprised him as much as it seemed to surprise Martin and the footman, whose eyes widened. If she only knew how human. She merely smiled, reaching out to return the kite to the boy.

"I think Lord Hartley would rather you keep the kite for now, Martin. I suspect he has had enough flying for today."

"Yes, thank you," Brandon said, relief washing over him.

Martin nodded his dark head. "All right. May I use it a bit more and then return it before we go home?"

Brandon nodded. Miss Prim nodded as well, then reached up to pat the footman on the shoulder in encouragement. "Ready, John?"

"Yes, Miss Prim," he said, still obviously a little unsure of Brandon's mood. "Call us when it's time to go." He jogged after Martin.

Brandon schooled his face as she turned back. "Thank you. I did not wish to lie to the lad any more than necessary."

"And I appreciate that. He has had to live enough falsehoods of late. And so have I." She raised her head at last and met his gaze. Up close, he could see that her eyes were a unique mixture of gray, blue, and green. Her black dress had made them appear darker.

"You have your father's eyes," he said, "just like Martin."

She cocked her head, a few honeyed tendrils escaping the cap to gleam in the sun. "How long have you known?"

"Only for a few moments. Your demeanor was odd; however, it seemed entirely too odd for a governess to have dainty footwear the color of roses."

She grimaced. "The real Miss Prim's feet were larger than mine. Even with paper in the toes, the shoes kept falling off."

"Then there is a governess of that name?"

She nodded. "Martin's governess in Somerset. She is devoted to us. I intend to keep her on once I am married."

He tried to picture Arlington with this strong-willed, outspoken woman and failed. "So is everything true? You are engaged to Mr. Arlington?"

"Guilty. And I did come to London to claim my inheritance. I met with the solicitors, and they had the gall to tell me my father left Martin and me penniless. Then I knew that Patrice had stolen the fortune."

"I see. And did it never occur to you that the solicitors were telling the truth?"

She raised her head and jutted out her chin. "Not for a moment. I may never have read my father's will, my lord, but I know his intentions and his worth. He set aside his fortune in four portions—one for Patrice, one for me, and a double portion for Martin. It should have been held in trust for the last four years. It could not have disappeared so easily without a great deal of help."

He could believe that part, but he thought it far more likely that it was the solicitors who had absconded with the money and said as much. She shook her head.

"They were reliable men. My father trusted them."

"And their names?"

He expected to hear the name of some nonentity deep in the bowels of the City. "Carstairs and Son," she said defiantly.

He started, and she frowned. "What is it?"

"Nothing, though I find it odd that your father used the same solicitors as mine. My fortune also rests in the hands of Carstairs and Son."

Her frown deepened. "I, too, find that decidedly odd, my lord. I do not know when my father started using them. Could it be that Patrice recommended them?"

"My cousin cannot recall her address, let alone the name of the family solicitor, Miss Rider. However, rest assured that I will look into the matter."

She planted her hands on her hips. "Your recollections must be just as faint. I did not ask you to rescue me."

"Neither am I rescuing you. You claim my cousin stole your fortune. She could not have done so without the aid of solicitors, and the solicitors who would have aided her oversee my fortune. This is not charity, Miss Rider; this is survival."

Her hands fell back to her sides, and she nodded. "Very well, my lord, I can accept that. You will remember your promise: you said you would not give me away."

"I swore not to reveal your location. However, my cousin thinks you have gone missing. What if she investigates?"

She chewed her lower lip a moment, then shook her head. "If she truly is forgetful, she probably cannot remember the conversation today. If she does think to ask after me, perhaps you can tell her that you learned I returned to Somerset."

"You want me to lie for you?"

She trilled a laugh. "So very offended, my lord? I had the impression that lies came easily to you."

"Then you thought wrong, Miss Rider."

She shook her head, sobering. "I truly did not mean to offend. And you must call me Miss Prim."

That he could not do, but she must never know it. "The name does not do you justice. If I must encourage the charade, I will continue to call you Lady Governess."

She nodded. "Very well."

He held up a hand. "However, if I learn the real situation surrounding your fortune, will you tell my cousin the truth?"

She paled. "It would be easier if I could simply reappear in Somerset."

"Easier for you; hardly easier for the lad and my cousin, not to mention Mr. Arlington. I achieve what I set my mind to. I will find your fortune. Will you honor my wishes?"

She sighed. "I suppose it is the right thing to do. Very well, my lord, if you learn the secret of my fortune before I do, I will tell my stepmother who I am."

"Then you intend to continue your inquiries? How?"

She regarded him with obvious suspicion. "You have your ways, I have mine."

"Which are?"

"None of your concern."

"Every inch my concern if you intend to involve my family."

"Stubborn," she muttered.

"Like knows like," he countered.

"Indeed it does. Very well, then." He listened with growing concern as she explained her intentions of searching the town house. He shook his head. "Lady Honoria will have you for dinner if she catches you."

"Then I shall take extra care that she does not catch me."

"Are you always this determined?"

"Always." She smiled. "Father used to say it was one of my most endearing qualities."

He ought to argue, but he was finding it too interesting. Instead, he changed the subject. "I want to hear how your search goes. We will meet again, tomorrow."

She shook her head. "Impossible. Word will likely reach Patrice and Lady Honoria soon enough that we were with you today. If we were to make a habit of this, one of them might suspect something."

Very likely they would suspect he was seducing the governess. The idea had merit, but he doubted she'd be as interested in the prospect. And she was far too unpredictable for him. "Very well. I will find a way to meet you tomorrow, and no one will know."

She cocked her head to look at him from the corner of her eyes, the picture of suspicion. "How?"

"That, my Lady Governess," he said, "you will find out tomorrow."

Six

Brandon knew exactly how to meet Celia the next day and what must be accomplished first. Unfortunately, it wasn't easy.

To check on the status of the Rider fortune seemed simple. However, when he called on the solicitors, Milford Carstairs, the aging senior partner, and his son James were out visiting other clients. Brandon made an appointment for the next morning, then had his driver go by Westminster to pick up his uncle and continue out to Pellidore Place.

His grandfather had spared no expense in building a home for his first bride in the country just outside London. The colonnaded portico towered three stories over the wide marble entrance stairs, and wings swept back on either side. The ten bedchambers were enough for a good-sized family. With three wives in succession, however, his grandfather had only managed to sire three children, one by each. The house had seen far more deaths than births. After the more intimate and rustic surroundings of the Scottish estate where he'd spent much of his life, he and his uncle rattled about the huge house like lead balls in a pistol case. He spent only as much time there as it required to change, eat, and sleep.

Edmund was silent most of the way, though Brandon caught his uncle eying him as if awaiting confession of some desperate act. Edmund was perfect to play the father confessor of an earlier age. Everything about him was spare, as if he begrudged giving any quarter. He was nearly as tall as Brandon, though leaner, a rapier to his cutlass. His thin lips and long nose were part of an angular face made gaunt and gray with years of diligent guardianship. His sandy hair was going gray as well, though it was still as thick and straight as Brandon had ever seen it. The only features that marked him for a Pellidore were his deep-set, dark eyes, button bright.

"A moment," he ordered when they reached the house.

Brandon turned slowly back to eye him. Edmund shook his head. "I know you too well for that practiced glower to work. Join me in the library; we must talk."

Gainsaying him would only raise questions in his mind. Brandon snapped a bow and motioned Edmund to proceed him. A moment later, they were seated in the brown leather armchairs among the tall walnut bookcases. Edmund waited until Mr. Openshaw, the butler, brought a tray with a pitcher of lemonade and two crystal glasses. Though Edmund poured himself and Brandon a glass, he did not speak until the servant had bowed himself out. Then he eased his tall frame back in the chair.

"I wish to know more about your search for Miss Rider. You were in late last night and out early this morning. I did not wish to speak near the servants. The less gossip the better."

Brandon inclined his head, feeling his tension lessening at the conciliatory tone. "I located the young lady and am satisfied that she is safe, for the moment."

Edmund raised his elegant brows. "For the moment? You make it sound as if her peril were imminent."

"She is in a difficult situation. Yet, she seems clever enough to work her way out of it." He took a sip from the glass.

"Then you are free to pursue other activities," Edmund said with an approving nod.

Heaven forbid that he get involved. Too many secrets, too much at stake. "I am not free just yet," he replied. "She raised some issues that I must resolve."

"Such as?"

He eyed his uncle. "What do you know of my cousin's dower arrangements?"

"Not a great deal, I suppose," Edmund admitted, rubbing his nose thoughtfully with a slender finger. "That was Lady Honoria's duty. Why? Does the girl ask for money?"

"Not exactly. She claims that her father left my cousin well off indeed. If that is true, why am I giving my cousin additional funds?"

Edmund frowned. "She must be mistaken. Lady Honoria requested the funds herself after Rider died. According to her, Patrice would be destitute if not for the allowance you give."

"My cousin seems to think so as well. Interesting. How long have you known Milford Carstairs?"

"All my life. The family fortunes have been under his administration since before he put out his own shingle. It was Trent, Macy, and Carstairs in those days. Why would he know anything about Patrice's finances?"

"My cousin seems to have him as a solicitor as well."

Edmund nodded. "Of course. Honoria would

want all the money kept within the family, so to speak. She favors young Carstairs. She always did prefer those with ambition."

"So he seeks to advance?" That could explain the theft of Celia's fortune, or negate its possibility, depending on the risks the younger Carstairs was willing to take.

"I merely speculate by the way he toadies up to Honoria. I have seen him at her bedside at least a dozen times in the last few months. Do not tell me you suspect him of embezzlement?"

"I will know more tomorrow after I talk with him."

Edmund shook his head. "Miss Rider must have made quite an impression for you to go to such trouble." He frowned at Brandon. "Are you feeling all right?"

"Stop," Brandon snapped, rising. He set the glass down on the table with deliberate calm, though a part of him wanted to smash the crystal in his irritation. "I am fine, Uncle. Thank you for asking. Excuse me."

"Wait." Edmund rose to lay a hand on his shoulder. Brandon straightened away from the touch. Edmund dropped his hand, sighing. "Forgive me. It is rare for you to show such an interest in strangers. But I trust your judgment in the matter. You are a gentleman, and a gentleman helps a lady in distress."

Brandon shook his head. "This lady wants no rescue."

"Neither did our friend from the country, yet you were kind to him as well."

"And will you tell me you see that, too, as a weakness?"

Edmund grimaced. "Not a weakness. You had to stop the scene he was making before others commented. I saw him in town, by the way. He seems a bit lost."

"He will survive," Brandon predicted. "As soon as I resolve this issue with the fortunes, I will connect him with Miss Rider and send the two of them home." Something whispered to him that sending her away was wrong, but he shook the voice off. Now was not the time to get mawkish. His only interest in Celia Rider was her connection to his family.

Brandon's reluctance to see the last of Celia was not the only hindrance to his plans. James Carstairs was still unavailable when Brandon called the next morning. His father, however, was delighted to see him.

"My lord," he proclaimed, coming around his desk to shake Brandon's hand when the clerk showed Brandon in. "To what do I owe this honor?"

"Curiosity," Brandon acknowledged. "I will shortly come into my fortune, and I need to know what debts I inherit."

"Debts?" Carstairs motioned Brandon to the polished armchair before the dark wood desk. Watching him take his own seat behind it, Brandon could see no sign that the solicitor's usual competent air had diminished. He was almost bald now, that was true, with only a few wisps of iron gray hair running around his head like a silver crown that had slipped. His frame was straight, the light in his blue eyes bright. The tan knee breeches and brown velvet coat with the lace peeping out at the cuffs might have come from an earlier age, but Mr. Carstairs appeared to be up to the moment otherwise.

"The Pellidore estate has always produced, my

lord," he answered Brandon. "In addition, the will allows for prudent investment in the funds and certain other secure ventures. Any expenses from your father's day have long since been paid."

"And Lady Honoria and her granddaughter? Do I fund them as well?"

"Her ladyship, certainly. Sadly, her husband brought no financial assets to the family. It was his connections abroad that were prized, though those were of less use after the hostilities with Napoleon."

"And my second cousin?"

"Mrs. Rider? Her father left her nothing—a matter of an unfortunate gambling problem. However, she has her own jointure from her late husband. She derives a tidy income from the five per cents, I believe. But my son could tell you more."

He would make sure of it. "Then I will not need to take care of her children either, a lad and a young lady?"

"No indeed," Carstairs assured him, leaning back so that the sunlight from the windows behind him made his bald head gleam. "The boy was given a double portion and will be quite well off when he reaches his majority. We are merely awaiting word from the young lady to award her portion."

Brandon cocked his head. "You have heard nothing from Celia Rider?"

"Not a word. James provided her instructions for claiming the inheritance, but she has not seen fit to do so. I assumed she and her mother agreed to let the money mature a while longer, but again, you would have to ask him."

"I would like nothing more. Have him available to meet with me at four the day after tomorrow. I have someone I should like him to meet."

Carstairs agreed, and Brandon made his farewells. Outside the office, he shook his head. What was he to make of the two stories? His father and uncle had trusted Milford Carstairs. Nothing in the older man's demeanor or words said Brandon should trust him less now.

Yet neither could he distrust Celia. True, she was even now playing his cousin for a fool, but she felt she had good reason. And there could be no question she was David Rider's daughter. The resemblance between her and Martin was too strong, and their affection for each other seemed real. Besides, he had seen how hard it was for the boy to lie.

Yet the boy hadn't claimed her as his sister.

Now, that was interesting. Why hadn't he realized it before? He had no one's word on her identity but hers. Was the admittedly false Miss Prim really Celia Rider or a by-blow of David Rider's attempting to lay claim to a fortune that would otherwise never be hers? It was either a grand mistake or a serious conspiracy.

He only had two days to find out which. Heaven help his lady governess if she should prove false.

Celia easily occupied her time until the meeting with Lord Hartley. As she and Martin had agreed that she would not attempt to fill the real Miss Prim's role unless someone was watching, she had no other duties but to entertain her brother and search for proof of the theft of their fortune.

Today, she had another purpose in mind in leaving the schoolroom. She needed to know whether she could trust Lord Hartley. She had admitted to Martin that she had told the man the truth. She hadn't intended to, even when he was so persistent. He was too cool, too sure of himself by half.

Yet when he had paused for a moment in the park, the oddest look had come over his face. His dark eyes had widened, and his breath come more quickly, as if something had shaken him. She'd been struck with the intense desire to gather him in her arms and stroke his hair until he calmed. It was ridiculous. What possible reason could he have for suddenly losing his confidence? Yet it had seemed right to stop her charade then, to gentle her tone, to help him. Now she could only wonder whether she'd made the right decision.

It was ever thus, she thought as she trooped down to the kitchen. She was always leaping to action before stopping to think. The trait had stood her in good stead any number of times. She wouldn't have plucked the ripest plum of a bachelor in Somerset if she hadn't been quick on her toes. But every plum had a pit, and Stanley had more than his share. Perhaps, if she had thought ahead, she would have seen them before she had agreed to his offer.

She must do better where Lord Hartley was concerned. She knew exactly how to ferret out his secrets. Servants, she had learned, had a different and often more accurate view of their masters than anyone else. According to what she had been told, her stepmother's servants were actually paid from the Pellidore estate. Surely, they had some impressions of Lord Hartley.

Of course, getting them to share those impressions might be another matter. As an upper servant and newcomer, she had been an object of wariness. She knew the folly of challenging the idea. Instead, she had spent the last three weeks offering helpful advice, sharing an occasional task, and being as congenial as possible. Compared to Sally's sour arrogance, her small kindnesses, she hoped, would seem large indeed. Now she sensed that while she was by no means an ally, she was no longer the enemy. She put her influence to work with a few discrete inquiries.

At the casual mention of Lord Hartley, Cook's mouth puckered in her pale, wrinkled face.

"Poor little mite," she muttered, rubbing an eye on her beefy shoulder as she stirred the soup for the evening's meal. "Left an orphan and in such a bad way."

"Bad way?" Celia encouraged, taking her time about arranging a snack for Martin, which was her ostensive reason for being in the kitchen.

Mr. Kinders and Mrs. Watson, taking a midday break, exchanged knowing glances.

"She hasn't heard the story, Mrs. Watson," the butler said, shaking his graying head.

"Comes from the country, don't you know," the housekeeper replied, smoothing back her own brown hair with one hand.

"We simply cannot get good gossip there," Celia said with a sigh. "You lead much more interesting lives."

"Not so interesting as when her ladyship lived at Pellidore Place," Mr. Kinders replied. He paused to take a sip of his tea, careful to let none spill on his ornate black jacket and knee breeches.

Mrs. Watson leaned forward, green eyes alight over her black bombazine. "I wasn't there when it happened. Do tell."

Celia stood rooted to the spot. The butler cleared his throat importantly. When he spoke, his voice was hushed.

"Over twenty years ago now, and I can still remember that dark night like yesterday. We should have known it was coming. Lady Honoria warned him that his own mother had gone off that way. But it came on so sudden. We heard him yelling something horrible. The coachman said the shrieks echoed to the stables. Once in a while something crashed. Later, we found he'd broken nearly every piece of furniture in the room. Lord Pellidore was there with him until the end. Can you imagine that duty? Watching your own half brother go mad and die, foaming at the mouth like a rabid dog."

Celia swallowed. "Lord Hartley's grandmother and father went mad?"

Mrs. Watson hurriedly put her finger to her plump lips. "Hush, now. We'd best say no more. It upsets her ladyship." She glanced toward the door to the upper stairs as if expecting to see Sally glaring them all to silence.

"And so it should." Mr. Kinders took a sip of his tea before continuing. "A horrible family trait to inherit. Luckily, Lord Pellidore came through a different line. We all know it's a matter of time before Lord Hartley begins showing the symptoms."

"Stammering, wildness, madness." Mrs. Watson shuddered.

Cook sniffed. "Poor little mite."

Celia stared at them. "You cannot mean the current Lord Hartley? But he is so polished!"

"Aye," Mrs. Watson replied. "Lord Heartless I hear they call him. Just as well he has no heart. Think how it would break otherwise."

"Only a matter of time," Mr. Kinders repeated.

Celia's hands shook as she finished setting up the tray. How horrible! He could not have been more than a child. If the stable hands had heard the sound of it, how much closer had he been? Small wonder he held himself so tightly!

She felt as bad as cook, pitying the poor boy. She must remember that he was no longer a child but a grown man with considerable power that extended to her future. The problem was, she wasn't certain she could face him knowing his history.

She had no idea how he intended to meet them the next day and found herself jumping every time she heard a foot on the stair, even when it was far too early for callers. Besides, she told herself, he could not possibly meet them at the house because of Patrice. She hadn't seen much of her stepmother except when Patrice came to talk with Martin in the evenings, but John had told them the woman had been asking after Lord Hartley as if expecting him to call. Her stepmother would surely grab him for herself if he showed up at the front door.

Celia was glad to escape midmorning to the garden behind the house. At least she would not fear finding him there. In fact, she and Martin sometimes had a hard time finding each other. The house was of an older style, dressed stone with its own walled garden behind. While the area was not extensive, it had been subdivided into smaller plots for particular plants and even had a miniature hot house for Lady Honoria's special plants. Between the hedges dividing the areas and the large shade trees sprinkled throughout, it was easy to lose oneself.

It was also the best place in the world for a rousing game of catch-me-who-can.

Today, she gave her brother to the count of twenty before going to find him. Then she moved down the central path slowly. The gravel crunched softly underfoot. She checked several of his usual places: behind the central fountain, along the trail of sun flowers, in the Grecian grotto. Oh, he'd outdone himself this time. She should at least catch a glimpse of his dark suit among the flowers and bright greens of late spring. She glanced about, searching for some telltale movement, ears tuned for any sound other than the drone of bees and the coo of the dove.

Something dark passed along the far wall.

Celia grinned. She darted back the way she had come. If she cut through the rose garden, she could catch him before he reached the house, where, by the rules they had agreed on, he would win this round. She picked up her skirts and dodged through the thorny bushes. Another flash of black showed her he made faster progress. She picked up speed and hurled herself over the last bit of hedge.

"Got you!"

Her arms caught on something significantly bigger than her brother. Lord Hartley gazed down at her, both brows raised.

"And just what do you intend to do with me," he asked, "now that you've caught me?"

Seven

Brandon watched as the woman flamed. She released her hold to stumble back.

Martin's laughter echoed from the hedge as he crawled out. "You should see your face, Celia! I tricked you!"

"You certainly did," she said, though Brandon could see the effort it cost her to appear so cool. He was more interested in the fact that young Rider had just called her Celia. He felt himself relax. "Your sister does not seem amused, Rider."

The boy's grin faded, but Celia shook her head. "Oh, I am terribly amused, at my own stupidity. I should certainly have been able to tell a gentleman from a boy."

Martin's grin returned. "Celia's usually pretty good at this game, my lord. I think you startled her. You can join us, if you like. It's her turn to hide."

Brandon felt a smile tugging but held his mouth firm. How very interesting that would be, to search through the blooming garden for the fairest flower of all. Unfortunately, every minute here increased the chance that he would be noticed. "I cannot stay long," he told the boy. "I only came for a few words with your sister."

"You may take my turn, Martin," she said. "Go find

another hiding place. When I search, I shall have no mercy."

Giggling in anticipation, her brother scampered away. She turned to Brandon. "How did you get past Patrice?"

"My Uncle Edmund lived in this house when he was younger. The ivy along the wall hides a rear gate."

"And it did not squeak from disuse?"

"Not at all. Someone seems to keep it in good condition." And he had wondered if she wasn't that person. "How goes your search for the fortune?"

She bowed her head in obvious frustration. Her cap must have fallen off during her dash through the bushes, for he could see that her hair was shiny and thick, crowning her head in dusky gold.

"I have yet to get into Lady Honoria's rooms," she admitted. "She is supposed to leave shortly, but I cannot trust that Patrice will stay out of my way." She glanced up at him, eyes narrowed. "You could help."

He raised a brow. "You want me to search her suite?"

"No, no. I want you to keep Patrice busy for me, but be careful. She fancies you to replace my father."

That came as no surprise. "She wastes her time and mine."

Her mouth widened in a smile. Did his disinterest in Patrice please her? She immediately disabused him of that notion. "Good. Then you will not mind keeping her busy."

Brandon hid his displeasure. He could visit with Patrice to see this mystery answered. "You have one hour. And I want to know the results of my sacrifice. I will have my carriage at the corner of Kensington and the lane at four this afternoon. Meet me there."

"But my brother," she started.

"May come, too," Brandon finished. "Now go, for if you let me think of what my cousin has in store for me, I could well change my mind."

Celia went. She found Martin, explained the situation, and ferried him back to the schoolroom, then hurried down the stairs. Every step, her senses were just as attuned as they'd been in the garden searching for her brother. Only this time, she watched for other servants or her stepmother.

Lord Hartley must have been keeping Patrice busy, for she was able to reach the suite safely. She tapped at the door, but when no one answered, she dared to peer in. The ornate furniture stood empty, with neither people nor papers to make it interesting. The thick carpet and heavy upholstery sucked in all sounds. It seemed almost a sacrilege to enter. She went in anyway.

A while later, she trooped back to the schoolroom. Martin brightened seeing her. She shook her head. "If her ladyship keeps records, she locks them up tighter than the monarch's crown."

Martin made a face. "Wait until Lord Hartley hears he had to visit Mother for no reason."

Celia swallowed. Somehow, she thought his lordship would be even less forgiving than her brother suspected.

The hours crawled by until it was time for them to visit the park. John did not question her when she led them along the paths that came out at Hyde Park Corner. Martin, who knew what was planned, was more than happy to claim the location was his wish. It allowed him to ogle the passing horses. Celia felt less comfortable. The corner was exposed to every vehicle, rider, and passerby from Park Lane, Kensington Road, and Piccadilly. Every eye seemed fixed on her and every look disapproving. She felt as if she'd placed a placard on her chest proclaiming her perfidy like a hired clown hawking pies.

"Look at those grays," Martin exclaimed as one particularly fine carriage slowed at the corner. "A matched set of four. I'll drive one of those someday."

"No day like today," the marquess said from the window. The crested carriage, shiny in its black lacquer, stopped before them. "Mr. Rider, well met."

Celia's heart leapt. As always, he was dressed in black, from his top hat to the waistcoat she could see inside his tailored jacket. Why was it black made him look debonair and her look like a frumpy raven?

Martin crowded closer, and she had to grab him to keep him from falling under the wheels. "Did you mean that?" he chattered, his formalities forgotten in the promise of handling the reins. "May I really drive them?"

"Whenever you like," Lord Hartley assured him. "I am in your debt after all. I was just heading home. Join me."

"To Pellidore Place?" Celia asked, remembering the name from the butler's conversation. She mentally calculated the time it might take to drive to the country estate and back, surely an hour either way. "Mrs. Rider would be concerned."

"Then we shall send her word. John, is it not?"

John stepped forward smartly. "Yes, my lord."

Lord Hartley flipped him a coin that glimmered gold in the sunlight. "Tell my cousin that I have Martin with me and will return him this evening."

John caught the coin and nodded. "Right away, my

lord." He cast Celia a glance. She shrugged as if to say she thought she ought to stay with Martin. John nodded again and set off toward the house. Brandon's groom jumped down to open the door.

"I thought I was going to drive," Martin said suspiciously as the groom lowered the stair for them to climb in.

"And so you shall," the marquess promised, sitting back to give them room to enter. "However, city driving is dull with all the stops and starts. Join me until we get out of the traffic."

Celia accepted the groom's hand to enter the coach. Martin scampered up after her and sat on the blue velvet upholstery with so much enthusiasm that he nearly bounced. The marquess, seated across from them, tapped the panel above his head, and the coach sprang forward.

Martin kept up a constant stream of conversation about the equipage and the horses they passed. Celia only half listened. How could she confess that she still knew nothing? Perhaps he would remain interested in her brother's chatter. Glancing up at him, she sucked in a breath.

He was watching her.

She raised her head and gazed back at him in challenge. He smiled, and her irritation melted away. Did he know how very attractive he was when he smiled? She could not help but smile back.

"If you look out that window, Rider," he said, "you will see the Kensington grounds. They have fine mounts. Let me change seats with you. The view is worse from your side."

Martin eagerly sprang across the coach, and Lord Hartley shifted to sit next to Celia. His thigh grazed hers, and she swallowed, feeling warmth flame up her side. If she leaned over, her head would be against his chest. Would she hear that his heart beat as quickly as hers? What was she thinking? She held herself perfectly upright. He leaned back against the squabs and stretched out one arm along the top of the seat. His fingers brushed the hair at the back of her neck.

She would never survive this!

Her only choice was to keep her gaze fixed on the scenery. However, the houses and shops failed to take her mind off the man beside her. She tensed when he crossed his booted legs, seeing the muscle ripple in his thigh. She jerked when he bent past her to point something out to Martin, teasing her senses with his sandalwood cologne. She closed her eyes listening to his deep voice explain the difference between curricles and gigs and marveled that such a trivial subject could sound wonderful simply because he was discussing it. She was surely lost.

When she dared open her eyes again, she found that the shops had changed to estates and traffic was thinning. The carriage slowed and then stopped. Martin looked at Brandon.

The marquess nodded. "If you wish to try your hand at the reins, Rider, this is an ideal time."

Martin immediately slid to the door, which the groom snapped open. Her brother didn't wait for the step to be lowered; he leapt out and scurried to the driver's side.

"Excuse me," the marquess said, climbing down more slowly.

Celia sighed, leaning back against the squabs. Thank God for horses. Perhaps the marquess and her brother would both be so amused they would forget about her. Then she needn't report her fail-

ure, and she wouldn't be discomposed by his lordship's presence.

The coach shook as he climbed in to sit across
from her.

"My coachman has Martin," he said to Celia's look
of surprise. "The lad seems clever; he should catch
on quickly."

As if to prove his words, the carriage started out
again, even more smoothly than before. He relaxed
on the bench.

"So, what did you learn in Lady Honoria's suite?"

Celia sighed. Might as well get it over with. "Nothing. Even though I have seen her working on
accounts there, I found no papers. You say you know
the house. Where would she keep them?"

"Mayhap the suite has a safe. Did you check the
walls?"

She grimaced. "I didn't think. What a poor spy I
am!"

"Do not fault yourself. Even if you had found a
safe, you could not have seen inside. What will you
do now?"

"I wish I knew. There must be some way to prove
my stepmother's guilt!"

"Or innocence."

Celia frowned at him. "You seem certain of that.
What did she tell you when you visited?"

"The usual—she admires me, she needs money."

"You see! She needs money."

"She would not if she had stolen your fortune."

"Possibly," Celia allowed. "But my father told me
her father gambled away his inheritance. Perhaps it's
in her blood. Perhaps she's spent everything and still
needs more."

"Mayhap. I have heard she frequents gaming houses."

He still sounded unconvinced of Patrice's guilt. "I begin to think you help me only to prove her innocent," she accused him.

"I assist you," he said, leaning forward, "for the amusement. Read nothing more into it, Miss Rider."

His face was only a foot away from hers. If she leaned forward, she could plant a kiss on those stern lips. Would they warm if she did?

The coach lurched, and she fell forward. He caught her shoulders as if to keep her from being flung into his lap.

"I think Martin just took the reins," he explained, setting her back in place. She could only hope he would think her flaming face was a result of the bump.

The carriage picked up speed only to jerk into a slower pace. The vehicle weaved from one side of the road to the other, following an erratic path that crossed carriage ruts and shook the coach.

"Forgive me," he said after the first few moments. "I thought myself so clever for managing a moment alone with you."

"You will pay the penance for your deed, I fear," Celia replied. She wanted to laugh at the irony, but her stomach knocked at the back of her throat with each jolt.

"The cost is worth it," he said. "Are you certain you wish to marry Mr. Arlington?"

Celia stared at him. His face betrayed nothing beyond casual interest, but were his eyes just the bit darker? Did he want her for himself? The wildest hope surged through her, but unfortunately her stomach surged with it.

"Stop the carriage," Celia told him.

He shook his head. "You cannot fend me off so easily. He seems an unlikely fellow for you. Why did you decide to wed?"

"Stop the carriage," Celia demanded. Then she clamped both hands over her mouth to keep from spewing the contents of her stomach all over his elegant waistcoat.

He must have understood at last, for he rapped sharply on the panel above him.

"Relax," he urged as the carriage immediately righted and slowed. "Take in air through your nose. That's right."

A moment later, the groom opened the door. Celia pushed past him in a tumble of skirts, pulled herself up, and dashed for the ditch, where she promptly cast up her accounts.

She started to wipe the bile from her lips with the back of her hand. Brandon offered her his handkerchief.

She shook her head, not daring to look at him. Did she appear as foolish as she felt? She heard Martin call her name in concern. She stepped back from the ditch.

Lord Hartley caught her elbow. "Easy. You may well feel faint. Can you walk?"

She nodded. "Yes, thank you."

"Mayhap I should take you home." His voice was warm with compassion, and she dared a look. His face was drawn in a sympathetic smile. As before, the day brightened.

"The road is unfortunately too narrow to turn the carriage here," he continued. "A little ways farther and I think we can contrive. I swear I will interrogate you no more today, only say you will meet me in the garden tomorrow alone. I want to reunite you with Mr. Arlington."

Stanley had never looked less interesting. However, agreeing would allow her a few more moments alone with the marquess. "Of course, my lord," she murmured.

Lady Honoria eased herself back in the chair before her desk. One of the few things she had inherited from her family was the gout that had killed her grandfather. Some days it was all she could do to get out of bed.

"My accounts," she ordered Sally, who hurried to a landscape painting and swung it aside. Lady Honoria closed her eyes and listened to the soft whir of the lock. No fear Sally would betray her. The maid relished her power over the other servants too much. Lady Honoria could tell. She enjoyed feeding that sort of hunger.

Ah, but how much more satisfying to feed her own. She sighed contently as Sally spread her papers before her and set about laying out the quills and ink as well. Now, what had James said about those investments this morning?

Someone rapped at the door, and she waved Sally to answer it. All those lovely numbers danced across the page. She simply couldn't have enough of them, particularly as each one on her side of the ledger meant one less on theirs.

She glanced up to find Sally standing before her.

"It's Miss Patrice," she said, nose wrinkled in obvious distaste. "Shall I tell her you're busy?"

"Miss Patrice," Sally called her granddaughter, refusing to acknowledge the marriage and the child upstairs who was the result of it. Silly woman. Martin was the future, as long as Patrice and her step-daughter did not interfere.

"No," Lady Honoria replied. "I can spare a moment."

As soon as Patrice entered, Lady Honoria could tell her granddaughter was worried. Her delicate hands fluttered more than usual, and she trembled as she made her curtsey. That was one of the problems with Patrice: she was so very obvious. The Pellidore subtlety was completely missing.

"What is it, child?" she asked, dipping her quill in ink and preparing to return to the accounts.

"I do not like Miss Prim," Patrice said, hand knotted in the skirt of her pink cotton gown. "I want her dismissed."

How typical. She was too flighty by half. "You liked her when she first came with Martin. What has she done now?"

"I think," Patrice replied, pausing to lick her lips, "that she is setting her cap at Lord Hartley."

Lady Honoria smiled to herself. "I rather think it is the other way around. I heard that my nephew has taken an inordinate interest in her."

Patrice glanced at Sally, who raised her head so that the tip of her long nose tilted upward. Shame on Sally! Did she want Patrice to suspect how she bullied the other servants into telling tales? Patrice turned to face her.

"Then you can see why she must be dismissed," she persisted. "I thought *I* was to marry Lord Hartley."

"I doubt he is considering marrying Miss Prim. However, you are right that he needs no distractions. Still, I am not certain dismissal is the right course."

Patrice frowned. "Then what?"

A good question but one she was not prepared to answer. Patrice was obviously ignorant that the woman posing as Miss Prim was not the stern-faced matron her steward had hired. Lady Honoria was fairly certain of her identity. She should have known the girl would come looking after Sally destroyed her letter to Patrice. Best to keep her busy and underfoot.

"I shall think on it," she told Patrice. "You see, I have grown fond of Miss Prim. She is cheerful company when Sally is unavailable, and she always has the most interesting anecdotes."

Patrice pouted. "But you would not countenance a liaison between Lord Hartley and Miss Prim."

Lady Honoria offered her a comforting smile. "Of course not. He is, after all, family. Now, you better go. I expect young Mr. Carstairs. He will stay to dinner, and you may join us. In fact, it would please me if you were nice to him."

Patrice blinked. "Nice?"

Ah, but that was one way her granddaughter could be useful. James must be kept on a leash a while yet. "Yes, dear. He has worked very hard for our family—helping me manage the trust, managing your late husband's estate. He is a clever man, and he has mentioned a keen appreciation of you."

Patrice put on what was obviously her best smile. "I would be happy to help you entertain, Grandmother. Let me go change."

Lady Honoria nodded her permission and returned her gaze to her accounting sheets. Some things in life were meant to be savored. Because of their sojourn in Scotland, she'd been forced to wait over twenty years. Revenge would be sweet.

Eight

Celia waited for him the next day as she had promised. She'd even gone so far as to change into the traveling dress she'd worn when coming up from the country. It was not as stylish as her stepmother's gowns, being made by a country seamstress, but she fancied the long stripes of the gray-and-white cloth made her look taller. It was certainly better than her governess's gown. She should look nice for Stanley, she reasoned. Her desire to look more attractive had nothing to do with the marquess.

If only she could say the same for the rest of her feelings.

The memory of his warm smile had teased her all evening. When she slept, his dark-eyed gaze heated her dreams. She obviously had no moral fiber, for here she was betrothed and all she could think of was another man!

"Having second thoughts, Miss Rider?" the marquess asked, moving out of the shadow of the trees.

He *could* read her mind! She shook herself at the silly idea and offered him a smile. "No, my lord. Just a bit melancholy. Perhaps I miss the country more than I realized."

"Then allow me to reunite you with some of that

country," he said, offering her his arm. "Mr. Arlington awaits."

She wasn't sure why, but the mention of Stanley only lowered her spirits further. She accepted the marquess's arm and let him lead her through the rear gate to where his coach stood.

"I trust you will find this ride more enjoyable," he said as she settled herself on the bench and the coach set off.

She smiled at the reference to their last trip. "With my brother away from the reins, I should be fine."

"How did you manage to evade your duties?" He crossed one booted leg over the other and clasped it with both large hands.

She felt her smile widen, remembering. "Martin is riding with a groom. He is in alt, and my stepmother grudgingly allowed Miss Prim a few moments to herself."

"Then you will not mind taking extra time in our meeting."

She cocked her head. "No. Why?"

"I intend to learn the truth of your fortune, as I said."

She laughed. "If you can do that, I will think you possessed of magical powers, Lord Oberon."

He raised a brow. "You see me as a fairy?"

Her laugh bubbled up again, but somehow she thought he liked the sound. Perhaps it was the smile that tugged at the corner of his mouth.

"Have you ever read Shakespeare's *A Midsummer Night's Dream*?" she asked. "Puck you may call a fairy. Oberon is definitely something more."

He crossed his arms over his chest. "Indeed. Arrogant, demanding, controlling."

"If the shoe fits, my lord."

"Only too well, Miss Rider. And do I take it you see yourself as Titania, queen of the fairies?"

She shook her head. "And fall in love with an ass? No, thank you."

"A shame," he replied with a decided twinkle in his eye. "I was growing rather fond of Mr. Arlington."

Celia burst into laughter and was rewarded to see the smile spread on his face. It was like the sun coming out after a storm. Given his history, however, it was no wonder the moment came so rarely.

Her face must have betrayed her thoughts, for his smile disappeared as quickly as it had come. "What is it?"

"Nothing," she replied with a cheeriness she hoped sounded more sincere than it felt. She thought he might question her further, but he seemed to want to keep the mood as light as she did. He changed the subject, and they conversed in trivialities until the coach came to a stop.

Brandon watched the emotions play across Celia's animated face. Did she know how transparent she was? Every thought, every feeling, showed from those changeable eyes. It was like looking into her soul. Was Patrice blind not to have guessed her game, or was this openness something Celia reserved for him?

He did not want the idea to buoy him as much as it did. He didn't want to be attracted to her—not here, not now. With his birthday only months away, Lady Honoria would be watching him for any change in his behavior. She would not surrender the fortune until she was certain of him. Falling in love was not in the cards.

Yet how could he resist Celia? She was everything he wished he could be: open, loving, giving, spontaneous. Dressed as she was in the striped traveling dress, he could see that her figure was as perfect as the rest of her—lithe yet softly rounded in all the right places. A part of him prayed she was a cunning fraud so he'd have a reason to keep her at a distance.

As the coach stopped in front of the stone office building, Brandon moved to help her down. Stepping to the curb, she glanced up at the building before turning to him.

"We are to meet Stanley here?"

He could not help but notice the use of the fellow's first name. His grip tightened on her elbow. "Yes. You were here earlier, were you not?"

She frowned, glancing at the building again. "No. Unless it was when I was a child."

The day seemed colder, but Brandon could not allow it to deter him. "My mistake. Shall we?"

She didn't move, frown deepening. "I doubt you make many mistakes, my lord. The only word to describe you is perfection. Tell me the significance of this building."

He put his hand on the small of her back and felt her resist. Between the grip on her elbow and the hand on her back, he could easily have forced her forward.

He could not bring himself to do it.

"Celia!"

Arlington's joyous cry saved him. Her head jerked around to gaze past him, and he saw her smile widen.

"Stanley!"

Arlington was on them in a rush and enveloping Celia in his arms. Brandon had no choice but to step back. How dare the fellow handle her like that! His fists balled at his sides, and he forced his fingers to open. He took a deep breath. Must he endure watching her respond to another man's public caresses? The cool gray stone of the building seemed enveloped in a red haze. He took another deep breath and dared to look.

Celia was thumping Stanley on the shoulder, beaming. "You big clod! What do you mean following me all the way to London? Did you doubt I could care for myself?"

Stanley grinned. "You're glad I came, admit it! Besides, when you didn't come straight home, Father grew worried."

Celia snorted. "I might have known. When are you going to stand up to him, Stanley?"

Brandon stared at them. She spoke to him in the same way she did Martin! Where were the loverlike caresses? The exchanged glances? If the woman he loved had been missing for four weeks and presumed dead, he wouldn't be standing on a city street talking about his father.

As always, the mere thought of his father sobered him. He stepped forward and nodded toward Arlington.

"Mr. Arlington, good to see you again."

Stanley grabbed his hand and pressed it. "Thank you, my lord. You were as good as your word. I wouldn't have believed it, don't you know."

"Stanley," Celia scolded. "And what is this I hear about your accusing Lord Hartley of murder? I told you my stepmother took the fortune. His lordship had no reason to do away with me."

"I suggest we go inside," Brandon put in as Stanley hung his head. "You will draw a crowd."

Celia blushed and allowed him to take her elbow.
Stanley fell into step behind them.

What a shame she could not call Lord Hartley by
his first name as she did Stanley, Celia thought as she
paused to let the marquess open an interior door for
her. Perhaps she would call him Brandon in her
mind. That would certainly be no reflection on Stanley. While she was delighted to see her fiancé, she
could not help noticing the differences between
them. In the country, Stanley was the most eligible
bachelor for miles. Next to Brandon, he was like a
gelded plough horse to a thoroughbred stallion.

Her feelings were also a contrast. Looking at Stanley's beaming face was like putting on an old
slipper—comfortable, comforting. Looking at Brandon's handsome features was like getting ready to
run a race—her body tingled with excitement.
Standing between them made her positively edgy.

"Carstairs and Son," Stanley read off the door.
"Aren't those the men you came to see?"

Celia started. Both Brandon and Stanley were
watching her. Stanley's frown was curious, but Brandon's look was intent, as if a great deal depended on
her answer.

"Those were the names of my father's solicitors,"
she replied. "But they have offices in the Port of London."

"Mayhap they moved since you were a child,"
Brandon said, ushering her through the door.

"No. I saw them at their offices when I came to
London."

Brandon raised a brow but said nothing.

A balding clerk hurried forward. "Lord Hartley,

welcome. The Misters Carstairs are expecting you. May I announce your guests as well?"

Now Brandon regarded the clerk with that intent look. "Certainly. Miss Celia Rider and her fiancé, Mr. Stanley Arlington."

The clerk merely nodded, offered them all a polite smile, and hurried toward the office at the back of the suite.

"My lord?" Celia asked.

"All will come clear in a moment," he replied. He put out a hand to wave her forward.

She wasn't sure what to expect when she entered the room. Two men stood at the sight of her. One was elderly, short, and nearly bald. Wrinkles feathered his eyes as he smiled at her. When he bowed, she noticed his clothes seemed to date from an earlier time.

The other was young, considerably taller, and handsome. His tailored clothes were stylish, and his blue eyes assessing.

"Lord Hartley," he greeted. "Miss Rider, Mr. Arlington. How may we help you?"

"You can clear away a mystery for us," Brandon said. "Miss Rider is the rightful heir to David Rider's fortune. I would like to know why you will not give it to her."

Oh, but he was magnificent! Celia gazed up at him in wonder. His dark head was high, and his eyes flashed lightning. His words were polite, but the solicitor would have had to be deaf to miss the power behind them.

"I say, Celia," Stanley piped up as if he suddenly realized the significance of the moment, "are these the fellows who told you your fortune was gone?"

Celia shook her head. "I have never seen these gentlemen in my life."

"You see my concern, Carstairs," Brandon said. "Someone seems to have taken advantage of Miss Rider."

"So it would appear," the older gentleman said. He moved forward to take Celia's hand and bring it to his lips. "Miss Rider, a pleasure to see you again. You may not remember me, but I certainly remember you. David Rider was extremely proud of both his children and showed them off at the least provocation. And those are certainly your father's eyes."

"Thank you," Celia managed as he led her to a chair. She felt rather than saw Stanley take a place beside her. Brandon remained standing by the desk.

"Then you can confirm her claim?" he asked as the older man took a seat behind the desk. His son also remained standing, watching them all with a polished smile that was just this side of too bright.

"That, of course, will be a more formal undertaking, Lord Hartley," the younger Carstairs answered. "We will need a copy of her baptismal record, letters of introduction from prominent citizens who knew her father, a signed statement from Mrs. Rider. . . ."

"All that is secondary," his father insisted with a wave of his hand. "Your word is unassailable, my lord. You must be certain of the young lady's identity, or you would not have brought her forward. Miss Rider, what would you like to know?"

Celia put a hand to her head and rubbed her temple. "A very great deal, I suppose. If you are Mr. Carstairs, who did I meet on Wapping High Street?"

"Wapping High Street?" Carstairs frowned in obvious confusion.

Brandon leaned forward. "Miss Rider wrote to

your firm, at an address she recalled from her father."

"Ah," Carstairs said with a nod. "We moved from that address many years ago, my dear. Letters are rarely forwarded. Your missive must have been misplaced."

"No, you answered," Celia told him. "Or rather someone did." She opened her reticule and pulled out the letter, which she kept with her lest someone in the house find it and suspect her. She opened it to hand it to the solicitor.

Carstairs took one look at the letter, and his face darkened. He thrust the missive at his son, who merely raised his brows as if surprised.

"You have indeed been the victim of a cruel prank, Miss Rider," the father said. "I am sorry to say that that is our stationery. However, that is not my handwriting."

"Nor mine," the son assured her.

"May I?" Brandon took the letter and read it.

"The man I met when I followed those instructions," Celia told them, "said that my father's fortune was gone."

"Ridiculous!" the older Carstairs exclaimed.

"Indeed," the younger added. "Your fortune is in good hands, Miss Rider. Your stepmother approved some excellent investments that increased the value significantly."

"My stepmother?" Celia stared at him in amazement. Before he could answer, Stanley clapped her on the shoulder.

"You see? Everything is fine. Your fussing was for naught."

She glared at him. "So it would seem, though I do not need a reminder of what a fool I have been."

"Hardly a fool," Brandon said before Stanley could do more than open his mouth to protest. "Someone went to great lengths to make you think your fortune was gone."

"But who?" Celia frowned. "And why?"

"We may never know the answers to those questions," James Carstairs said. "We should simply be grateful to Lord Hartley for bringing you to us so that we might rectify matters."

Gratitude was the least of the emotions she felt toward Lord Hartley. At the moment, it was impossible to sort them out, though she could not deny her relief in knowing the money was still available to her. She did notice, however, that Lord Hartley had pocketed her letter.

"Never mind all that," Stanley said beside her. "Let's get down to business. How much is she worth?"

"Stanley!" Celia scolded, feeling her face heat.

Carstairs smiled, though his son looked less amused. "A logical question, Mr. Arlington. James, if you would be so kind?"

"Of course, Father. Excuse me a moment."

"You shall see that he has taken very good care of you, Miss Rider," Carstairs said as his son left and they waited for his return. "Your father's estate was his first major task as a solicitor. He's worked very hard to be worthy of it."

The younger man returned with a thick portfolio. He set it on the desk, chose an accounting sheet, and handed it to Celia. Stanley looked over her shoulder and whistled.

"What does this mean?" Celia asked.

"I haven't a clue," Stanley admitted, "but I like all those zeros behind the numbers."

"Allow me." Brandon moved to look over her

shoulder as well, bending to put his head beside hers. His breath was a caress on her cheek. She could barely concentrate on what he was saying.

"This is your father's initial investment in his firm," he explained, long finger pointing at a set of numbers. "And here is where he sold it."

"Patrice insisted on it," Celia said, remembering. "A gentleman should not be in trade, it seems, even in shipping."

He nodded as if in understanding, and a curl of his dark hair brushed her temple as softly as the kiss of a butterfly.

"Down here," he continued, "is the series of investments Mr. Carstairs mentioned. Interesting choices—easy to sell when money was needed."

She felt him glance up and followed his gaze to James Carstairs. The young solicitor inclined his head as if in agreement. Brandon returned to his perusal of the accounts.

"Even considering that your share is a quarter of the value, I see that Mr. Arlington's whistle was merited. You are a wealthy young woman, Miss Rider."

He sounded a bit surprised by that fact. Hadn't he believed her when she'd told him her father was rich? Or did he suspect that the money was still a sham somehow?

He straightened. "And I take it my second cousin's quarter is still available to her?"

The older man glanced up at his son. James held himself still. "Mrs. Rider is in charge of her portion, my lord. You would have to ask her. Client privilege, you understand."

His father frowned, but Brandon inclined his head graciously. "What is next for Miss Rider, then?"

Carstairs senior recovered himself. "We will, of

course, go through a more formal process as my son mentioned. I am certain I can count on your cooperation, Miss Rider."

"Of course," Celia said readily. If these gentlemen were willing to hand over a considerable amount of money, she would certainly go along with the game. "But I gave my identification papers to the other Mr. Carstairs. I shall have to write to Somerset for another copy."

"Allow us to do so," the younger Carstairs said with his polished smile. "It is the least we can do after what you have been through."

Celia agreed. They spent a few more minutes in pleasantries, with both Carstairses going out of their way to assure her that her troubles were over.

It was not until she left the building with Stanley and Lord Hartley that she realized her troubles were just beginning.

Nine

Stanley could not seem to believe her good fortune. "How can I thank you, my lord?" he said as they neared the carriage. "First you find Celia and then her fortune. You work magic!"

"So I have heard," Brandon replied, but she caught that hint of a smile and knew that Stanley's enthusiasm amused him. A shame she was not so easily amused at the moment.

"My father can say all he likes now," Stanley continued. "Let him push Violet Thornhill at me. I shall snap my fingers in her face. *I'm* to marry an heiress."

"Leave off, Stanley," Celia snapped. "You do neither yourself nor your father a service with such talk."

He stopped to gape at her, pale green eyes wide. "Well, I like that. Find yourself an heiress and take on airs. Perhaps I don't need you either."

"Oh, Stanley, honestly." She stopped to face him. "I cannot see this situation as such a blessing. For one thing, someone wants to keep the fortune from me, and I will not be easy in my mind until I know who and why. For another, I appear to be stuck in London until all the papers are found acceptable. You, however, can certainly go home."

She recognized the set of his jaw and resigned herself to a row. "Perhaps I will," he said, "and perhaps

I won't. Strikes me I've spent my time here all wrong. Instead of worrying about a pert young miss who is obviously smarter than I am—even though I was the one to tell her nothing was wrong—I should have been kicking up my heels. After all, I am *supposed* to be leg shackled soon."

"Excellent idea, Mr. Arlington," Brandon said quietly before she could snap a response to his ridiculous threat. "Allow me to make a few suggestions. Excuse us a moment, Miss Rider, and then I will see you home."

Celia nodded, not trusting herself to speak. She watched as he led Stanley a short distance away. She could hear nothing, but Stanley paled, nodded shakily several times, and promptly took himself off. Brandon returned to her side.

"What did you say to him?" she asked as the marquess led her to the coach.

"Nothing of any significance."

She doubted that. The marquess was a man of few words, she'd noticed, and he made those few count. Whatever he'd said, she hoped Stanley would take it to heart. She had too much on her mind to deal with him at the moment.

She waited until they had climbed in and the coach set off before questioning Brandon further. "How did you know about the fortune?" she asked as he leaned back against the squabs.

"I realized that you and Mr. Carstairs had conflicting stories of your father's fortune. It made sense to connect the two of you and see how to rectify the situation."

"What of the false Mr. Carstairs?"

His look darkened, and it was as if the air had chilled. "I will look into the matter."

"Is that why you kept my letter?" she asked with a frown. "You certainly proved your ability to solve a mystery, my lord, yet I cannot see why you should involve yourself further. You said you wished to be certain Mr. Carstairs was legitimate. He appears to be. Your duty is done."

"And if I choose to do you a service, why would you argue?"

"Because I am perverse?" She grinned at him. "Besides, I am already in your debt. Help me further and how can I possibly repay you?"

He was silent, watching her across the coach, and she was suddenly aware that they were all alone. No one would know if they offered sweet words of longing, if they touched, if they kissed. Her heart sped, and she swallowed.

He leaned forward, and she waited, hoping, praying, that his lips would meet hers. Just once, just to remember, just for the shivering, heated pleasure it would surely bring.

"You can start," he said in his deep, slow, rich voice, "with the truth. Tell my cousin who you are."

She blinked. He held her gaze as if trying to elicit a promise. As her heartbeat slowed, she managed to find her voice. "I . . . I suppose there's no reason not to."

"None that I can see. She has handled your fortune well, against all odds. She is guilty only of forgetting that you are grown, which seems a failing of all those who rear children. You cannot fault her for it."

He was being reasonable, and she was in no mood for it. "Can I not? You did not live in exile for four years."

"Mayhap I did not." He stopped for a moment and frowned. "Why are you smiling at me like that?"

She immediately felt foolish and dropped her gaze. "Forgive me. I simply enjoy the way you speak—slow, warm, rich. It puts me in mind of melted chocolate." Dear God, was that the best she could do to flirt with him? She sounded insipid! She glanced up and found he was trying not to smile again. A sense of power curled up from her toes to her top. She could, at least, make him smile. She didn't think she shared that distinction with many others.

"You are right, of course," she offered. "I will tell Patrice as soon as I return to the house."

"Good." He settled back against the squabs once more.

The conversation was no more than pleasant all the way back to Mayfair. She watched her opportunity to touch him slip away as sand through an hour glass. Perhaps it was just as well. Nothing could come from her attraction to him. She was promised, after all. It was not until the carriage drew up to the rear entrance to the garden that she realized this might be the last time she saw him. If the imposter solicitor was merely a prank, Lord Hartley had no more reason to call on her.

"Will I see you again?" The words came out in a panic, and she clamped her mouth shut lest something else pop out as well. What, would she cry out her admiration like a love-struck schoolgirl? She was engaged to Stanley. She had no business dreaming of how it would feel to kiss Lord Hartley.

He was watching her again. "If I learn anything concerning your false solicitor, I will send word. Otherwise, we may meet, through my cousin."

Socially, he meant. No more secret meetings. No more murmured conversations. No more having him all to herself. "Of course. Silly of me."

"You will return to Somerset shortly, will you not?"

Did she hear a suggestion in those words? She searched his face, all but begging him with her eyes. *Say you want me to stay! Tell me you need me more than Stanley does.* His face was as still as ever. She dropped her gaze to where her hands clenched in the lap of her gown. "Yes, of course. Somerset."

"Then I wish you every joy. May I kiss you farewell?"

Her gaze flew up to his once more. It was customary, after all, to kiss the bride, and he would not be coming to Somerset to the wedding, for she would never have the courage to invite him. She nodded mutely and turned her face to offer him her cheek.

His hand came up to cup her chin, the leather of the glove warm against her skin. Gentle pressure turned her to face him. His eyes were as intense as midnight. Before she could ask his meaning, his mouth descended on hers.

It was as warm and sweet as eating sun-drenched strawberries from the vine. Like an eager child, she wanted more. She wanted him to fill every nook and cranny of her being until she wasn't sure where she ended and he began, and she didn't much care. Surely if there were such a thing as perfection, it was this closeness she felt with him.

When he broke from her, she had to take a deep breath to regain her senses.

His eyes were stormy, his breath rough. By God, she had affected him! She, little Celia Rider, had rattled the great Marquess of Hartley. What had happened to Lord Heartless? To the omnipotent Lord Oberon? Her hand flew to her swollen lips in wonder.

He fumbled with the door latch. "You must go."

Was it her imagination or was his voice even deeper than usual? Could it be he truly cared? She could not let things end like this. Launching herself at him, she returned the kiss he had given her. Her hands tangled in his dark hair, feeling his curls tumble like skeins of silk through her fingers. His hands gathered her close, pulling her onto his lap. The hard, long length of him pressed against her, his breath as ragged as her own.

"Celia." Her name was a groan against her lips. He pushed her back. "This is madness."

As soon as he said the word, all color drained from his face, and she saw the unmistakable pall of fear cloud his eyes.

"My fault," she said breathlessly, pulling back from him. "I am too impetuous. Any gentleman would react that way if a young lady threw herself at him. You are not to blame."

He caught her shoulders. "Stop. I wanted this as much as you did. Mayhap more. However, I am the older and wiser and once your guardian. This is wrong."

Then why did it feel so right? She tightened her mouth to keep from asking. She knew why. She was engaged. She nodded and sucked in a breath. "Forgive me. Thank you again for all you did for me. Good-bye, Lord Hartley."

She sprang from the coach before he could stop her.

Brandon sank back against the cushions. He heard the door snap shut behind Celia. He could not, would not, go after her. If he did, they would both be lost. He tapped on the panel and told his coachman to take him home.

Had any woman ever moved him so? He could not remember letting one close enough to find out. A kiss had seemed so trivial, but the moment his lips met hers, he knew that a kiss was the least of what he wanted from her. When she'd flung herself at him, it had been all he could do not to make love to her then and there. He wanted to taste her, to touch her, to feel her touching him. His desire was so overpowering, it scared him. The only chance for peace was to forget he'd ever met Celia Rider.

Yet thoughts of her teased him all the way home. She was betrothed. He could make Stanley disappear. She was related. The church would not disapprove of the union. He was named as her guardian. She was of age. He dared not let anyone close until the fortune was his. Try as he might, he could find no argument to counter that.

When he reached the seclusion of his bedchamber, he leaned his head against the post of the bed. Why was it so hard to find that place of stillness inside? He'd learned long ago to isolate himself there, his dreams, his feelings, his soul. Now it eluded him, and he knew he would have precious little time to find it. Gregory, his valet, would appear any moment to help him change for dinner.

All his staff saw to his every comfort with alacrity and deference. A few who had been there when his father died still tiptoed past him as if expecting him to fly up in a rage at them for doing no more than their normal duties. He was thankful he didn't remember seeing his father that way. They'd kept him away that night for fear of what the man might do to him.

God save him from such a fate.

He needed air. Going to the window, he jerked it open and stuck out his head, letting the breeze cool his face. The smell was crisp, clean, pure. It reminded him of Celia.

"What are you doing?"

Brandon turned to eye his uncle, who stood in the door. His long face was pale above the dark blue of his jacket.

"Just letting in the light, Uncle. We have entirely too much darkness here, don't you think?" The last phrase sounded exactly like Stanley Arlington, and Brandon grimaced.

Edmund moved into the room, steps slow and stately. "I find the house well lit for our purposes. You were absent from Parliament again today. It was remarked on."

"How did they get on when I was in Scotland?"

"You offer no explanation?"

"I was detained elsewhere."

"How long do you intend to dance to Miss Rider's tune?"

Brandon blew out a breath. "I swear, Uncle, you are worse than a Cheltenham gossip. Will you leave me nothing to myself?"

Edmund shook his head, easing himself onto the armchair by the fireplace. "I cannot. I promised your father to see you inherit. I have done what I must to keep that vow, even to taking you to another country. You cannot begrudge me a scold, however little I relish it."

Brandon chuckled wryly. "You scold me too often for me to think you truly hate the role."

His uncle sighed. "I hate the fact that I anger you. Anger is not something you can afford."

"Is that why I work so hard to maintain this fiction of a life? So that I can 'afford' anger?"

"You know as well as I do what good your behaving to perfection can do. Honoria controlled the fortune all these years. I am ashamed to say I let her do it. Now she seems to think of nothing else. Sometimes I think she hated your father and me for coming along after her. But for us, she would have had everything."

"She seems to have done well enough," Brandon pointed out.

"She has amassed considerable power. Why do you think young Carstairs sniffs around her so? He smells a seat in the House and from there a title."

"He is welcome to them so long as he manages our estate."

"Perhaps, but you will never see a penny if we are not careful. Less than three more months, Hart. Is that so much to ask when we have come so far?"

"No." Brandon leaned against the windowsill. "Yet I tell you, at times, even a day longer seems an eternity."

His uncle rose to come lay a hand on his shoulder. The touch was light but firm. Brandon stood a little straighter under it.

"I know, my boy," his uncle murmured, dark eyes warm and bright. "But you have studied and trained for this time. You have no reason not to hope for victory. You have spoken before Parliament; you have gambled at White's; you have danced at Almack's. Never once have you betrayed yourself. No one knows you well enough to even guess."

"You see that as a comfort. I assure you, it is a curse."

His uncle sucked in a breath. "You cannot think to tell her. She cannot mean so much to you."

"No, she cannot, even if I might wish her to mean a very great deal."

The warmth vanished from his uncle's eyes, leaving his face gray, cold, and implacable. "You are not the type to seduce a schoolgirl."

The words knifed him. Anger pounded in his temples. "I did not seduce her, and she is hardly a schoolgirl. Did you have me followed?"

"I pay the servants well," Edmund replied, but his gaze did not meet Brandon's outraged look. "Your sudden obsession concerns us all."

"Does it indeed?" His voice came out icy, and he balled his fists at his sides. "Then feel free to assure your creatures that I am not . . ."

"Obsessed?"

"Don't give me words!"

"Even when I know you cannot say them?"

"Even then. I have assisted Miss Rider in finding her fortune and ensuring that mine is in good hands. However much I might wish to do otherwise, I am sending her home. I know my duty, Uncle. I am no fool."

"And you think she will give up so easily? It seems to me that she has you where she wants you. Was not her tale of a lost fortune simply a way to pull you into her orbit?"

"Enough." Brandon's hands were shaking as the emotions surged through him. "You know nothing of her, her cleverness, her kindness, her joy of life. You cannot judge her."

"And you can after a visit in the park and a few drives?"

"More than you think." He brushed past Edmund before his anger swallowed him whole. There was only one place to escape in this house. He yanked off his coat and strode from the room.

On his way up the stairs, he passed a maid and nodded. She squeaked in dismay, but whether it was from something in his face or his state of undress, he didn't know. He unbuttoned the waistcoat and pulled open his cravat as he walked down the corridor. By the time he reached the door to the training salon, he could drape both over the waiting dumb valet. His shirt followed.

His footsteps echoed on the hard wood of the floor. In the corner hung the stuffed leather bag, tall, bulky, a bit uneven from previous sessions. He had heard of few like it in England. It was a Scottish farmer who had shown him the secret. The same man had kept Brandon's secret, that he slipped away from the estate from time to time and joined the village men in their friendly brawls. Then Edmund had not been quite so jumpy and less likely to have him followed.

Now he jabbed at the bag and set it swaying. Bringing up his other hand, fisted to protect his face, he moved around the bag, driving his punches home. The rhythm came naturally, focusing him, shutting away other pains, other dreams.

Jab, jab, right cross, left cross, right upper cut, left. The chains groaned as the bag ricocheted off the wall behind it. Again. That for the servants who were so afraid of losing their positions they spied on their master. That for an uncle who remembered a promise of survival but chose to ignore the affection that prompted it. That for a man who couldn't allow himself the luxury of telling them all to go to hell.

Sweat ran down his bare chest, his breath came in gasps, and blood dribbled from cracked knuckles.

The poison in his system didn't lessen. He'd let it go too long this time, kept too much bottled up. Small wonder he couldn't resist Celia's openness.

The thought of her stayed his fists. The bag swung to a stop. He leaned his face against it, the leather cool against the damp of his skin. Edmund was wrong about Celia. He had to be. She had never set out to trap anyone. All she had wanted was her fortune.

So that she could marry Stanley Arlington.

He leaned back and slammed his fist into the bag, ramming it into the wall behind. Plaster cracked, and wood splintered. Brandon turned and walked away.

Ten

Celia's evening fared even worse than Brandon's. She had barely managed to get through the rear gate and into the garden before her feelings overwhelmed her. What was wrong with her? A bargain was a bargain. She was going to marry Stanley, and he would logically expect his bride to come to him a virgin. Yet she'd actually courted seduction! One simply did not throw oneself at Oberon without repercussions. She was lucky he was such a gentleman.

Why couldn't she have met him sooner? She could have had a real London season, and they could have met properly. He could have courted her, met her father, charmed her chaperone. She would have been dressed in something far prettier than black bombazine, and she could have met him at the park, at parties, and at the opera without fear that someone might see them. They might have had a chance to fall in love.

She took a deep breath. She was not one for might-have-beens. What was, was, and it was up to her to make the best of it. She would keep her promise to tell Patrice the truth. Then she would get on with her life.

Unfortunately, her stepmother was out, and Martin had returned. With John needed for dinner preparation, she was forced to play governess for a while longer. They had just finished dinner when John appeared in the schoolroom door. She thought he must have come for the dishes, but he moved to her side and bent to speak quietly to her.

"Her ladyship asked for you," he said. "Watch yourself. Mrs. Watson says she's in a temper."

Celia grimaced. If Lady Honoria was in a bad mood now, how much worse would it get when she learned Celia had been running about London masquerading as a governess?

Murmuring her thanks to John, she hurried to her ladyship's suite. The sneer on Sally's face told Celia that Miss Prim was in terrible trouble. She supposed a whole afternoon off was a bit much. How ironic that Lady Honoria would sack her now that she no longer had to pretend she needed the position.

Lady Honoria sat at the polished desk before the window, her rose silk gown a splash of color against the dark. Papers lay scattered across the desk top. Celia caught herself trying to read them upside down. She barely deciphered the word "liquidate'" before she remembered she no longer needed to be concerned about the fortune. She hastily dropped a curtsey. "You called for me, your ladyship?"

Lady Honoria looked her up and down. Celia held very still, praying that nothing about the striped traveling dress was out of place, worn, or dirty. Perhaps she still had time to reinstate herself in the lady's good graces. She was going to need all the allies she could get.

Lady Honoria sniffed. "I certainly hope you wore something else when you ran off today. Patrice should dress you better as her stepdaughter."

Celia's head snapped up. "You knew?"

Lady Honoria glanced over her shoulder at Sally. "I told you she would not try to lie."

"Yes, ma'am," Sally said with such arch superiority that Celia wished she *had* thought to lie.

Lady Honoria affixed Celia with a narrow-eyed glance. Her ladyship's eyes were as dark and disconcerting as jet buttons on a christening gown. Lie to Lady Honoria? What was she thinking? That would be as bad as lying to Lord Oberon. Both would surely know instantly.

"Why would you do such a thing?" her ladyship demanded. "Do you delight in plaguing your family?"

"No, ma'am," Celia replied, mind whirling. Though she'd feared discovery, she'd never actually considered what she could say if she was caught. She could hardly tell Lady Honoria she'd thought them all conspiring to steal her fortune. "I was unsure of my welcome," she tried. "You had not called me up from the country after my father's death."

"Thought you might see something of the world, eh?" Lady Honoria said. "Much as I admire your spirit, I must deplore your methods. I must also deplore the fact that you were alone with my nephew several times over the last few days."

No reason to lie about that either. The old woman would surely enjoy putting her to the rack and screws. "Yes, ma'am."

Lady Honoria waved a beringed hand. "You may stop acting like a servant. You are my great-granddaughter by marriage. I expect you to call me 'Grandmother' as Patrice does."

She would surely gag. "As you wish," she managed.

"What do you think of Hartley?"

Now there was a loaded question if she ever heard one, ready to blow up in her face whatever way she answered it. If she said she disliked him, Lady Honoria would be certain to know she lied. If she said she adored him, Lady Honoria would likely read far more into the statement. She stood straighter.

"Lord Hartley is a fine and noble gentleman," she said.

Lady Honoria rolled her eyes. "And very fine weather we are having today and praise God the Regent has good health. If I wanted such bland platitudes, I could have called for your stepmother. I want to know what you think of him as a man."

She could feel the heat in her cheeks. "I am certain I have no business thinking of his lordship as a man. If you know who I am, you also likely know that I am engaged."

Lady Honoria puffed out a disdainful breath. "I heard some such nonsense. Who is he?"

"Mr. Stanley Arlington, of the Arlingtons of Somerset." That ought to give her pause. Stanley's father was well respected, across several counties. He'd been a magistrate. His estates were expansive. He knew people in Parliament.

"Never heard of them," Lady Honoria said. "Besides, you did not have my permission to accept his offer; therefore, the engagement is null and void."

Celia's spirits soared. Could it be that easy? She could simply say she hadn't known what she was doing and beg off? Immediately her conscience nagged. She'd made her choice. It had been a good one at the time. She couldn't help it that she was now of a different opinion.

"I am of age, your ladyship," she said, "however much your granddaughter wishes to forget that. I can enter into a marriage contract without your permission."

Lady Honoria's eyes narrowed again. "Look at her, Sally. I do believe she is proud of herself."

"Like a peacock, your ladyship." The abigail shook her head so that her iron gray curls bounced. Celia bit her cheeks to keep from uttering a sharp retort.

"You told me yourself, girl," Lady Honoria said, "that Hartley had no interest in Patrice. Could that be because he is already interested in you?"

She could only wish as much. "I would not presume to guess Lord Hartley's feelings. You will have to ask him yourself."

"I may do that. Does he frighten you?"

At the moment, the only thing that frightened her was that she might show her growing temper to Lady Honoria. "No, ma'am."

"Good." She cocked her head. "Do I frighten you?"

Another question where the wrong answer would likely see her roasted. "Yes, ma'am."

Lady Honoria laughed. "You see, Sally. Celia is a good girl. She knows what is best for her. Send someone for my granddaughter."

Celia stiffened. Much as she disliked Patrice, her stepmother deserved better than to have Lady Honoria break Celia's news. As Sally hurried from the room, she humbled herself to go to Lady Honoria's side. "Please, your ladyship, let me explain the situation to Patrice."

"I should like to hear you do that. She fancies him for herself, you know."

"Yes, ma'am. But as I told you, he does not return her sentiments."

"Doubtless. What were you thinking, to meet my nephew in secret, repeatedly?"

"Hardly secret meetings if you discovered them so

easily," she pointed out. "And until today, I had Martin with me."

"A small child is hardly a chaperone."

"Have you ever tried seduction with one watching?"

Lady Honoria's mouth quirked, and for a moment Celia thought she might laugh. Instead, she shook her head.

"You may joke all you like, but the fact of the matter is that I have let this situation go on far too long. You should not even be living in this house."

Celia gasped. "You would cast me out?"

Before the woman could answer, Sally returned with Patrice. Her stepmother was dressed to go out for the evening, lavender satin gown rustling with each step. White ostrich plumes waved from the pile of golden curls atop her head. She looked torn between annoyance at the interruption and fear of Lady Honoria. Lady Honoria's wrinkled face, however, was drawn in censure.

Celia's mind raced with her heart. What was she to do if Lady Honoria threw her out? Would Mr. Carstairs advance her living money before he had her papers in hand? Would her reputation be damaged if she was forced to live in a hotel? She stepped away from Lady Honoria feeling as if she walked to her execution.

"You wished to see me, Grandmother?" Patrice asked, frowning at Celia as if surprised to see her there.

"I most certainly did. Your 'Miss Prim' has a confession."

Patrice gasped, hand going to the lace bodice of her gown. "She married Lord Hartley."

Celia blinked. "No. Not that." Patrice relaxed, but Celia could feel them all looking at her. She squared her shoulders. "Mrs. Rider, Patrice"—she swallowed her pride,—"Mother, I lied to you. I'm not Martin's governess Miss Prim. I'm your stepdaughter, Celia."

Patrice's frown returned. "You are?"

"She is," Lady Honoria said with finality. "And I have forgiven her for not trusting us with her identity. However, I hope you can see that her masquerade presents us with a problem, Patrice, a problem I am counting on you to help solve."

The problem of a suitable punishment, Celia was sure. She held herself still, waiting.

Patrice turned her frown on her grandmother. "You are?"

"I am. Celia has come of age. You know what that means."

Patrice looked blank for a moment, then brightened. "Certainly. She must marry."

Celia grimaced. Why didn't Lady Honoria get on with it? "I am engaged already," she told her stepmother.

"You are?"

"She is," Lady Honoria insisted. "And we must do something about it."

"As I have explained to Lady Honoria," Celia said, seeing the growing excitement on her stepmother's face, "there is nothing to be done. I intend to hold to my word."

"Why, of course," Patrice agreed, clasping her gloved fingers before her as if to keep them from trembling in her glee. "But something most certainly must be done. There are betrothal breakfasts to host, the trousseau to be gathered, a wedding to be planned. I know all about those things!"

Celia shook her head. "I need none of that. Stanley and I plan a quiet ceremony in the village church in Wenwood."

Patrice looked ready to protest, but Lady Honoria spoke first. "My great-granddaughter," she said, "deserves better. Patrice, I will stand for nothing less than a full come out."

Celia stared at her. A come out? Was she mad?

"She needs a new wardrobe," Lady Honoria declared. "And I want her installed in the bedchamber next to yours, Patrice. And, Sally, I insist that you do something about that hair."

Sally's eyes glinted. "With pleasure, your ladyship."

Celia's hands flew to her head. "Now, wait a moment . . ."

"No time to wait!" Patrice declared joyfully. She hurried forward and enveloped Celia in a maternal hug that nearly knocked her off her feet. "Oh, welcome home, daughter! I cannot wait to bring you out in style!"

Patrice almost didn't go out that night. Celia was home from school and ready to be married! She was so excited she could barely think. She didn't understand why Celia had pretended to be a governess, but that didn't really matter. What did matter was that Celia didn't seem nearly as affected. In fact, the girl seemed a bit distant when Patrice took her up to the schoolroom to see Martin and gather her things.

"We shall fix this chamber up just the way you like it," she promised Celia when she conducted her to the room next to her own. "Those blue hangings will be down tomorrow. I am certain we can find something pink on Bond Street."

"Blue will be fine," Celia said. Silly thing. As if the

bed hangings mattered now that she had her daughter with her.

She'd attempted to have a civilized conversation, but Celia seemed tired and asked merely to be allowed to retire early. With the evening stretching before her, it was only natural that she call for the carriage and go out.

And just as natural for her to go to Madam Zala's.

She liked the establishment. There were always more men than women, and usually people were kind to her. The air hummed with a warm murmur of conversation, and even the smoky air seemed comforting as it wrapped around her.

James Carstairs had first introduced her to the place when Grandmother had insisted she allow him to escort her. She was still fascinated by the soft shush of the cards sliding across the table. Tonight, however, she could not seem to keep those cards in the right order. She watched as the last of her allowance disappeared. Whoever contrived such a silly game as trying to make twenty-one points out of a set of cards anyway?

"Perhaps something to drink, Mrs. Rider?" The owner of the establishment was at her elbow and steering her away from the vingt-et-un table. Patrice felt a moment of pique. It simply wasn't fair. All her life she'd done everything her grandmother asked of her—worn the clothes she picked, flirted with the men she dictated, lived in the houses she preferred. She'd more than done her duty, and where had it gotten her? Her mother was long dead, David was dead, her Martin seemed unsure of her devotion, and her Celia couldn't be bothered to talk to her.

And here was Madam Zala, tall, successful, beautiful even if her golden hair color came from a bottle. She needn't marry for money. The black silk dress spoke of wealth to spare. Patrice was willing to wager that the woman played by no one's rules. Unfortunately, she had nothing left to wager.

The woman poured her a glass of Madeira. Only men drank Madeira; everyone knew that. Patrice arched a brow.

"I fear we are out of negus at the moment," Madam Zala said smoothly. "I could get you a glass of champagne if you prefer."

Patrice shook her head. "No, thank you. I suppose I should leave. I seem to be out of funds. Unless you would wish to advance me credit again?"

She glanced at the woman hopefully. Madam Zala's smile was tight. "I would not be in business if I let advances go so high. However, I may know of a way you can earn money."

Patrice drew herself up to her full height. "A lady does not earn money. She marries it."

Madam Zala's painted mouth quirked. "Then I wish you the best of luck, Mrs. Rider."

"Mrs. Rider?"

Patrice turned to see a tall, broad-shouldered young man standing behind her. His clothing was not in the first stare of fashion, but the brown coat and tan breeches were acceptable. He had a long face with a nose that ended in a flat little knob. It only added to his charm. She felt her pulse quicken, but she kept her head high. "Have we been introduced?"

"Allow me," their hostess put in. "Mrs. Patrice Rider, may I present Mr. Stanley Arlington. Mr. Arlington, Mrs. Rider."

He grinned. "I knew it as soon as I heard the name. I'm to be your son-in-law, don't you know."

As Madam Zala drew away, Patrice frowned. "No, I know no such thing. You must have me confused with someone else."

His grin faded. "By your leave, I truly doubt that. I have seen you before, from a distance. My father always said David Rider married the most beautiful woman in London, and I doubt there can be two such beauties named Patrice."

"Why, thank you." Patrice beamed. "How very nice to make your acquaintance, Mr. Arlington. Do I understand, then, that you are to marry my Celia?"

"I am," he said proudly. Then he bent to offer her a green-eyed wink. "Though if I had seen her mother up close before I offered, I might be marrying someone else entirely, don't you know."

He was flirting with her. How very delightful. She loved flirting; it was one arena in which she felt confident. "And if I had met you before Celia did, you might be marrying elsewhere as well," she said, gazing up at him from under lowered lashes.

Stanley stared at her as if she had struck him over the head with a mallet. She'd seen that look before, from gentlemen who were too shy to flirt. She'd frightened him. She offered him a gossamer giggle. "Come now, Mr. Arlington. I vow a gentleman of your charm is rarely tongue-tied. Surely you can speak with me. We are, after all, nearly related."

He nodded, seeming to recover himself. "Why, so we are, don't you know." He glanced about. "Are you here alone? Or is Lord Hartley escorting you?"

She smiled up at him, fluttering her lashes. "I appear to be all alone, Mr. Arlington, and I could certainly use an escort. My carriage will not come for me for another hour, and I seem to have run out of funds."

He snapped her a bow. "Your servant, ma'am. It would be my pleasure to escort you until your carriage arrives. And my pockets are open to you."

Patrice gazed up at him. She knew she still didn't have everything straight. Celia was supposed to be engaged to a young man from Somerset, not a presentable gentleman from London. Mr. Arlington's tale could be designed to trick her. However, he did have the loveliest smile, and his offer to fund her gambling was the nicest thing anyone had ever done for her. She liked nice men.

She accepted his arm. "I would be delighted, Mr. Arlington. Lead me where you wish."

Eleven

Someone was after Celia's fortune. Brandon could reach no other conclusion. He visited the address on Wapping High Street and found an empty office. Scars in the wood beside the door showed where something had recently been pried away. A name plaque, perhaps? The brass plate around the door knob and lock was also scarred. Had someone forced an entry?

He spoke with the shopkeepers on either side. One vaguely remembered someone taking the space for a short time. He took the name of the building owner, who was incensed to learn that someone had used the space without his knowledge. He promised Brandon to secure the door more strongly in the future.

The perpetrators had covered their tracks well, which said to him that the work was far more than a prank. The reason, however, eluded him. With no direct access to the funds, what would anyone have to gain by tricking Celia into thinking herself penniless? It was possible a local rival thought to keep her from marrying Arlington, but he could not see how someone from Somerset had gotten a blank piece of old stationery from Carstairs and Son or set up an elaborate charade in London.

He also could not see how Celia could be hurt further. The Carstairses were aware of the incident and working to grant her the fortune. It appeared that his service to her was over.

With no news, he had no reason to visit her. He should be pleased to so easily avoid temptation. Unfortunately, his good intentions began eroding immediately.

For one thing, he was entirely too aware of the scrutiny of others. Grooms attended him while he rode or drove. Gardeners watched from the shrubbery as he strolled the grounds. Inside, the various maids and footmen seemed to keep him under constant surveillance. His mood became so black that he barked at Stanley Arlington to leave him alone when he happened to run into the fellow twice in one evening. He had then, of course, been forced to apologize.

"Think nothing of it," Stanley said with a wave of his large hand. "I wished to speak with you, don't you know, and this gave me the chance."

Brandon stiffened; however, having all but insulted the man, he felt compelled to hear him out.

"How many rooms do you have out at your country retreat?"

Brandon eyed him. "My estate is well favored. Why?"

"As much as we seem to be running in the same pack, it makes sense to combine forces, don't you know. As it is, I have to trust to luck to hook up with you in the evening. If I were to stay with you, think how much easier it would be."

The thought did not survive its birth. "Were you not intending to return home soon?"

"I was, but circumstances have changed."

His tone was sufficiently cryptic and uncharacteristic that Brandon felt obliged to probe. "And these circumstances?"

Stanley leaned closer. "I am not at liberty to say, don't you know. However, they may well surprise you."

Could Arlington have been part of the prank? He had appeared in London shortly after Celia arrived. Could he instead have come ahead? To what purpose? He crowed his good fortune in marrying an heiress. And his friendly face hid none of his emotions. He must have some other surprise in mind.

"You continue to amaze me, Mr. Arlington," Brandon told him. "However, I doubt you would enjoy my estate. It is some distance from town, and there is my uncle to consider."

Stanley wrinkled his nose. "He is a stickler from what I've seen, by your leave." He brightened. "But you and I can work together to thwart him. When the two of us put our heads together, we shall prevail. What do you say?"

His uncle would have Stanley for dinner with a little plum sauce. Brandon almost smiled picturing it. The idea that he and Stanley might together thwart the network of spies surrounding him, however, had merit. His uncle might even come to see Stanley as a sort of bodyguard. The fact that Brandon could hear how Celia was doing and perhaps see her had nothing to do with his inclination to accept.

"Collect your things in the morning, Mr. Arlington," he said. "I shall have a room made ready for you."

Lady Honoria smiled as James Carstairs made an elegant bow before her in the sitting room of her suite. Such a handsome fellow. She'd always preferred dealing with beauty. Vanity frequently accompanied it, and that was a helpful trait to manipulate. Besides, she liked pleasant surroundings.

He moved forward to lay out the most recent accounting sheets, spreading them before her as if they were silver serving platters at a banquet.

"As you can see," he said, satisfaction evident in the gleam in his blue eyes, "everything is going according to plan."

She perused the numbers, tallied them in her head, and nodded. "Well done, James. And my great-granddaughter?"

"Is awaiting her confirmation."

Was that pique she heard in his voice? Glancing up, she noted the gathering of his blond brows, the tensing of his thin lips. "You do not approve of the way I am handling the girl?"

"I would not presume to criticize, your ladyship. It is only that she seems so strong-willed."

"And this disturbs you."

He perched on the chair across from her and leaned forward, as if he needed to be confidential when she'd dismissed even Sally from this conversation. "It disturbs me a great deal," he said in a low voice. "What if she should suspect that we are manipulating her father's fortune?"

"And why should she do that? I know the man who impersonated you. He will be silent."

"I agree that we would have succeeded, if your nephew had not involved himself."

"A decided shame. However, you recovered nicely with that business about requiring papers for her confirmation."

"A temporary measure, I fear. It is only a matter of time before she presses her case."

Lady Honoria waved a hand, keeping the motion gracious. At moments such as this, he reminded her of a skittish colt. How much worse would he react if he knew financial ruin was only part of her plan? "I shall keep her much too busy to care about her inheritance," she assured him.

"Then you have decided to marry her to the marquess?"

His voice had risen even as his gaze probed her. Trying to get ahead of her? Couldn't have that. "Perhaps," she purred.

He licked his lips. "So you have given up on marrying him to Mrs. Rider, then?"

Ah, so that was his game. Quite a hunger he'd developed for her granddaughter, it seemed. A shame she was not ready to release Patrice. "He was uninterested," she said carefully. "But that is no matter. I decreed his fate from the moment he was born. His sojourn in Scotland delayed my plans. If my great-granddaughter cannot behave to perfection, she may well share them. I trust you will not argue that point."

He smiled. "I try never to argue with you on any point, your ladyship."

She returned his smile, with the same amount of sincerity.

"Where are we going tonight?" Arlington asked, bounding down the grand staircase of Pellidore Place after Brandon.

Edmund, in the act of putting on his evening cloak, spared Brandon a glance. "I do not know what possessed you to offer that idiot a place with us," he murmured, "but keep him away from me."

Brandon hid a smile. "Certainly, Uncle." He raised

his voice. "We are invited to an event, Arlington. Come along."

They were out the door before Edmund could ask them their destination. It was a short-lived victory, Brandon knew. His uncle had perfected the art of following him.

Stanley chattered away as the carriage rumbled back toward the city proper. Brandon answered as needed. It amazed him how well things were working out. Once he got beyond the peppered phrases and belligerent country air, he was surprised to find that Arlington was actually coherent. The fellow was well versed in a number of topics, rode like the wind, and played cards better. He also had a keen appreciation for beauty, whether in architecture, art, or the female form.

Most evenings found him at least for a time in Stanley's company, though Arlington also liked to slip away occasionally. Brandon wasn't sure what he was up to, but the respite was less welcome than he would have thought even a few days ago.

Even with Stanley at his side, he felt his thoughts drifting to Celia. Contrary to Brandon's hope, Arlington had shown no interest in visiting his betrothed. Brandon could hardly insist. Yet he longed to see her, once more. Would that he were the Oberon she named him, able to come and go as he pleased, able to command nature at a word. Would even that he could confide in someone. Of necessity, he had never developed any close friendships. Now he had no one in whom he could share his feelings save Edmund. Given his uncle's recent behavior, he had no interest in doing so.

"So do I understand we are attending the Borin ball?" Stanley asked.

"A required event," Brandon explained. "Our families have known each other for years." He decided not to mention the fact that the viscount, though of an age with him, had ever been too chipper for Brandon's taste. Luckily, the event was a decided crush, and Brandon could do little more than greet his host and hostess before being swept up in the crowd.

Stanley continued to chat amicably to him as Brandon moved about, seeking a place where he could safely observe without having to interact. He thought he'd lost the fellow at least twice, but like a faithful hound, Stanley sniffed him out again. He couldn't help noticing that Arlington had acquired a bit of town bronze. Like Brandon, he had taken to wearing black. Tonight Arlington's coat and breeches were nearly as impeccably tailored as Brandon's.

Finding an excellent vantage point on the far wall overlooking the large ballroom, Brandon settled in for a long night. Beside him, Stanley blew a breath and fanned himself with his hand. "I don't know what possesses these ladies to cram their ballrooms. The candles are melting, and so am I."

"Feel free to take a walk," Brandon said, watching the crowd milling. Lady Borin had rented assembly rooms for her grand ball and chosen an Egyptian theme. Tall pillars stood draped in sheer muslin, and potted palms hung heavy branches over the dance floor. Somewhere off to his right behind a screen painted with hieroglyphics, a string quartet began to play, and his host and hostess moved out to start the dancing. He would be expected to do his duty shortly. Why else invite bachelors?

"Looking for a likely chit?" Stanley asked, having made no effort to remove himself. "You might try Miss Dalrymple. She seems a nice sort."

Brandon eyed him. "Nice? My dear Arlington, what makes you think I need settle for nice?"

Stanley chuckled. "Oh, very good. How about Miss Emily Turner, then? Excellent carriage, flashing eyes, pouting lips, and, by your leave, a fine figure."

Brandon glanced across the room to where Stanley indicated. A tall, dark-haired beauty, Miss Turner did indeed have a fine figure. Her Forester's green gown with its high waist and deep neckline guaranteed that her figure would be noticed. Brandon nodded. "An excellent choice, Arlington. Thank you."

"Happy to be of service, don't you know. I thought I might try my luck with Miss Mitchell." He nodded to where a statuesque blonde held court.

"Daring man," Brandon replied, noting her proud head.

"Bit high in the instep," Stanley agreed. "I generally make it a practice never to approach a lady buried in beaux, but with my time limited, I thought I might as well try."

Brandon stilled. "You leave shortly, then."

"Oh, not as soon as all that," Stanley replied airily. "The papers still haven't arrived from Somerset, so Celia has to wait a while yet. Wish me luck, old man. I want to grab my lady before the next dance starts."

He clapped Brandon on the shoulder and strolled off. Brandon frowned. Now that he thought on it, surely a fortnight had passed since he'd kissed Celia good-bye. Any necessary papers should have arrived from Somerset by now. Why was she still in London?

The music ended. He must move to get a partner. Miss Turner appeared to be just as buried in beaux as Stanley's intended lady, for the corner where she had been standing was deep in gentlemen. He decided to try his luck anyway.

The knot of gentlemen, however, was thicker than he expected. It was only the judicious use of his shoulder and elbow that finally won him a privileged place in the innermost circle. His pleasure in making it there was short-lived. The first sight that met his eyes was his cousin, hands raised in entreaty before her pink satin gown.

"Gentlemen, gentlemen," she pleaded, violet eyes wide. "We are overcome by your attentions. You will put us to the blush."

Since when did Patrice help other debutantes? He glanced about and noticed the absence of Miss Turner. Was all this for his cousin, then?

"I shall accept Mr. Darby's offer," she proclaimed, taking the arm of a dapper blond fellow, "and Celia will accept—"

"Celia?" Brandon spoke without thinking. All heads swiveled in his direction.

"Lord Hartley," Patrice said, blinking.

Standing to one side, Celia saw him staring at his cousin as if dazed. She could scarcely believe he was here as well. Each one of these balls she had attended with Patrice, each one little different from the last, she had hoped against hope that he might appear. Stanley she'd seen several times, but the one man she prayed for eluded her.

Now she stepped forward eagerly to take advantage of Patrice's surprise. "Indeed, I would be honored to be your partner, my lord." She held out her hands. Could they all hear the pounding of her heart? She prayed Brandon would hear it and be moved, at least to pity. She didn't think she could stand being on display another minute.

His emotions showed in no more than a flicker of his dark eyes and a quirk of his brow. Was he surprised to find her here? Why didn't he move, say something, say anything? Patrice would recover her composure soon, and Celia would be lost.

Suddenly he swept her a bow. "I am the one honored, Miss Rider." Straightening, he offered her his arm. Her breath nearly exploded from her chest in relief as she accepted it.

He led her into the line of dancers and took up his place opposite her. His face was taut, his eyes narrowed. Whatever he was thinking, it did not appear to be pleasant. Though the room remained stifling hot, she shivered.

Thank God it was one of the dances she knew. So many movements had come out since she had left school that she feared she would embarrass her partners. She also wasn't too certain of this artistic pile of curls Sally had fixed to the top of her head. And then there was the insipid pink gown Lady Honoria had insisted upon with its yards and yards of flounces at the hem, making her feel like a rose gone nearly to seed. She was beginning to be thankful she had never made her London debut.

The movement of the dance called for them to meet in the center of the lines and circle shoulder to shoulder, though her shoulder only reached the center of his chest.

"You keep staring at me," she murmured as they passed "Do I look so horrible?"

Taking her place, she saw him shake his head. He stepped forward to lead her down the lines. "You are as lovely as ever," he said. "I am merely amazed to find you here."

They parted to weave in and out among the other dancers. She darted a look and found him frowning. Her heart sank. Part of her had hoped he would appreciate the changes, particularly as she didn't seem to have a choice in the matter. The other part had hoped he'd hate them as much as she did and demand that Patrice and Lady Honoria return her to her normal life.

They met at the bottom of the set to repeat the movements. "I thought you intended to collect your fortune and return to Somerset," he said as they circled.

"I had," she promised. "But Patrice and Lady Honoria had other ideas. You told me to confess."

He nodded. They continued through the dance; but he said nothing further, and she found her tongue tied. He obviously regretted his time with her and was acutely embarrassed to find her haunting him. Likely he would bow and take himself off as soon as the dance ended. Likely he would never have danced with her if she hadn't tricked him into it.

As soon as the music stopped she steeled herself, but to her surprise, he seized her hand and threaded it through his arm. "Walk with me, Miss Rider."

She didn't like the order, but she liked less seeing him walk away. She allowed him to lead her to the edge of the floor.

But a promenade proved to be impossible with the number of people at the ball. Brandon muttered something that sounded like a curse. Tightening his grip on her hand, he pulled her toward the door.

His uncle intercepted them. "Now then, my boy, you cannot expect to keep the belle of the ball to yourself."

Brandon's look darkened. "I thought you intended to find other amusements tonight, Uncle."

Lord Pellidore smiled. "And slight Lady Borin? No indeed. And then I saw Miss Rider and took the liberty of asking your cousin for her hand in the next dance. We should become better acquainted."

Now what was she supposed to do? She couldn't very well accept his offer without offending Brandon, and she couldn't insist on staying with Brandon without making it appear as if she had proprietary notions. As if Brandon understood the position she was in, he released her and snapped her a bow.

"Another time, Miss Rider," he said.

"Most certainly, Lord Hartley," she replied, transferring her gloved hand to his uncle's arm. Lord Pellidore led her into the set.

Twelve

"You look lovely this evening," Lord Pellidore said as they began the dance.

She smiled her thanks for his compliment. He moved slowly, reminding her of an elderly courtier from an earlier age. They had been the last to join and were the first to stand out. Unlike his nephew, he had no trouble stating his thoughts.

"I saw in the paper that you were presented at court."

She grimaced at the memory of the hoop skirts and ostrich plumes that were still required. "Lady Honoria insisted on it."

"You do not like the attention, then."

"Certainly not! I once dreamed of a Season, but I can see that I missed little."

"Then you will not be on the marriage mart."

What a revolting term. "No, I am already engaged."

"Indeed, to Mr. Arlington, I believe. He seems to have attached himself to my nephew."

"Has he? How odd."

"Odd indeed. Odder that he does not go about with you."

Was he censoring her? His long, angular face showed nothing unkind. But perhaps he was just as good as his nephew at masking his emotions. "Mr. Arlington is making the most of his final days in London, and I am chaperoning my stepmother while I await the awarding of my fortune." That, at least, was a close approximation for her purpose here.

"Ah yes, a pity it is taking so long to confirm. I suspect it might keep you here for some time."

"I certainly hope not!"

Her vehemence must have impressed him, for he raised a brow. "Then you wish to return to Somerset."

"Eagerly, my lord, I assure you."

"Perhaps I might see my way clear to assist you."

"I would appreciate whatever assistance you might offer."

The dance required their attention then, and he did not speak to her again until they finished. Then he squeezed her hand. "Remember, Miss Rider, if you need assistance, come to me first. I will see that your difficulties are solved."

"Thank you," she said, though she could not understand his insistence. He had less reason to help her than Brandon did. What would motivate him to such generosity? She let him return her to Patrice and curtseyed to his bow. Patrice curtseyed as well, though her violet eyes were huge.

As he left, she visibly swallowed. "What did he wish?"

"Merely to offer his help in confirming my right to the inheritance," Celia informed her, bemused.

Patrice frowned. "He offered help? I have not known him to be kind. He was so insistent that you dance with him. I thought he meant to scold you for dancing with my cousin."

"Why scold me? I only danced with him once."

Patrice spread her hands. "Silly of me. Lord Pellidore has more reason to be angry with Miss Turner."

"Why?"

Patrice pointed to the dance area. "Lord Hartley took up with her the moment you left him. There, he leads her out in the waltz."

Despite herself, Celia felt her gaze drawn to the couples on the floor. Brandon partnered a dusky beauty, who gazed up at him adoringly. She was tall and curvaceous; they made a striking pair. Celia sighed.

"Did you want him so much?" Patrice asked.

She tore her gaze away with difficulty. Her stepmother's face was concerned, and she seemed sincere. "I suppose I did," she replied.

Patrice nodded. "Well, do not give up hope. My cousin is a difficult man to know. He may yet come around. And something tells me Miss Turner will not last the Season."

Brandon endured two dances with the lovely Miss Turner, though he scarcely remembered them. Immediately afterward, he located Stanley.

"If you wish to ride home with me, Arlington," he said, "you will leave now."

"Most certainly, don't you know," Stanley replied. They bid their host and hostess good evening and decamped.

"Miss Turner put a spike in your wheel, did she?" Stanley asked as he settled himself in the coach.

Brandon kept his gaze on the darkness outside the window. "The lady is charming. My mood is not."

Stanley stretched. "Pity. I was doing rather well with Miss Dalrymple. Though, mind you, she cannot hold a candle to a certain other lady in our fair metropolis."

"A shame I did not see you dancing with the lady, then."

"She was otherwise engaged." Stanley eyed him. "Is it Celia that put you in this black mood, then? You must pay her no heed, Hart. She hasn't learned how things are done in London."

"Oh, I think she has learned quite well," Brandon replied.

His dark mood must have finally defeated Stanley, for Arlington curled up in the corner and closed his eyes. Brandon shook his head. Why was he letting this situation concern him? Celia was in town waiting for her fortune to be awarded. She had every right to enjoy herself while she did so.

Unfortunately, some part of him did not agree. He did not shake the black mood until shortly before he called at his aunt's establishment two days later. Coming upon Celia at the ball had been a shock, he reasoned, but he had weathered worse. The larger issue was Celia's future. If there was some reason she had failed to be awarded the fortune, he needed to know it. If there was another reason she was still on the ton, he needed to know that as well. He did not want to see her as the temptress Edmund hinted at, but he was hard pressed to explain her sudden transformation into the belle of the ball.

And it was a transformation. When she was wearing that awful dress and cap and cavorting with Martin, it was easy to overlook her beauty. Seeing her last night, he had nearly been struck dumb in admiration. She moved with the eagerness and light of a brook sparkling in the sun. Between her looks and her fortune, any number of fellows would be only too happy to ignore her more humble roots. Celia was on the marriage mart, and the bidding would be fierce.

All that remained was for him to decide whether he could stand to see her go to another.

A part of him had never really believed she would marry Arlington. While he was growing fonder of the fellow, he could not see the man wed to Celia. She would never be completely happy with him; his will was too weak for her, and she would lose respect for him soon enough. However, it did not stand to reason that she would be any happier with him. In fact, given his situation, she would likely be significantly less happy. Yet would he ever attain a modicum of happiness imagining her in anyone else's arms but his?

He had reached no conclusions but had resolved to approach the matter logically. He would meet her and learn why she had stayed on. She had intimated that Patrice and Lady Honoria had forced her into it. He could not see his cousin creating competition, or Lady Honoria offering a Season when she counted every penny. Surely, however, a calm, reasoned conversation would answer his questions. One look in the forward salon, however, and reason flew out the window.

Every gentleman in London had come calling.

Celia, dressed in a fetching spring green gown that made her creamy skin glow, was surrounded on the sofa. A dark-haired fellow with Byronic curls leaned on the arm beside her, angling for a better view down her décolletage. A burly blonde perched on a footstool before her, reading his latest poetic composition to her beauty. A balding peer with a heavy paunch had been so bold as to sit beside her and take hold of her hand, stroking it as if it were a pet tabby. Lord Leslie Petersborough stood beside him with a plate of sweet meats, looking ready to lob one over his rival's head to the fair maiden, and Chas

Prestwick was leaning against the mantel with such a glare from his emerald eyes that Brandon wondered the coals didn't flare.

"Join the crowd, Hartley old man," Arlington proclaimed from across the room. He sat next to Patrice on the piano bench. Balancing himself with one arm behind her, he waved to Brandon with the other hand, then turned the page of music. Patrice paused from playing quiet strains of the music and welcomed Brandon with a smile.

Celia did not seem to notice he existed.

Straightening his shoulders, he strode to his cousin's side and made her a bow. "Cousin. I see you have as many admirers as usual."

Her smile widened, but she kept her eyes on her hands as they smoothed down the skirts of her pink sprigged-muslin gown. "Oh, no, we have a lot more gentlemen callers of late. I cannot even remember all their names."

"Neither can Celia, I wager," Stanley said, and Brandon was surprised to hear the ring of pride in his voice. "She's the most popular girl in town, next to Mrs. Rider, of course."

Patrice simpered.

The room seemed to be getting smaller. "I actually came to visit Lady Honoria, so I will make my farewells."

"Lady Honoria?" Patrice frowned. "But you never visit Grandmother unless she calls for you."

"All the more reason to do my duty. Excuse me." He turned and fled. If Celia noticed, he did not want to know. He made his way to his aunt's suite.

Sally let him in immediately. Lady Honoria seemed pleased to see him. She ordered a chair brought over to the bedside and insisted that he sit and talk with her. She asked after Edmund and other acquaintances, lamented Parliament's recent stand on feeding the poor, and cautioned him against investing in coal. Brandon's mind kept wandering to the scene in the forward salon. Was Celia happy in this new role? Did she like such fawning attentions? Did she miss secret meetings in gardens and private carriages? He did.

"I trust you saw my granddaughter and great-granddaughter."

Brandon nodded. "And their visitors."

"Yes, I hear we recently became the home for indigent dandies. I also hear they are a sorry lot."

"Actually, Lord Hastings's son is an excellent catch."

"Petersborough? For Patrice or Celia?"

He swallowed. "Either," he tried to say, but it came out, "My cousin."

Lady Honoria wrinkled her nose. "Ah, but he must wait for his title, and who knows how long that father of his will last? I prefer them to marry men who have already gained their titles. What do you think of this Arlington fellow?"

"He's as loyal as a hound."

"And about as bright, I gather. How large is his estate?"

Brandon shook his head. "We have not discussed it. I gather from Miss Rider that it is one of the largest in the area. His father certainly seems to think his son should merit a sizeable dowry from the woman he weds."

"Which lets Patrice out. And I cannot see him with Celia."

A thought so like his own intrigued him. "Why?"

"The girl is strong-willed, high-spirited, and short-tempered. She needs someone with intensity and spirit to match. Mr. Arlington has as much spirit as an ill-stuffed pillow."

A smile tugged. "Mayhap he has hidden strengths."

"Perhaps. Unfortunately, I think Patrice has other ideas."

Brandon had a sudden vision of Arlington, sitting close to Patrice on the piano bench, one hand behind her back to balance himself as he turned the page. Was this his secret pastime, wooing Celia's stepmother? Surely even Arlington had more sense than that.

"What do you mean?" he demanded.

Lady Honoria sighed. "My granddaughter has an inordinate interest in money. I fear she may seek to ally Celia with someone who will promise her an allowance for the privilege."

She had a point. Patrice did not seem to understand that she was well off. He'd seen his cousin's obsession with money. He'd also known some men to promise anything to marry into something as large as the Rider fortune. Carstairs could tie up the principle, but by law the interest would go to the husband to manage. That alone would be a princely sum.

"Mayhap my cousin and I should discuss the matter. I learned recently that her jointure is sufficient for her needs, yet she still demands money from the estate."

Lady Honoria shook her head. "She spent her jointure on fripperies, no doubt. It does no good to talk to her."

"You have a great deal of influence over your granddaughter. Mayhap you can convince her to manage her funds, and to find Miss Rider another suitor."

"Why do you do that?" Lady Honoria demanded. "It is not 'mayhap' but 'perhaps.' Surely your tutors taught you better."

"You must allow me some whimsy." He rose. "And I have overstayed my welcome."

"Mayhap you have," she said with a sniff. "And if you dislike Patrice's choice for the girl, tell her yourself."

"Mayhap," he said, "I will."

Celia wasn't sure whether to laugh out loud or scream in vexation. News of her fortune must have spread, because every jackadandy in London wanted her hand. The perfume from the bouquets she'd been sent was making her nose run. If she ate another candy she was certain she would break out in hives. And if she was forced to listen to another sonnet rhyming Celia with Ophelia, she would happily have burned every copy of *Hamlet*.

Martin was the only one who sympathized. He hated the fact that she had no time left for him except an occasional breakfast. Celia thought the real Miss Prim might be sent for, but so far, her brother spent his days with John or one of the maids. She'd even seen Sally called in to duty. She felt for him, but she couldn't seem to shake off these social duties.

Her stepmother was no help. Half the suitors penned her praise as well, as if trying to get in Celia's good graces through her. Patrice seemed to take the hackneyed phrases as sincere and enjoyed every one of them. When Celia complained, she merely said, "But that is courting," and refused to throw anyone out. Celia was getting tired of reminding everyone that she needn't court at all.

She had thought she might at least have help from Stanley, but he seemed to think her popularity reflected well on him. "Eleven callers in one hour. Wait until Father hears." He was equally bad at toadying up to Patrice, as if Celia would actually require her stepmother's blessing to marry. If it weren't for the fact that she was in Lady Honoria's home, she would have thrown him out with the rest of them.

Her spirits had risen momentarily when she'd spotted Brandon. Perhaps he didn't loathe her as much as she had thought the other night. But he'd merely paid his respects to Patrice and left with no word to her. He had obviously been more interested in her problem than her person. She wanted to burst into tears, but she was afraid Mr. Summers would see that as a sign his wretched poetry moved her.

As it was, she was in a foul mood when Brandon reappeared in the doorway. She tried to attend to the conversation Lord Petersborough had begun, but she could not help noticing that Brandon had begun a conversation of his own, with another of her suitors. In fact, as he made his way around the room, they all found reason to leave. Lord Petersborough was continually interrupted as she was forced to bid them farewell, until at last only Mr. Prestwick, Lord Petersborough, Stanley, and Brandon remained.

"How delightful," Petersborough drawled, settling back against the arm of the sofa. "Hart, I owe you a favor."

"Actually, he owes us one," Prestwick corrected him, patting the young lord on the shoulder. "Come on, Les. There are greener pastures."

"Never," he swore, but his friend's touch must have been persuasive, for he climbed to his feet to eye Brandon.

"So that's the way the wind blows, is it? I might have known. Always a suitor, never a groom. Farewell, Miss Rider."

She bid them both good day and cocked her head to eye Brandon as Lord Petersborough had done. "Impressive magic as always, Lord Oberon. I am only surprised you did not have Puck here do your bidding."

"What's this?" Stanley asked with a frown.

"A literary allusion," Brandon explained, only to earn him looks of confusion from both Stanley and Patrice.

"It does not signify," Celia told them. "I was merely attempting to thank Lord Hartley for once more rescuing me."

His face went stiff. "I am certain you give me too much credit, Miss Rider. The day is late. No doubt your admirers found they needed more sustenance than a kind word from you."

She felt equally stiff. "You would know, my lord."

Patrice glanced between them. "Is something wrong?"

"No," Celia chorused with Brandon, then glared at him.

"It seems I was of less use than Miss Rider thought," he said. "I shall take my leave. Arlington, do you wish a ride?"

"By your leave." Celia watched as Stanley bowed. "Mrs. Rider, your eternal servant. Good afternoon, Celia."

She shook her head as they started for the door. Stanley loped along as if he hadn't a care in the world; Brandon walked as if he carried the world itself on his broad shoulders. She was losing them both, and she had no idea what to do about it.

Patrice watched them leave as well, brows drawn together with concern. Brandon had come calling, but she didn't think he realized it. If he intended to woo Celia, he was doing everything wrong, and Celia wasn't helping. But Celia was supposed to be engaged to Stanley, or so he said. Yet Stanley was so very nice to her that it made her heart happy. It was all very confusing.

She was supposed to be the mother. She had forgotten her own mother for the most part, so she had no ready reference as to how she should behave. Stepmothers in books were often horrid creatures; she certainly didn't want to be one of those. Besides, she didn't feel old enough to arrange Celia's marriage. Perhaps Lady Honoria could do all the paperwork. Her grandmother was good at paperwork. She certainly spent enough time at it. Patrice was glad that all she had to do was sign the occasional piece of vellum James Carstairs handed her.

But she did know how to court. She was good at courting. She liked courting. She knew any number of ways to get a gentleman to offer. She would find a way to get Celia married.

If only she knew who the groom should be!

Thirteen

As soon as Brandon and Stanley were out the door, Celia decided she had had enough. She should have stopped this socializing long since, but in truth, she had felt a certain thrill at first to find herself so very sought after. Now that she knew Lord Hartley would not be among those admirers, she was just as glad to give it up. She missed Martin.

Lady Honoria refused to let her stop so easily when she told the woman her decision that evening.

"You cannot simply hide yourself away," her ladyship said as Celia and Patrice dined with her in her suite. "Your father would never have wanted that."

"My father hardly expected me to come to London for a Season."

"I disagree. Did you never stop to wonder why your father settled on Patrice?"

Celia cast a glance at her stepmother, who was watching Lady Honoria over her baked ham. "I suppose it was because she was beautiful."

Patrice dimpled and popped her pork into her dainty mouth.

"Beauty was only the sauce. The meat was her social connections. Your father wanted his children to walk at the highest levels of Society. If you return to

Somerset with your Mr. Arlington, you will never achieve his dream."

"I like Mr. Arlington," Patrice said with a pout.

"Yes, dear," Lady Honoria snapped, "but Celia could do far better." She returned her dark gaze to Celia, who sat straighter under it. "You can beg off. It has been done."

"A bargain is a bargain," Celia replied, knowing she sounded stubborn. Sometimes, however, stubbornness was the only appropriate response to Lady Honoria's demands.

She refused her stepmother's invitation to the theater. Dismissing John, she spent the evening playing games with Martin. As always, time with her brother helped her focus on what was important to her. She had come to London on a mission—to find their fortune. It was time she got back to it.

She asked Patrice about the matter the next morning.

"Finances are difficult," Patrice answered with a wrinkle of her nose. "Better leave them to those who know them well."

"Gladly," Celia replied. "Let us go into the City and meet with Mr. Carstairs."

Patrice shook her head, setting her golden curls to swinging. "No need. Young Mr. Carstairs comes to see Grandmother nearly every day. We have only to catch him."

Celia did just that. But when she drew him into the forward salon to express her concerns about the delay, he merely smiled his polite little smile that so infuriated her.

"I realize the wheels grind slowly, Miss Rider. However, you must understand that there are other matters to consider. Your rector may be too busy to copy the papers immediately."

"Surely that is moot," Celia protested. "My stepmother and Lady Honoria vouch for me, and you already have Lord Hartley's word on the matter. Why do you need a copy of my baptismal record? It states that a child named Celia Rider was baptized on that date, not that I am she."

He tugged down on his burgundy-striped waistcoat importantly. "Estate management is a complicated process, Miss Rider. I would not expect you to understand the nuances."

His arrogance only fanned the flames of her temper. "I, however, expect *you* to understand them," Celia informed him. "And I expect you to explain them to me until I understand them as well."

"Perhaps Lady Honoria would be of some assistance in that area. She manages the Pellidore estate."

"My father did not pay Lady Honoria to manage his estate. He paid you. And if you expect me to do the same, you will learn to deal with me."

He frowned. "Perhaps we should make an appointment with Mr. Arlington. I am certain he could explain—"

"Hang Mr. Arlington," Celia exploded, rising in a rustle of green taffeta. "Mr. Carstairs, I have been lied to, put upon, and manipulated. You either produce my fortune or explain to me why you cannot. If you can do neither, I shall find myself another solicitor. I trust you understand *that*."

He bowed. "You have been most clear, Miss Rider. I did not bring your portfolio with me today. I would need some of the papers in it to explain things to you properly. May I call upon you at this time, the day after tomorrow?"

Celia agreed, and he bowed again before leaving the room. She watched as he climbed the stairs to the upper floors. On a whim, she quietly followed.

The door to Lady Honoria's suite snapped shut before she reached it. Sally certainly let him in quickly enough. Celia had no reason to interrupt, and Sally would likely bar her way even if she did. She glanced both directions and, seeing no one, put her ear to the door. She could hear nothing.

She sighed, leaning away. She should stop seeing collusion everywhere she looked. Still, something in his demeanor troubled her. He acted as if he expected her to be as helpless as Patrice, yet if he dealt with Lady Honoria regularly, he had to know that some females were made of stronger stuff. Was he behind her original problems with the fortune that he now refused to talk to her?

If only she had someone with whom she could validate her impressions! Martin was too young, and she didn't want to worry him. She would only confuse Patrice. Stanley would tell her she was borrowing trouble. Lord Hartley would be ideal; unfortunately, she refused to make him think she needed his rescue.

She started for her room, only to find Patrice in the corridor outside it, a piece of fabric in her hand. When she held it up eagerly, Celia could see that it was a domino.

"What do you think?" Patrice asked, sliding the folds of the long, hooded cloak across her fingers. "See how the material looks green one moment and blue the next? It matches your eyes!"

Celia smiled, fingering the satiny fabric. "It is lovely. Are we to attend a masquerade?"

Patrice nodded. "At Lady Brompton's, tomorrow

night. I considered more elaborate costumes, but a domino seemed perfection."

Celia would have preferred something more original, but she decided not to say so this time. "It will be fine."

Her stepmother puffed out her chest as if she was well pleased with herself, and Celia was glad she had not protested. Besides, the fabric did come close to matching her eyes. And a masquerade was sure to be fun.

"Will Lord Hartley be there?"

She grimaced as soon as she said the words. Patrice would certainly think she was pining for him. To her surprise, her stepmother beamed.

"Yes, he will. We must make sure we find him. Even in costume, he should not be difficult to spot."

Celia had to agree with her there. No matter what he wore, she thought she'd recognize Oberon anywhere. And in costume, perhaps he wouldn't feel the need to be so formal. She might even be able to get him to smile again. Perhaps even laugh. She felt her mouth turn up at the prospect. This masquerade might be even more enjoyable than she had thought.

Brandon was just as certain the masquerade would be a nasty affair. Lady Brompton's reputation was shocking. Few received her. Her parties were rumored to degenerate far too often into gaities no gentleman admitted attending. He could not imagine what had possessed her to invite him. He was penning a polite refusal when his uncle strode in. He cocked his head as if to read the invitation Brandon was answering.

"What is that?" Edmund asked.

"Do you read my mail as well now, Uncle?" Brandon sanded the note and blew off the dust.

"If necessary," Edmund said with infuriating calm. "I actually came in because I heard a distressing rumor."

"And you felt you must share it with me? How delightful."

His uncle eyed him. "You appear in rare form today. However, you will earn that awful appellation of Lord Heartless if my tale does not move you. Miss Turner and her entire family have come down ill. The physicians are uncertain whether she or her mother will survive."

"Good God!" Brandon stared at him. "Typhus?"

"The physicians are uncertain there as well. The symptoms are similar to cholera."

Brandon shook his head. "Hideous. I shall have flowers sent."

His uncle continued to eye him, dark gaze thoughtful over his long nose.

"What?" Brandon asked. "Have you more?"

"I do. Does it not strike you as odd that the one woman in whom you showed an interest suddenly falls ill?"

Brandon snorted. "No. It strikes me as just my luck."

"And you do not see the connection with Miss Rider?"

Brandon felt himself go still. "I do not see a connection for the reason that there is no connection."

"You think not? Perhaps you also failed to note the look on her face while you danced with Miss Turner."

Celia had watched him? Had she been jealous? If so, she had given no indication when he'd visited the house yesterday. Her frosty reception still stung.

"Whatever you saw, Uncle, I assure you it had nothing to do with Miss Rider's feelings toward me."

"I disagree. The girl was green. You have heard the expression, if looks could kill?"

"You will not have me think that a single look sent an entire family into a serious decline. You go too far, Uncle."

Edmund shook his head. "She has blinded you. She invented that story of her defrauding to play upon your emotions."

"I am Lord Heartless, if you recall. I have no emotions."

"You were skilled at hiding them, until she appeared. Beauty is a more potent weapon than all Napoleon's guns combined. She used hers to lure you into the role of protector. When you were clever enough to resolve her problem, she became more open in her attempts to ensnare you. Perhaps, when you refused her, she sought to eliminate her rival."

Brandon held up his hand. "Enough, Uncle. Continue with this farce, and I shall think *you* have succumbed to the family curse."

"It came through your father's mother, not mine. I am not mad, but the girl is scheming to trap you. See for yourself."

He held out a folded sheet of paper, addressed to the Marquess of Hartley. The sealing wax had been broken.

Brandon accepted it from him with a sigh. "You really are reading my mail. Is this how low we have sunk?"

"We shall sink lower if you agree to her request."

Frowning, Brandon read the letter.

"Dearest Lord Hartley," it read. "I have something of the utmost importance I must share with you and no one else. I understand you are to attend Lady Brompton's masquerade. Please, please meet me there. I shall be dressed in a domino that matches my expressive eyes. Do not fail me. Yours in devotion, Celia Rider."

"You see?" Edmund said, crossing his arms over his chest. "She obviously plans to lead you into a compromising position. She knows you will offer if she does."

Brandon stared at the note. "This is ridiculous. Celia Rider did not write this. It sounds nothing like her. I wager she would fall ill to use such groveling language. And she would hardly remind me vainly of her eyes."

Edmund snatched the note from his hand and read it again. "You are certain?"

"As certain as I am that you like interfering in my life."

Edmund handed him back the note. "I would like to see this Miss Rider as the angel you call her. Allow me to accompany you to the Brompton masquerade. If she behaves to perfection, I may be convinced."

His uncle was clearly giving Celia enough rope to hang herself. But Brandon had other ideas. He set the note aside. "No, Uncle, I will not attend this masquerade. Someone continues to interfere with Miss Rider's life, and in doing so interferes with mine as well. I understand your reasons for doing so; you are motivated to keep your vow to my father. This mysterious other must have a different motivation, one I cannot trust. I intend to find him."

"Or her," his uncle put in.

"Or her," Brandon agreed. "And I swear I will force that interference to end, even if that someone is you."

* * *

Patrice put on her best smile the next afternoon as Stanley stepped through the door into the marble-tiled entry of her grandmother's house. Seeing her waiting, his smile widened. He hurried forward to take her hand and bring it to his lips.

"Mrs. Rider. The days pass so slowly after I leave here, yet I could swear I only left a few hours ago."

Patrice dimpled, lowering her gaze. "You are too kind, Mr. Arlington. Please, come this way."

She boldly kept his hand as she led him up the stairs. Her flounced pink dress brushed his calves. His fingers were long and thick. She felt so safe with them curled around her own. He was so tall, so strong, so sturdy in his dark coat and trousers. Oh, she must make this come out right!

"Celia is out," she told him as they entered the rear salon.

He gazed about the little room, which was decorated in yellows and blues. She had chosen it because it was much more intimate than the larger forward salon. Besides, she liked yellow.

"A shame I missed her," he said. "I say, this isn't our usual room, don't you know."

"No. Forgive me. I wanted to be certain we were not interrupted."

Stanley blinked as he returned his gaze to her. "Mrs. Rider?"

Patrice rubbed the toe of her plum-colored slipper against the Grecian key pattern of the thick carpet. "You will think me forward, Mr. Arlington, but I must ask you some questions."

"Anything," he assured her. "I am at your disposal."

He sounded so sincere that she could not help but smile. "Have you enjoyed your time in London?"

"Very much. You are kindness itself to show me around."

"Then you also enjoyed my company?"

"More than I can say. More than you can know."

"But that is just it," Patrice murmured, raising her eyes in entreaty. "I must know, Mr. Arlington. I must know how you feel about me."

She could see him swallow. "My dear Mrs. Rider, I . . . I don't know what to say, by your leave."

She put a finger to his lips. "Then say nothing, Mr. Arlington. Merely listen. My stepdaughter and I will be attending Lady Brompton's masquerade tomorrow night."

His lips moved against her finger, like the wings of a butterfly against a flower. "By your leave, I received just such an invitation this morning."

She smiled. "That was my doing. I have known her ladyship since we attended finishing school together. People say she runs with a faster crowd. That has troubled me in the past. However, for your sake, I am willing to overlook it."

She lowered her finger. He licked his lips as if to taste her scent. "I would not see you put in danger."

"I would brave any danger to know your heart, Mr. Arlington. Besides, I will be perfectly safe as long as I have a strong male escort, someone I trust. I can trust you, Mr. Arlington, can I not?"

"Of course," he stammered, "certainly. I am your willing servant."

"Good, for I am counting on you to attend. I have even procured you a domino." She took the package from the table near the door to the room and handed the domino to him. He hugged it to his chest.

"You will have to find us in the crowd," she explained. "If events transpire as I suppose, you will likely have the opportunity to escort only one of us. Celia and I will be dressed in dominos that match the colors of our eyes. I trust you know the color of her eyes."

"Yes, by your leave, a sort of mixed-up blue and gray and green, but—"

"Shh. I want to make sure you know the color of mine." She stepped in front of him, took a deep breath, and stood on tiptoe so that her eyes were nearly on a level with his. She held his gaze for several moments, watching the emotions dart across the green of his eyes. Surprise, good. Interest, excellent. Ah, desire. She felt it curling through her as well. He reached for her, and she dropped down and stepped away.

"Remember, Mr. Arlington," she said. "Two dominos, one choice. I trust you will make the right one."

Fourteen

To Brandon's mind, only Patrice could have sent him the note supposedly from Celia. Either she thought to lure him to the masquerade to trap him herself, or she thought to make Celia available for him to compromise into marriage. He could allow her to do neither. He played out several scenarios to teach her a lesson, but finally decided that the best revenge was to reveal her to Lady Honoria. With this in mind, he slipped in the rear gate of his aunt's establishment the next day and made his way to Lady Honoria's suite.

She rolled her eyes when he told her of his suspicions.

"A masquerade," she said, "a dark night, a hostess known for letting her guests get away with murder, how very typical. But what else could I expect from Patrice?"

Brandon wasn't sure he liked the description. "Then you will talk to my cousin, tell her to stay home tonight?"

"Perhaps." Lady Honoria's dark eyes gleamed. "Or perhaps I have a better idea. I think you should attend this masquerade. It may be the only way you can thwart her."

"But I came here to thwart her. I wish her schemes ended. Immediately."

Honoria shook her head. "But think! You were not the only intended victim of this prank. You do not know what mischief she hopes to inflict on poor Celia. I tell you, she is jealous of the girl. I think Patrice may even have designs on Mr. Arlington, God help us. I have no doubt that she intended the girl to be compromised tonight. If you do not attend, I shudder to think whom she might get to take your place."

Brandon felt cold. "You think Miss Rider is in danger?"

"I do not think Patrice would see it as danger. She is intent on marrying the girl off. You know the types who frequent Lady Brompton's events. Can you imagine what one of them might do alone with the girl?"

He could indeed, and his chill intensified. "Tell my cousin and Miss Rider they cannot attend."

"I could, but that will not stop Patrice. She may well try the same trick another time. How would we know? If you go, you can discover what she has in mind and prevent poor Celia from coming to harm."

At the time, her argument was persuasive. As he dressed for the event that night, after sending a note to accept after all, he realized he had let himself be convinced. He could have found any number of ways to prevent the situation. He simply wanted an excuse to be of service to Celia again.

The ache to see her had been growing for some time, he admitted to himself as his coach set off the short distance to Lady Brompton's. Their meeting the other day had not helped. He didn't want to argue with her or compete for a moment of her

Get 4 FREE Books!

We created our convenient Home Subscription Service so you'll be sure to have the hottest new romances delivered each month right to your doorstep—usually before they are available in book stores. Just to show you how convenient the Zebra Home Subscription Service is, we would like to send you 4 FREE Kensington Choice Historical Romances. The books are worth up to $24.96, but you only pay $1.99 for shipping and handling. There's no obligation to buy additional books—ever!

Save Up To 30% With Home Delivery!

Accept your FREE books and each month we'll deliver 4 brand new titles as soon as they are published. They'll be yours to examine FREE for 10 days. Then if you decide to keep the books, you'll pay the preferred subscriber's price (up to 30% off the cover price!), plus shipping and handling. Remember, you are under no obligation to buy any of these books at any time! If you are not delighted with them, simply return them and owe nothing. But if you enjoy Kensington Choice Historical Romances as much as we think you will, pay the special preferred subscriber rate and save over $8.00 off the cover price!

llı..lıı.llll....llılı.lılı..lllı.lı.lı..llılı.llllı..l

KENSINGTON CHOICE
Zebra Home Subscription Service, Inc.
P.O. Box 5214
Clifton NJ 07015-5214

PLACE
STAMP
HERE

time. He wanted the days of teasing camaraderie and stolen kisses. He wanted her at his side and in his arms. As he could have neither, he would settle for keeping her safe.

Lady Brompton's home was less than a mile from his, perched on a slight rise. Her gardens resembled a miniature Vauxhall, complete with waterfall, colonnaded walks, and leafy alcoves. Certain the masquerade would be held out there, he wasn't surprised when he was conducted through the house to the rear, where he was effusively greeted by his vivacious hostess.

Unfortunately, the masquerade was as bad as he feared. Though he was one of the earliest to arrive, already poorly dressed satyrs chased barely dressed nymphs down graveled paths. Anthony was seducing a willing shepherdess near the waterfall, while Cleopatra waltzed with an overgrown tin soldier to music from a string quartet. Most of Lady Brompton's guests had enough imagination to invent costumes that displayed significant amounts of flesh. Luckily, the number of dominoes was limited.

He stationed himself just outside the door from the house to keep watch for Celia. Her domino was supposed to match her eyes, but as he had never been able to decide on the exact color, he wasn't sure whether to look for gray, blue, or green. Glancing about, he spotted someone in a silver domino, emerging from the maze. Brandon made his way forward, fending off suggestions from an unlikely angel, a plump harem girl, and something that resembled a large, uncooked rutabaga. He hadn't even reached the hooded figure before he realized that the person was far too tall to be Celia.

The figure turned then, and even with the mask,

Brandon recognized Stanley Arlington's soft-tipped nose. Stanley apparently had just as little difficulty recognizing him, although Brandon had thought the hooded black domino with its matching silk mask was appropriately anonymous.

"Evening, Hartley," he greeted with a grin. "I say, but I didn't realize you were coming."

"It was a late decision," Brandon replied, glancing about hopefully. "Is Miss Rider with you?"

Stanley's grin tightened. "No, not really. In fact, I have yet to find her or Mrs. Rider, don't you know."

Someone jostled past him, and he stepped closer to Brandon. "I say, Hart, can you spare me a moment? I tried to catch you earlier, but we seem to have been at cross purposes lately."

Brandon's gaze kept roaming the growing crowd. "I really should find my cousin. Can it wait?"

Stanley cleared his throat. "No, not really. You see, it has to do with your cousin."

Brandon met his gaze at last and raised a brow. What he could see of Stanley's long face was pale, and his shoulders were slumped. Somehow Brandon didn't think the change was entirely a result of fast London living. Stanley knew something about Patrice, and the secret was killing him. Brandon jerked his head toward the far hedge. "This way."

He had barely settled himself in a position where he could see the door to the house when Stanley launched into his tale.

"It is the most deuced luck, don't you know. I am in love, and the situation prevents me from doing a thing about it."

Brandon grit his teeth. "Arlington, I have no time for this. You will have Miss Rider's fortune soon enough."

Two Grecian water bearers wandered past. One winked at him—the male one.

"That is just my fear," Stanley lamented. "What will Father say when I tell him I no longer want it, er, her?"

Brandon frowned, focusing on him at last. His long face sagged in misery.

"What do you mean," Brandon demanded, "that you no longer want Miss Rider?"

His tone must have been sufficiently harsh, for Stanley held up his large hands as if in protest. "Celia is a great gun, don't you know. I have the highest admiration for her. It is simply that I found a woman who is so much more! I tell you, Hart, she ignites my passion!"

Brandon reached out and pushed down his hands. "I would not say that too loudly here if I were you. So, you find yourself wishing to cry off from your engagement to Miss Rider, do you?"

"I do." Stanley hung his head. "But it isn't done. Besides, Father will say I whistled a fortune down the wind."

"I take it your lady love is less favored in that area."

He nodded. "Far less so, by your leave. And she is older than I am as well—a widow with child. Yet I have always gotten on well with Martin."

Brandon stared at him. "Martin? Good God, Arlington, you cannot mean . . ."

"That I love your cousin? Yes. I will not blame you if you cast me out. My perfidy is dastardly. But truly, how could I help myself? She is as sweet-natured as a dove, as lovely as a rose, as soft as—"

"Yes," Brandon said to stop him. "I can see you are smitten." He shook his head. "Have you told my cousin of your feelings?"

Stanley drew himself up to his full height. "By no

means. I am a gentleman, sir." He sagged again. "Only I suspect she knows. She took great pains to tell me what she and Celia would be wearing tonight. I think it was a test."

"No doubt." Brandon shook his head again, but the thoughts tumbling through it refused to settle. What game was his cousin playing? Certainly she had skill enough to infatuate the innocent Mr. Arlington. Lady Honoria said Patrice coveted him, but would she really go so far as to steal her stepdaughter's fiancé? And why invite Brandon? What was Patrice planning?

"I say, Hartley," Stanley said, "I am not at all certain of this event. I think I just saw a gentleman with his hand up a lady's skirt."

"You will see more than that if we do not leave soon," Brandon assured him. "I came tonight for one reason: to safeguard my cousin and Miss Rider."

Stanley's eyes widened. "By your leave, do you think them in danger here?"

"I do, and it strikes me you have just as much reason to fear for them. You said you knew what they were wearing?"

He nodded. "Celia will likely be in gray. Mrs. Rider is in a delightful shade of violet that shimmers between blue and purple." He smiled as if remembering, then flushed. "Their hooded cloaks and masks match their eyes."

"Good," Brandon said, refusing to quibble over eye color. "We will divide the garden. You take the maze and the lower walks. I will search nearest the house. Meet me here in a quarter hour."

"And if we do not find them?"

"Then we will take stronger measures, Arlington."

* * *

Celia was intrigued the moment she crossed Lady Brompton's threshold. A darkly caped footman escorted them down a long corridor toward the back of the house, past lamps turned far below what she would have expected for a party. The soft glow gave her the briefest glimpses along plastered walls. She sighted paintings of naked cherubs surrounding scantily clad goddesses and alcoves hiding statues without fig leaves. Her feet sank into the thick Turkish carpet so that her walk was hushed. She could barely make out the group ahead of them or behind them. Coming to the double doors to the garden, however, she heard voices and laughter, the strains of music, and the falling of water.

"The party is *al fresco*, then," she whispered to Patrice, who walked at her side just as wide eyed.

"It is out-of-doors," Patrice whispered back. "Your mask is slipping. Wait, let me fix it."

She stopped just inside the house. The footman stopped with them. Patrice tugged the shimmering cloak more fully about Celia's curls. She'd escaped Sally's petty ministrations and left off the complicated knot work for the night. Her honey-colored locks hung in soft ringlets inside the hood, tickling her cheeks as she moved.

"Am I covered?" Patrice asked, letting her hands fall back to her sides and standing straighter. She gave a little shudder in obvious excitement.

Celia smiled. Patrice was so eager, it was hard not to like her. Martin had told her only that day that he thought his mother was really a child like him. It was his way of seeing her immaturity, she supposed. At moments like this, she certainly felt as if she was the more motherly of the two.

She gave her stepmother's violet cloak a tug for

good measure. "You look delightful," she assured her.

Patrice dimpled, then turned to the footman. "You may announce us."

"We cannot announce, madam," he said formally. "It is a masquerade." He led them through the doors, Patrice's pink cheeks clashing with the color of her cloak.

They were introduced as the ladies mysterious to their hostess. Lady Brompton was square and squat, with impossible black curls tight about a round face. She was dressed as a cherub, tiny feathered wings and all, and Celia was glad their hostess wore more than the ones in the paintings.

Lady Brompton directed them to avail themselves of the festivities, waving a plump hand to encompass the garden, which was lit by glimmering lanterns in the shape of butterflies. The clear, dark night, with stars shining overhead, the soft music coming from near the maze, and the murmur of voices lulled Celia with a sense of peace. She had decided she liked masquerades very much indeed when a fat satyr strode up to them.

"I have room at my table for two more nubile lasses," he proclaimed in a booming voice. A sour smell washed over Celia, and she frowned.

Patrice went further. She reeled away, dragging Celia with her. "We must find Mr. Arlington."

Celia dug her heels into the gravel to slow her. "Stanley is here?"

Patrice tugged harder. "Yes, he promised. We must find him, before it's too late."

"Too late for what?" Celia asked, but at that moment a pair of Grecian water bearers approached. As they passed, one of them patted her posterior. Celia wheeled. The woman of the pair glanced over her shoulder to grin at her.

"Patrice," Celia said, "where have you brought us?"

"We must find Stanley," she repeated, but Celia could hear the panic rising in her voice. "He will protect us. Look for his silver domino."

She did not question how her stepmother knew what Stanley was wearing. Very likely he had told her himself, they had their heads together so often. She scanned the area, her heart sinking as she saw how crowded the grass was growing. Then someone bumped her from behind, pushing her forward. A troop of fairy folk, gossamer wings fluttering behind them, pressed laughing and chattering around them. It should have been delightful, but the glint in their eyes held a dark menace.

She tried to break away from them, but she was swept up and carried along as easily as a twig in a flood. She was being pulled toward something unknown, but she knew it would be unpleasant. She reached out to keep hold of her stepmother, but her gloved hands slipped on the slick fabric of Patrice's domino. As she struggled against her captors, Patrice disappeared behind them. Celia was dragged alone into a sea of milling, cavorting humanity.

Patrice pushed away from the throng and pressed her back up against a hedge. Clinging to the plant, she glanced about for Celia. The faces of strangers, made more strange by the masks they wore, looked back at her. A hand touched her arm, and she jerked away. Another caught her domino as if trying to pull it from her, and she snatched the fabric to her. She broke from the hedge and stumbled up the path, only to collide with a tall man in a black domino.

"Caught in your own net, Cousin?" he drawled.

Surely that was Lord Hartley's voice. She wanted to feel comforted, but the tone held menace. Backing away, she peered up at him. She had never seen him angry, but the stillness of his face below the black mask and the stiffness to his shoulders told her he was furious with her. He reached for her. She turned and ran.

Panic drove her through the milling groups. She dodged and wiggled her way past grasping fingers. Her hood fell back from her hair, sending the golden waves tumbling down in her face. She thought she heard her name being called, but it was hard to hear anything over the pounding of her pulse.

Then someone caught her arm, pulling her up short. She lashed out with her feet.

"Ow!" Stanley dropped his hold to hop back.

"Oh, Mr. Arlington!" Patrice fell into his arms, voice cracking. "Save me! He is out for my blood, I can feel it!"

She hid her face in his chest and felt his arms come around her. "There, there, Mrs. Rider." His voice sounded like a deep rumble under her ear. "I am here now. No harm will come to you."

She cuddled closer, basking in his strength. "There are so many people, and they were touching me, and then my cousin confronted me, and I am so very glad you found me."

His hand touched her hair lightly, as if he were afraid he might frighten her further. "You are safe now. I shan't let you go, ever."

She sighed. "Oh, how lovely."

The noise around them seemed to recede, and

she let her eyes close for a moment. His voice was
so gentle, his touch sweet. He even smelled good,
like hot chocolate on a cold day.

"Stanley?" she said.

"Mmm?"

"May I call you Stanley?"

"Of course. And by your leave, I shall call you
Patrice."

She smiled against him. "I should like that." Something tugged at her mind, and she felt her smile
fading as she concentrated. "Stanley?"

"Mmm?"

"Celia is out there alone. We should find her."

He pulled back to eye her, and she thought he
might protest; but something in her face stopped
him. He took her by the shoulders and pushed her
back against a tree.

"Very well. Only promise me that you will not
move from this spot until I come for you."

Patrice nodded. He started to go, but she pulled
him back against her. "Stanley?"

"Yes?"

"You did choose me, did you not?"

His tender smile melted her heart. He put a hand
to her cheek. "Always, love, and forever. Back in half
a mo."

Fifteen

Celia told herself not to panic. She truly wasn't alone in this mass of debauchery. Somewhere among the nymphs, satyrs, and rutabagas were Patrice and Stanley. She wasn't sure Patrice would be much help, but surely Stanley's size alone would deter the more ardent lechers. All she had to do was find him.

A strapping squire's son in a silver domino should have been easy to spot, but as she made her way through the crowds, she could not catch sight of him. Perhaps he hadn't arrived yet. Patrice said fashionable gentlemen often attended several balls each evening. Stanley certainly didn't qualify as a fashionable gentleman, but she wouldn't have been surprised if he aped one. After all, he had recently begun dressing in black like Lord Hartley. So, had he yet to arrive at the party, or had he come and gone? Was she truly alone?

Her steps faltered, and her breath quickened. She shook her head. She could count on Stanley. Theirs might not be a love match, and he often forgot her needs in preference to his own, but he loyal. Patrice said he would meet them here. Surely he would not depart without doing so. She had to continue her search.

Of course, Patrice also said Lord Hartley would be

in attendance, and that had been a lie. Celia could not see him at such an event. Just imagining him, eyes alight with passion, hands reaching to caress her, set her face to flaming.

A Roman senator, laurel wreath crowning a balding head, put himself in her path.

"Ah, a lady in gray." He squinted as if he could not quite focus and waved at her domino with the wine goblet in his plump hand. "Allow me to put more color in your cheeks."

He leaned forward, mouth pursed. She tried to sidestep him, but an arm snaked out to encircle her waist. There was more hair on it than on his head. Shuddering, she twisted out of his grip. The wine splashed upward into his face and down the front of his toga. She heard him curse her as she sped away.

Her feeling of satisfaction lasted only a moment. There were far too many of his ilk here. She and Patrice were both in danger. She needed to find Stanley, and quickly. Schemes tumbled through her mind, but none of them seemed suitable for polite society.

She stopped with a grin. No one else here was bothered by propriety. Why should she be? She glanced around and located a small stone fountain with a bench before it. Making her way over, she climbed up on the bench and surveyed the garden.

Lady Brompton's guests were no less salacious viewed from her vantage point. Many were already weaving with drink. Those that were not either pursued or were being pursued. Color and shape blended and parted. It was difficult to make out any single individual. Suddenly, she spotted a tall fellow in a silver domino.

She cupped her hands around her mouth. "Stanley! Stanley Arlington! Over here!"

He glanced about wildly. A skinny Marc Anthony sidled up to her bench and entwined his arm around her leg. "I came as Anthony, I saw as a man, I would be delighted to conquer as a Stanley."

Celia wiggled her leg to dislodge him. "Take your hands off me. And you are paraphrasing Caesar, not Anthony, and doing it badly."

He looked ready to protest, but Stanley arrived just then. He seized the would-be politician by a shoulder and spun him neatly back onto the grass. Laughter echoed on all sides, and Lady Brompton hurried forward to placate the fallen hero.

"What are you doing, Celia?" Stanley demanded, putting out a hand to help her down from her perch. "Do you wish to make a spectacle of yourself?"

"Everyone here wishes to be a spectacle," she informed him. "I prefer to leave. We must find my stepmother."

"She is safe," he assured her. "I will take you to her, but first I must speak with you."

She rolled her eyes. "Not now, Stanley. I cannot endure another minute of Lady Brompton's hospitality."

He shook his head. "But you will see the evidence as soon as we reach her. Indeed, I am surprised it does not shine from my eyes, throb in my voice, gleam from my limbs. Birds should be circling me, singing, 'Patrice, Patrice, Patrice.'"

Celia stared at him. "What on earth are you talking about?"

He took her hand and patted it. "Celia, dear Celia. I shall always be fond of you. In fact, I daresay you will become as a daughter to me. In any event, I shall always remember that you brought us together. How can I express my gratitude?"

She grabbed his hand and pulled him toward the door to the house. "You can get me out of here."

He balked. "No, no, you misunderstand."

Celia tugged. "Then you can explain on the ride home. Now take me to Patrice."

"In due time. I do not like leaving her alone in this crowd either, and I would be eager to return to her side regardless. But it is vital that I speak with you. This way."

Thinking he meant to talk as he escorted her to Patrice, Celia allowed him to lead her away from the fountain and down the grass. Her suspicions grew, however, as he started into the maze. He took the first right, then a left. He started to go right again, then jerked away. Pausing, he peered back in that direction and grinned.

"Stanley," she said in warning.

"A moment," he assured her, leading her onward. He seemed to find what he was looking for and pushed her back into a small boxed alcove set in the hedge. Another of the stone benches sat at the back, a torch flickering beside it.

"Stanley," she started again, but he held up a long finger.

"Now, now. If you will listen to me for once, this will only take a moment."

Celia sat and crossed her arms over her chest. "Very well. Get on with it."

He took a deep breath. "Celia, I must ask you to release me from my promise of marriage. I wish to marry your stepmother instead."

Brandon felt his panic growing with each step. Where was she? Patrice had fled before he could ask, and he was hard-pressed to catch sight of the violet domino in the darkness. Neither could he catch sight of Celia's. Each group he parted, he expected to find her under attack, or worse. The behavior around him degenerated by the minute. He had already found two couples in full copulation. It would only worsen.

He could not count on Patrice to protect her. Even if Lady Honoria was wrong about his cousin's jealousy, he questioned Patrice's reliability as a chaperone simply by the fact that she had brought Celia to such an event. He wasn't even certain Arlington could be relied on, infatuated as he was with Patrice.

He felt as taut as a bowed string and very nearly snapped when he sighted Stanley hurrying past alone. "Arlington!"

Stanley jerked to a stop, then rushed to his side. "Hart! Thank God! Now we can leave."

He started forward again, and Brandon grabbed his arm. "Wait! Does that mean you found them?"

Stanley nodded. "I was just going to fetch Patrice." He elbowed Brandon with a grin. "She gave me leave to call her by her first name."

"Marvelous," Brandon drawled, resisting the urge to make him swallow that grin. "Where is Miss Rider?"

Stanley's face fell, and Brandon's gut tightened. His grip must have tightened as well, for Stanley continued in a rush. "She's in the maze. She needed a moment alone after I told her our engagement was off."

"You jilted her?" Brandon's fist slammed up under the domino to knot in Stanley's cravat. He jerked up, nearly lifting Stanley from the ground. "Here? How dare you hurt her like that?"

"Easy, Hart." Stanley's eyes were wide and his face

pale. His hands tugged uselessly on Brandon's. "She's all right, I tell you. I was a gentleman, I swear."

Brandon released him, and he stumbled back. Righting himself, he tried to straighten his neck piece with fingers that trembled.

"Not like you, Hart," he mumbled. "By your leave, I think the night air has addled your senses."

The night air turned to ash in his mouth. He could feel the emotions surging through him and fought to still them. Yet how could he be calm? Did this imbecile have no idea how he must have hurt Celia? Brandon had seen no sign of passionate love between them, but even if they had been good friends as it seemed, Celia had to feel betrayed. To hear such news in the midst of debauchery would only have added insult to injury.

Dear God, but his hands were trembling nearly as badly as Arlington's. He swallowed and straightened, looking Stanley in the eye with all the coolness Edmund had taught him. Stanley blinked and lowered his gaze.

"Go get my cousin," Brandon said. "Meet me at my carriage. I will fetch Miss Rider. Tell me where to find her."

"Take the first right in the maze, then a left, then right again, no, left, yes left, and keep going until you see a turn to your right. Or was it left?"

Brandon could barely resist the urge to grab him by the throat again. "Which is it?"

"Left," Stanley said with a shaky nod. "Only you must face to the right where you'll see a small boxed alcove. She awaits there."

Brandon set off without bothering to see whether Stanley did as he was told. At the moment, all he could think of was getting to Celia.

The maze was dark as he entered it. What torches he sighted had been extinguished. As soon as he made the first of Stanley's turns, the noise faded from the main party on the grass.

But other noises grew louder. Laughter echoed ahead as couples chased each other through the tall laurel hedges. Someone rushed past him in a flutter of white, only to disappear around the next turn. A woman shrieked off to his right, but in terror or delight, he wasn't certain. Glancing back, he saw another figure trailing not far behind him. As the person slipped through a patch of moonlight, he caught a glimpse of a white skull mask and a gleaming scythe.

Brandon shook his head. How appropriate, he was being followed by the Grim Reaper.

He stopped to let the man pass him, but the Reaper slowed as well. Brandon frowned. That stretch of path held no turns. Why did the fellow hesitate? Was he looking for someone?

Was he looking for Celia?

Brandon pressed himself against the hedge, feeling the bite of a branch through his gloves. His dark costume would hide him well in the uncertain light. Unfortunately, the Reaper's cloak hid him just as neatly. Brandon held his breath and listened. Fading laughter in the distance obscured closer sounds, but in a moment of silence, he heard the rustle of fabric, coming closer. Moonlight glinted on the edge of the scythe where it lanced up above the bushes. He could hear Death's breath, short, sharp, harsh, as if the man were trembling with anticipation.

Just who did he think he was chasing? And why?

* * *

Celia paced the leafy alcove, insides churning. What was Stanley thinking? Or better, was Stanley thinking at all? Her stepmother was years older, an avowed city dweller, a woman with a child for pity's sake! His father would murder him the moment Stanley announced his intentions.

A giggling medieval princess attempted to bring a middle-aged Adam around the corner. Celia's scowl alone was enough to send them scampering along. This was seduction, that's what it was. Patrice must have thrown herself at him. Never mind that Celia had more than once wondered whether she was wise accepting his offer. He had offered, and she had accepted. A bargain was a bargain.

A burly gentleman with heavy bands of fur wrapped around his waist and calves strode into her alcove, a knotty club over one bare shoulder. By the patch over his left eye she could only guess he was supposed to be a Cyclops.

"Aha," he crowed, "I find the prize of the maze at last. Prepare to face your penalty for making me hunt for you."

Celia put both hands on her hips. "You haven't found the prize; you've found the penalty itself. Take yourself off before I give it to you."

He shook his head. "Just my luck. Dozens of willing females, and I find the unwilling one. If you are truly intent on remaining pure, leave now. This maze will shortly become a wanton's paradise." He stomped back down the path.

Celia didn't hesitate to follow. As far as she knew, the only entrance to the maze was from the grass below the house. Surely Stanley would have to use that entrance to find her. She would simply wait for him there.

The Cyclops evidently took another turn, for she lost sight of him immediately. However, she had no doubts that his words were true. All around her came sounds of lust—groans, panting, cries of ecstasy. Face heating, she hurried down the path. She tried to count the turns that Stanley had made to get her to the alcove, but so many torches were extinguished that she could hardly tell what was a turn and what a shadow of the maze.

Out of the darkness rushed a woman dressed in white. She plunged toward Celia, hair streaming out behind her like the flag of a sailing ship. Celia fell back against the hedge, branches grasping at her cloak. The woman did not stop, dashing past to be swallowed up in darkness once more. Shaking herself, Celia pulled herself upright. Part of the hedge came with her.

She shook off the branches that clung to her, then felt a limb drop behind her. "When God closes a door, he opens a window," she murmured, bending to pick up the branch that had fallen with her. Holding it before her like a sword, she continued cautiously down the path.

Ahead, another figure moved in the darkness. She raised the branch in front of her. "I am in no mood for seduction," she told him. "Leave while you are still ambulatory."

"Celia, watch out!"

It was Lord Hartley's voice, but before she could even turn, she was grabbed from the side and pulled up against a dark figure. Somehow, she knew it was him. Ahead, something fell with a clatter. The rattle of gravel told her the other figure was fleeing. Lord Hartley evidently realized it as well, for he released her to step away. Even with the small space between them, she could hear his ragged breathing.

"What is it? Who was that?" she demanded.

"I have no idea; however, I cannot like him waiting for us ahead. Is there another way out of this maze?"

She shook her head, willing her own heartbeat to slow to something approaching normal. "Not that I know of. And it only gets worse the deeper you go, from what I can tell."

"Then we shall have to return the way we came." He reached out to take her hand. "Are you all right?"

Just his touch calmed her, even though her pulse quickened again. She nodded, then realized he probably couldn't see her in the dark. "I am unhurt. I was waiting for Stanley, but things were getting too busy." She paused to eye him. "And what are you doing here? Have I misjudged every man I know?"

"I cannot answer the second. As to the first, this event is no more in my fashion than it is in yours. I will tell you how I came here later. For now, we must get you out of here." He peered down the path, head cocked as if listening. The black cloak nearly blended into the shadows.

She clung to his hand, feeling safer just having him near. The noises seemed less dangerous. Far more dangerous were her feelings. She was no longer engaged. If she wanted to flirt with Brandon, or more, she had only to make the choice. It would be easy to give herself to him . . . but he was right. Now was no time for talk or anything else.

She bent to peer around his arm. She could see nothing ahead but moonlight spearing down onto the path. As he turned, she straightened.

"Let me go first," he ordered. "And watch your-self." He started out, and she fell into step behind him, clutching her branch in one hand. Almost immediately he stopped, and she bumped against his back. She scrambled away, face heating.

"What is it?" she whispered.

He bent as if to pick something up, then straightened and stepped into a patch of moonlight. Celia caught her breath. The light shimmered off the long black cloak, giving him a supernatural glow. She had been right—he was Oberon. Power and grace, strength and vitality, seemed to pulse around him. She reached out a hand to touch his brightness. Even brighter, however, glowed the light on the scythe in his hand.

She gasped, yanking back her hand. "Where did that come from?"

He turned, face in shadow. "Our friend Death left it for us. Considerate of him, was it not? Stand away."

She backed obediently against the hedge. Brandon lowered the hook and swung it back. For a crazy moment, she thought he meant to use it on her, and her heart jerked in her chest. Then he swung it forward and hacked it into Lady Brompton's hedge. The sound echoed through the maze, silencing the other noises. The blade sliced through the lighter limbs neatly, lodging finally in a thicker branch. He tugged it back out and stood, head bowed, as if considering its power.

Celia swallowed. "Do you intend to cut our way free like an African explorer?" she tried joking.

He raised the scythe. "As I am uncertain how far we are from the entrance, that would seem foolhardy. However, I reserve the right to change my mind. Come along, Miss Rider."

Sixteen

Arlington and Patrice were waiting for them at Brandon's carriage. Stanley eyed the scythe, but Brandon merely nodded toward the door to the coach. "Get in. We are going home."

Patrice sucked on her lower lip as if trying to hold back tears, but Brandon couldn't be bothered to care. If she felt his tone scolding, so much the better. She had no business bringing Celia to such a place. He handed the scythe to his groom with instructions to treat it with care, then climbed in after his forced guests.

Celia ought to have the most to complain about, yet she was the least vocal as they set out. She had pulled the hood and mask from her face as they left the house, and the lamplight coming through the window burnished her honey-colored curls with gold. Her eyes were dark, her face still. But by the way her hands were clasped tightly in her lap, he thought she behaved with such perfection only with difficulty.

"Good of you to rescue us all, Hart," Stanley said, shifting on the blue velvet upholstery beside him. He had removed his silver domino and now wadded it up to set it behind him like a pillow. "By your leave, that scene was getting a bit out of hand, or in hand, as it were."

Brandon did not smile at the feeble joke. "None of you should have attended."

Patrice sniffed. She alone remained in her costume, although she had seen fit to remove the mask. "We were escorted. How can you malign Mr. Arlington?"

"Mr. Arlington is new to London, madam," Brandon replied as Stanley sat a little straighter. "You are not. You must have known of the lady's tendencies. You are also the oldest of this group. You should have refused the invitation."

She burst into tears. Arlington shifted again, eyed Brandon, then shoved his way across the coach to take Patrice in his arms. He squashed Celia against the side of the carriage in the process.

"There, there, my darling," he cooed to Patrice. "Of course you could not have known what would happen. Such depravity is foreign to your tender soul."

Celia moved to plunk herself down next to Brandon. "If I must listen to this all the way home, I think I shall be ill again."

"We are not going to London," Brandon said aloud, for the benefit of all. "When I said we were going home, I meant to my home. It is closer."

Stanley nodded as if he thought that wise, his hand still stroking Patrice's hair. "We have been through a great deal. Thank you for your hospitality, Hart."

Patrice muttered something that could have been thanks as well. Celia cast him a glance and tightened her lips.

It was his turn to lean over. "You do not like the idea, Miss Rider?" he murmured in her ear. A wisp of hair teased his cheek, and he resisted the urge to wrap it around his finger.

She moved a little away from him. "I would not presume to gainsay Lord Oberon at his most imperious."

"Very wise," he murmured, and straightened away from her before he became as besotted as Arlington.

The drive was mercifully short. Mr. Openshaw, his butler, quickly dispatched an army of maid servants and footmen to make up the necessary rooms. Brandon was thankful Edmund had not yet returned from London. His uncle would have apoplexy when he heard about tonight's adventure. With any luck, Brandon would have them all safely in bed before his uncle arrived.

He played host in the withdrawing room, where his footman Timms hastily lit the lamps, until Openshaw announced that the rooms were ready. Patrice rose wearily, eyes still brimming with tears. Stanley offered her an arm, which she accepted with a sad smile. Celia rose as well, nearly as wearily. No one offered her help.

"Miss Rider, stay a moment," Brandon said. "We must talk."

Patrice sighed. "I will wait, then."

Celia seemed to sense his need. "That isn't necessary."

She put up her head. "Of course it is necessary. You must have a chaperone. It is only proper."

"Out!" Brandon commanded.

Patrice shrieked and fled the room. Stanley stiffened.

"I say, Hart," he started.

"And you as well," Brandon said. "Out. We will talk in the morning."

Stanley seemed about to say more, then thought better of it and left, feet dragging as he shuffled across the thick Oriental carpet. Brandon turned to Celia.

"We are surrounded by idiots," she said.

"For which I am grateful," he replied. "If they had any more sense, we might have had our hands full tonight."

"I suppose so." She sank back onto the striped-satin chaise. "What did you wish of me, my lord?"

What did he wish? So many answers offered themselves. But he had let his wishes rule him far too often that day. "I said I would tell you how I came to the masquerade tonight. I received an urgent invitation to attend, from you."

"What!" She jumped to her feet. "I sent no invitation!"

"I did not think you had. Someone is interfering again."

"Who would be so dastardly—Patrice! She was intent on getting me married. This was her doing!"

"My original guess as well. However, I think we have another enemy." He paced to the window, trying to decide how much of his concerns to share with her. She hardly needed more burdens to carry, but she could not protect herself if she weren't fore-warned. He turned to find her watching him. The glow of the candles behind her silhouetted her lithe figure in light. She looked as ethereal as an angel, yet she had proved herself determined and able. He should not seek to shelter her.

"The figure who fled in the maze may have come for something other than an orgy," he said. "The scythe was sharp."

She frowned. "Perhaps he merely wanted an authentic costume and borrowed the implement from his gardener without realizing how dangerous it was."

"Or mayhap he took the scythe with the idea of using it."

She shivered. "You talk of murder. Who would gain by having either of us dead?"

Who indeed? He still could see no advantage to anyone in harming Celia. Patrice's portion would not increase, and Martin already had a double portion. Besides, the boy was too young and isolated to be manipulating his elders like this. As for who would like to kill Brandon, Lord Heartless had doubtless made a considerable number of enemies. However, none, he thought, that would not prefer the satisfaction of a duel. He could think of no one who would either hide behind a mask or send a hired killer after him.

Not even the woman in front of him.

Edmund seemed so sure she was a cunning adventuress. Surely she had not staged the whole thing to prove she needed Brandon's help? He didn't want the light in those eyes to be avarice. But was he merely seeing what he wished to see?

He was silent so long that she frowned. "My lord? Will you answer my question? Whom do you suspect?"

"No one, Miss Rider. I am still at a loss for the moment. However, I intend to learn more. In the meantime, you should turn in. It is late."

She rose and came to lay a hand on his arm, the light touch surprisingly soothing. "Not before thanking you. You looked out for me tonight. I appreciate it." She stood on tiptoe and pressed a kiss against his cheek. He pulled her to him to kiss her properly.

At least, those were his intentions—a proper kiss to show her he cared. Anything else after tonight's escapade would be unthinkable. However, the moment his lips touched hers, he knew he was lost. She kissed him as she did everything else—with enthusiasm, with determination, with a wild abandon that excited him. Her hands slipped around his waist, and long fingers kneaded the muscles of his back. His hands seemed to have a will of their own, caressing her soft form, drawing her to him. All he needed, all he desired, was to feel her against him.

But as he continued to revel in her kisses, he realized he had another need. It surprised him so much, he very nearly didn't give in to it. Then she pressed a kiss against his earlobe, teasing him, testing him, and he knew he had to have it. As her mouth withdrew, he whispered, "Say my name."

"Hartley," she whispered back, silken smooth, breath soft against his cheek.

"My first name, my given name."

"Brandon."

God, it was sweet, like a prayer on her lips, the word forever denied him. "Again."

"Brandon, my love."

He closed her mouth with his own, kissing her again and again, breaking from her only to kiss her cheeks, her hair, her neck. She trembled in his arms, and his name became a request, a plea. "Brandon, please, more."

His hands slid over her hips to cup the soft contours behind and press her against him. She moaned in his arms, her hands caressing his chest, his shoulders, the back of his neck. He swept her up in his arms, lips claiming hers once more. As he raised his head, he saw her eyes close, her lips part as if in sheer desire. He had taken two steps toward the door when he saw Edmund standing framed in the opening.

His heart stopped beating.

His uncle merely turned and walked away. Brandon took a deep breath.

Celia raised her head from his shoulder and opened her eyes. "Brandon?"

"Forgive me." He carried her to the sofa and set her gently down upon it. Her hair was wild about her face from where he had dislodged the curls. Her eyes were a misty green, her cheeks pink, her lips red and swollen.

"What happened?" she murmured, watching him. A tremor went through her, and he gathered her in his arms and held her against his chest.

"Forgive me," he repeated. "I have no right. I admire you too much to treat you like that."

She hiccoughed a laugh. "If your admiration is what holds you back, I promise to give you a hardy disgust of me. Only please, stay with me."

He released her to take her hands. They were growing cold. "I must. This is wrong. I nearly forgot that."

Her lower lip trembled. "You do not care for me?"

"I care for you too much." He could see tears coming to her eyes and cursed himself for putting them there. "Celia, you deserve to hear a declaration of marriage after a demonstration like that. I cannot give you one. I cannot marry until I gain my inheritance."

She shook her head. "Why? You have your title. Surely you reached your majority."

"I have. However, my father's will ties up the monies that fund that title until I reach the age of thirty. I shall do so near harvest. Until then, I dare not commit myself."

"But I have a fortune. You need not wait."

"I would not marry you for your fortune."

She made a face. "That is not what I meant. I understand yours would come later. I merely meant that if funding is what holds you back, that should not be an issue."

He sighed. Much as he admired her strength, he did not think she could stand under the weight of his problems. And he could not bear to see her face contort in disgust when he told her. "It is more than the money," he tried. "My father's will requires that I meet certain criteria. Marriage, even engagement, might keep me from doing so."

She cocked her head, eyes narrowing in a frown. "Criteria? What kind of criteria?"

He took a deep breath. "My sanity."

He watched as her pupils dilated. "Then the stories are true."

Now he felt cold. "I should have known someone would tell you of my father. The story is much too good not to share."

She shivered as if her chill were growing as well. "Not too good. Too tragic. I am so very sorry you had to go through that."

"Thank you. If you understand the situation, you must understand why marriage is out of the question."

"Not really. You say you must satisfy certain criteria to prove yourself sane. Who judges you? By what standards?"

"Lady Honoria and my Uncle Edmund are the judges and jury, although my aunt's vote counts twice Edmund's. They will decide whether I show any of the traits that my father and grandmother showed as they died, and if I do not, they will grant me control of my life."

"And if you do exhibit these traits?"

"They are to consign me to a mental ward for the short time I shall have until the illness claims me."

She closed her eyes as if he had struck her. A part of him died inside. He stiffened. Better she know

now than when she had foolishly chosen to marry him in the heat of passion.

She opened her eyes. "I am so very sorry," she repeated, and a tear rolled down one cheek. "I love you, Brandon."

He stared at her, unable to speak. She leaned forward and pressed her lips to his. The kiss was solemn, a promise, a pledge. With a groan, he pulled her to him. Dear God, but he could feel tears in his own eyes. He had to gain control of himself. He pushed her away and struggled to his feet. Turning his back to her, he drew in a breath and blinked the moisture from his eyes. He heard her skirts rustle as she, too, rose; then a hand pressed on his back, gentle, reassuring.

"I do not understand why you must wait. I tell you I love you. Let me stand beside you."

He shook his head, hating himself for being unable to look at her. "You cannot know what you are saying. I could die tomorrow, foaming at the mouth, tearing at my own flesh."

"You have shown none of the symptoms so far, have you? How do you know that this disease will not pass you by?"

He could not tell her. Like all her decisions, her declaration of love came too quickly, too easily. Oh, he was certain she believed it, and would go on believing it until something forced her to do otherwise. He could not be that something. He could not tell her that he had been suffering the first symptom since the day his father died.

"Even if this disease leaves me alone," he said instead, "I live in a netherworld until my judgment. I would not see you share that shadow life. You have all of London at your feet."

She pushed her way in front of him so that he was

forced to see her and made a show of peering down at her toes. Then she glanced up at him with a smile. "If all of London is at my feet, the gentlemen appear a sorry lot. Even the ones I knew in Somerset cannot hold a candle to you."

He shook his head. "Arlington is an ass to choose my cousin over you."

She tugged on his arm to lead him back to the chaise. "You will get no argument from me. However, I find I cannot care. In truth, I have wished to be released from my promise for some time. Since the moment, in fact, that I met you."

He refused to sit, buoyed by her words. If he so much as touched her, he'd lose all power over his emotions. "Celia, think. You have suitors to fill a house. Any of them would give you more of a future than I can."

She cocked her head, letting her curls fall to one side in a tumble of gold. "I think I shall take the gentleman I love."

He sank down beside her and buried his head in her neck. She stroked his hair, the touch soft, comforting, infinitely satisfying. He thought he could stay here forever.

But Edmund would be waiting.

He raised his head. "I want you with me, Celia, for the rest of my life. However, my life will not start until I am cleared of this legacy. Can you wait that long to hear a declaration from me?"

"I am not very good at waiting," she said, the same smile playing across her lips. "But for you, I will make an exception."

He gathered her to him then, and it was a very long time before he was willing to let her go again.

Seventeen

A sleepy-eyed maid was waiting when Celia finally reached her bedchamber for the night. Under the domino, she wore a lavender silk gown, hopelessly wrinkled now. She felt her face heating remembering how that had happened and cast the maid a glance as the dark-haired woman helped her out of her things. But the maid merely smothered a yawn and went about her duties as if it were perfectly normal to be undressing rumpled females at odd hours of the night at Pellidore Place.

That it was not a normal occurrence was evidenced by the nightgown, yellowed with age, lying on the gold canopied bed.

"It belonged to the last Lady Pellidore," the maid explained when Celia asked. "Mr. Openshaw thought his lordship wouldn't mind having you and Mrs. Rider wear his mother's things, seeing as this is an emergency."

Not an emergency, Celia thought as she fingered the delicately embroidered cambric, but certainly a time of need. She assumed Patrice had planned to return home after the event, for they had packed no overnight bags. Or had her stepmother planned all along to stop at the estate? Had Patrice counted on

Celia's impulsiveness to land them a spot in Brandon's home?

She'd been beyond impulsive tonight, but she could not regret it. Though Brandon had not said the words, he must love her. She could wait. A bargain was a bargain, even if it was only acknowledged through a pledge of one's heart.

She had barely settled herself beneath the soft down comforter when there was a tap at her door.

"Celia?" Patrice's voice came muffled through the panel. "Are you all right?"

Celia sighed. "I am fine. Good night, Patrice."

Apparently her answer was insufficient, for her stepmother tiptoed into the room as if afraid her footfalls would be heard by others. She perched on the edge of the bed. Celia could feel her watching in the light of the dying coals.

"You were very long with Lord Hartley," her stepmother murmured. "Did he offer marriage?"

"No, but it does not signify."

Patrice shook her head vehemently, her gown fluttering in the dark. "It signifies a great deal! You were alone for well over an hour, in the dead of night. He must offer."

Celia sat upright. "He must not!"

"But the gossip," Patrice protested.

"There will be no gossip. Only Stanley, you, and I know of this."

"Servants always talk," Patrice reminded her.

"Not nearly as much as their masters and mistresses, I warrant," Celia replied. "You make a mountain from a molehill, Patrice. Do not belabor the point further."

In the dark, her stepmother's pout sounded in her voice. "I wish you would let me guide you! I may forget important dates and the like, but I know about courting!" She leaned closer. "You can still have him. The setting is perfect."

Celia frowned. "What are you talking about?"

Patrice waved a hand. "The late hour, the strange house, your brush with danger. Who could blame you if you wandered into the wrong room and could not find your way out until morning?"

Celia gasped. "You want me to trap him!"

"Of course," Patrice said. "Why do you make that sound so awful? That is the way it is done."

"I will not force him to offer! When he asks for my hand, it will be because he is ready to admit he loves me."

"Silly," Patrice chided. "Of course he loves you. All we need do is help him admit it." She rose and took Celia's hand. "Come, let me show you how easy it is."

Celia snatched back her hand. "Never! Is this how you got Stanley to propose?"

Patrice sat back on the bed. "No. I merely gave him a choice. It appears he chose me."

She sounded completely satisfied, and even though Celia was now certain she could never be happy with Stanley, she could not help the pain that bit at her. Stanley blithely committed himself elsewhere without a thought of the hurt it might cause her. It appeared to bother Patrice even less.

"I am certain Lord Hartley would choose me as well, if the circumstances were similar," she said, then winced at the defensive tone of her voice.

"I am certain as well. I only wish the gentlemen could appreciate how much effort we go through to manipulate them into the appropriate circumstances."

Celia closed her eyes. "Tell me you did not forge

an invitation from me to entice Lord Hartley to tonight's event."

She heard Patrice sniff and opened her eyes to see that her stepmother had straightened. "Of course I did not forge an invitation from you. How vulgar! A lady does not invite a gentleman to meet her at a party. I merely asked Lady Brompton to include him on her invitation list."

Her explanation made sense, in the strange way her stepmother thought. So Brandon was right that Patrice was not behind the interference in their lives. Who, then? Could Stanley have decided ahead of time to push Celia at Brandon while he pursued Patrice? It hardly seemed his style.

"And it all worked out beautifully," Patrice continued blithely. "Even if you decide not to encourage matters tonight, I am certain he can be made to offer. He barely has enough money to keep his estates going until he inherits. He told me so. Your fortune would be very welcome."

"He will not marry me for my fortune. He said as much."

Patrice shook her head, rising. "Gentlemen always say such things. It salvages their pride. You must be guided by me in this. If you want my cousin, he can still be yours."

She patted Celia's hand and tiptoed back out.

Celia sank under the covers with a sigh. Most likely Patrice was right—if she went to Brandon's room that night, she would not come out until morning. The idea sent a jolt of excitement through her. His caress, his kiss, his whispered praise of her, made her long for more. She could imagine slipping into his room, sliding the gown from her shoulders to let it pool at her feet, and stepping into his embrace.

Would that be so wrong when they were all but promised to each other?

But they weren't promised. She sighed again and turned on her side, burrowing deeper under the covers. Perhaps if she wrapped herself closely enough, she would no longer be tempted. Perhaps if she closed her eyes tightly enough, she might not see the tender light in his eyes when he'd spoken of the future, the fire that smoldered when he had at last let her go.

Perhaps sleep would come before she changed her mind.

Brandon walked slowly down the corridor for his uncle's suite. He had no idea what to say to Edmund, but he knew he had to get his emotions in order before he attempted conversation.

He tapped at the door and heard his uncle's gruff call to enter. Edmund had not changed his clothes, Brandon saw as he stepped inside. His uncle was standing by the fireplace, gazing down into the dying coals, the glow turning his dark evening wear to rust. One of his beloved cigars burned in his hand. He glanced up as Brandon entered.

"Tell me without roundaboutation. Did you offer for her?"

"No," Brandon said, "and yes."

Edmund straightened away from the fire. "I am too old for such games. Will you make me beg for an answer?"

"Sit down," Brandon replied, moving to suit word to action. He settled back in the armchair by the fire. Edmund did not move. Brandon leaned forward.

"Someone is trying to trap me into seducing Celia."

Edmund snorted. "Certainly. Celia. And she is doing a fine job of it."

Brandon shook his head. "You recall the invitation. I am convinced she did not send it. If you could have seen her at the event tonight, you would know she did not stay willingly."

"So you say. But I cannot see her as the angel you do."

"Neither can I see her as the devil you see. I think someone may have tried to kill her tonight."

Edmund stiffened. "What?"

Brandon explained about the figure in the maze. Edmund shook his head. "The fellow was no doubt merely looking for a willing partner. You have no evidence he was after Miss Rider. And if he was, it may have been because she asked him. Was it only a coincidence that he appeared as you moved closer to her?"

"Not in the slightest. Mayhap he was following me to her."

"You see what you wish to see."

Now Brandon stiffened. "Of what do you accuse me, Uncle?"

Edmund eyed him, taking a drag from the cigar before answering. "I daresay paranoia would be too strong a word."

Brandon shook his head. "You cannot rattle me so easily. I know what I saw, and I am confident that more is at stake than we originally thought. Unfortunately, I have no answers."

Edmund sat at last, facing Brandon leaning with his elbows on his knees. "Very well. I will attempt to see your side of the issue. It is possible that Miss Rider is in some kind of danger. You suspect the same person who lied about her fortune?"

"I do. What eludes me is the motive."

Edmund was quiet for a time, nursing the cigar. Brandon heard the enameled clock on the mantel tick off the minutes. "Someone must want the fortune," Edmund said at last. "Who has access?"

"My cousin, and Milford and James Carstairs, if only second hand."

"And Celia."

"And Celia," Brandon conceded. "At least, once she is confirmed. Why would she stage the fortune's theft?"

"To meet you so that she could force you to offer for her."

"Uncle," Brandon said in warning.

Edmund puffed out a cloud of smoke. "I evaluated your side of the argument, and it makes no sense. Will you at least consider mine?"

"No." Brandon leaned back, stifling the urge to walk away. "I love her."

Edmund closed his eyes. "God help us."

"Is love so very horrid, Uncle?"

"It is if it causes you to lose sight of your goals."

"It did not. I told Celia that I could not marry until the fortune was safely in my hands."

"You told her about your father?" He opened his eyes to stare at Brandon. "You told her the truth?"

Brandon turned his gaze to the fire. "Enough so that she would understand. She agreed to wait."

"Did she?" Edmund's voice was skeptical. "Interesting."

Despite himself, Brandon leaned forward again. Edmund's brows were drawn together, and his lips pursed thoughtfully.

"Then you will give her a chance?" Brandon asked.

"A small one," Edmund acknowledged, then took another draw from the cigar. His puff of smoke drifted toward the ceiling. "If you insist on investigating this business, I shall help. And if she continues to wait patiently for you to offer, as a young lady should, I will rethink my initial impression. However, if she persists in throwing herself at you, I will have no choice but to stop her."

Brandon's eyes narrowed. "Do not threaten her."

"Warn me all you like. I know my duty. I will not let you lose all for a conniving chit from the country. If she is the title hunter I think, she will not be difficult to run off."

Brandon chuckled, causing his uncle's brows to raise. "The more you insist on her surrender, the more she will fight you. I know Celia."

"You *think* you know Celia. In the next few days, we shall see just how well you know her. Until then, be careful. I would not see you give your heart to a jade."

Celia wasn't certain what to expect the following morning. The maid had pressed her silk evening gown, so she wore that down to breakfast. She found Stanley and Patrice there ahead of her. They were smiling into each other's eyes with so much longing that she very nearly walked right out again.

Brandon was not as effusive when he entered the room. Gone were any signs of the importunate lover. He was no more than polite. She felt a distinct lowering of her spirits.

She hoped he might spare her a moment before they departed, but he seemed just as disgusted with Stanley and Patrice's display of affection and left the room after only a greeting and a cup of tea. It was only when they had gathered in the front entry and

Stanley announced his intentions of escorting them home that Brandon pulled Celia aside.

"Are you all right?" he asked.

She felt his gaze linger on her face like a caress and held that look to her heart. "I shall survive. However, I would be delighted if you could come with us."

He shook his head. "I have duties that take me elsewhere. Another time."

Another time. Another young lady, she was certain, would have let matters stand at that. She couldn't be that proper. "When may I see you again?"

His gaze narrowed, but in thought or annoyance, she couldn't tell. "If all goes well, I will call on you tomorrow."

He sounded less courteous than James Carstairs and about as personal. She wanted to pull his head down and smooth his brow with kisses. After their physical closeness last night, surely they should speak more easily today. Yet, if anything, his manner was even more distant. It was as if he had exposed his soul to her and now would do anything to cover it back up. Only the curious gazes of Patrice and Stanley nearby prevented her from demanding an explanation. She dropped a formal curtsey.

"Until tomorrow then, my lord."

If he noticed how stiffly she walked beside him to the waiting coach, he did not show it.

A part of her was afraid that the day would pass too slowly. Another part wanted not to care. His distance cut. Had she misunderstood him last night after all? Or did he see waiting as something so passive that she was not even allowed to tell him how much she admired him? That, she knew, she would find untenable. They would clearly have to reach agreement on the issue when he called.

He had sent a servant last night to tell Lady Honoria of their situation. She expected to hear a ringing peal from her ladyship when they returned and was not surprised when Mr. Kinders instructed them to be taken to the lady's suite straightaway. She thought Patrice had more reason to dread the interview, as her stepmother had been the one to accept the invitation to an event she knew would be shockingly inappropriate. However, she positively glowed with happiness.

"May I tell Grandmother of our news?" she asked Stanley, who had accompanied them into the house like a doting puppy.

He brought her hand to his lips, setting her to blushing. "By no means. I intend to join you and tell her myself."

Celia was almost willing to be scolded for the opportunity to watch that little announcement. She stepped back to allow Stanley and Patrice to lead the way.

Lady Honoria was at her writing desk as they entered, though Celia could see no sign of the papers that normally occupied it. The older woman still looked in command in her gray silk gown with the black military trim. Her emotions only grew more evident when Stanley launched into his tale. As he blundered along, her face turned decidedly pinker, as if she held her temper with extreme difficulty, and her dark eyes flashed lightning. When he finished, she placed both hands on the shiny desk and narrowed her eyes at them.

"And I suppose you expect me to wish you happy?"

Patrice gazed up at Stanley adoringly. "Yes, Grandmother, for I am certain I shall be."

Stanley squeezed her hand where it lay on his arm. "And, Celia, have you nothing to say in this matter?"

Celia shook her head. "What is done is done. They seem to know their minds."

Lady Honoria nodded. "They do indeed. Unfortunately, that is impossible as I am convinced neither of them have the brains they were born with."

Stanley stiffened. Patrice bit her lower lip. Lady Honoria held up a hand as if to warn them against speaking.

"Patrice, you brought this on yourself. Two visitors stopped by this morning to tell me how shocking it is that Celia would attend such a reprehensible event. Celia's reputation is in shatters."

"*My* reputation!" Celia cried. "I had no knowledge of the event before I attended."

She gazed pointedly at Patrice, who blinked away the tears that were starting and stood straighter.

"Surely no one would slander either Patrice or Celia," Stanley said loyally.

"Sadly, Patrice seems to have escaped all notice," Lady Honoria said with a distasteful curl of her upper lip. "As she was not seen with Celia by the gossips, no one seems to know whether she attended that fiasco."

"And just how do they know I attended?" Celia demanded. "We were in costume."

"You," Lady Honoria said, "apparently stood on a chair or some such thing and shouted your intended's name. He was apparently equally stupid to call yours back. There are few couples named 'Stanley' and 'Celia' about the ton. Even idiots such as those you associated with last night are not that stupid."

"This is terrible," Patrice cried. "Celia will be shunned!"

Celia shrugged. "I have no more interest in courting."

"Do you not?" said Lady Honoria. "How very fortunate, as I doubt I shall get a single offer from an appropriate gentleman." She turned her dark gaze on Stanley, who shrank under it. "Mr. Arlington, I blame you for this. You had an agreement with Celia, one you apparently felt comfortable breaking with no more thought than required to change a cravat."

"By your leave," Stanley protested, "it took considerably more thought than that. I agonized for hours!"

"Stanley!" Patrice lamented.

He groaned and patted her hand again. "By your leave, forgive me, my love. I didn't mean it that way. I do not regret my decision. However, I hate leaving Celia in such a bad way."

"I will not allow you to leave her," Lady Honoria said. "I do not release you from your agreement. You will marry my great-granddaughter, as soon as we can procure a license."

Eighteen

As soon as Celia and the others were safely on their way, Brandon went to see Lady Brompton. The interior of her home was far more proper than last night's entertainment, if the soft blue carpet or the gilded chair he was led to in the withdrawing room was any indication. Lady Brompton, however, was definitely the worse for wear. Her eyes were puffy and bloodshot, her face blotchy, and she had developed a decided wheeze. A number of her guests were apparently still in residence, for Brandon thought he heard the sound of retching from down the corridor.

While her demeanor was bleary, she seemed to think her memory was sharp. At Brandon's subtle questioning, she insisted that he must be mistaken.

"I greeted all my guests, Lord Hartley, and I can safely say that none of them came dressed as Death. If you indeed saw someone dressed in that manner, he was an interloper."

She was also effusive in her apologies to Lady Honoria. "I always invite Mrs. Rider, for old time's sake," she confessed. "She always refuses. How was I to know she would accept this time or bring her stepdaughter with her?" She brightened and fluttered her lashes at him coquettishly. "Of course, I would not have had the pleasure of your company had she not insisted that I invite you as well."

So, Patrice had attempted to manipulate his attendance. Perhaps she had sent the note after all. Brandon thanked the woman and returned home with much on his mind.

Edmund was waiting. "I have news about your new toy."

Brandon raised a brow. "Toy?"

Edmund nodded, then turned to lead him to the library. The scythe stood braced against a bookcase. His uncle hefted it in one hand. "Your groom asked what should be done with it. I suggested we return it to its owner—our head gardener."

Brandon stared at him. "It is one of ours?"

"It is. I recognized it immediately." He upended it to show Brandon the initials of their man burned into the butt.

"How could one of our scythes end up on another estate?"

"This one," Edmund replied, "apparently had help. Mr. Neighbors, the gardener, remembers taking it with him to town to clear an area Lady Honoria wanted replanted. He has not seen it since."

He knew what Edmund wanted him to think. Here was proof that Celia had staged the affair. He had another theory. "Then my cousin had ready access to it. Our hostess last night tells me my cousin insisted on an invitation for me."

His uncle set the scythe back in place. "Interesting. Yet I cannot see Patrice being so clever as to arrange such a threat as your brush with Death. I fear that though we have pieces of this puzzle, we have yet to fit them to the true picture."

At least the picture Edmund wanted to see, Brandon thought as he and his uncle prepared to head into town for that afternoon's session of Parliament. Brandon could not deny that Patrice seemed incapable of masterminding all the threats to Celia. Yet who else did they have? This not knowing made him feel so damned impotent! He refused to tell Celia that he had failed her. If she could wait for his sake, surely he could find her tormenter. He might not be able to express his love publicly, but he would let her know in the things that counted.

Like saving her life.

Celia attempted to argue with Lady Honoria, to no avail. She only received a further scold for her behavior.

"You even left the younger Mr. Carstairs standing this morning, when I gather you had demanded the meeting in the first place," the lady said. "He shall have to make a special trip to see you tomorrow. What a sad state of affairs it is when a young lady is so rude."

She thought a little time cooling his heels would do James Carstairs good, but she decided not to argue the point with Lady Honoria. They had enough to disagree over already. By the time she left the dowager's company, she felt as frustrated as Patrice and Stanley looked.

"Do not listen to her, Stanley," Celia told him. "I could not give a fig about my reputation in London."

"By your leave, but I could not agree." Stanley's long face was pale. "I seem to have done you a great disservice. Perhaps we should wed after all."

Patrice burst into tears and ran off down the corridor. Stanley's shoulders slumped. Celia patted him on the back. "Go to her, Stanley. You love her. You should be with her."

Nodding, he shambled off.

Celia's fists balled at her sides as she strode off to her room to change. What right did Lady Honoria have to tell her how to behave? It was one thing to fault her actions; it was another to tell her how to remedy them. She could take responsibility for herself.

The best thing she could do, she decided as she dressed in a green sprigged muslin gown that Patrice swore was all the rage, was spend the rest of the day with Martin. She could take her mind off Brandon, and her brother could be counted upon not to censure her.

She was proved wrong on both counts. Martin greeted her with a cheery, "When is the wedding?" which served to stop her in her tracks.

"Wedding?" she managed.

He nodded, setting aside the slate on which he had been writing. She could see neat rows of numbers marching down the face of the black board. "You are to marry Stanley immediately. Lady Honoria said so."

Celia frowned. "When was this? I only just left her."

"She told me yesterday evening," Martin said, beaming as if pleased that he was the one to be best informed for once.

Yesterday evening? While they were at the masquerade? How had Lady Honoria known of the gossip before Celia had even given cause for it? The devious thing! Had she been the one to send the note to Brandon in Celia's name? But why if she was intent that Celia marry Stanley?

Unless she was intent that Celia step out of the way so that Patrice could marry Brandon.

"Excuse me a moment," Celia told Martin.

"But, Celia," he started. She held up a hand and left.

She marched down the stairs and through the corridor for Lady Honoria's suite. Tapping smartly at the door, she didn't bother to wait to be bidden to enter.

Sally scooped the papers off the desk onto the chair behind it and glared at her. "What do you want? Lady Honoria cannot be disturbed."

"Lady Honoria is thoroughly disturbed," Celia replied, heading for the bedchamber, "if she thinks she can tell me whom to marry."

She cast about the room, only to find it empty. She stalked back into the sitting room in time to see Sally stuffing the papers into a wall safe that had been concealed behind a pretty landscape. Sally slammed the door as she approached.

"Where is she?" Celia demanded.

"Wouldn't you like to know," Sally sneered, crossing her arms over her skinny chest. "You have no rights here. Take yourself back to your room and be thankful her ladyship is willing to give the likes of you a roof over your head."

"I might give you the same advice. Maid servants have more polish where I come from."

"There are no maid servants where you come from," Sally replied, nose in the air. "You smell of the shop."

"And you smell of yourself." Celia turned and walked out before she could answer.

She checked with Mr. Kinders, who told her that Lady Honoria had called for the coach. Celia hurried to the front door, just in time to see the coach pull away from the curb.

Where was her ladyship going in such a hurry? And why did Celia have a sinking feeling that she wouldn't like the answer?

Brandon and Edmund had started toward the House of Lords when Timms came hurrying after them. One glance at the footman, and Brandon knew something was wrong. The tall man was ever confident; now his hands positively trembled before his auburn and gold livery.

"What is it, Timms?" he asked, putting out a hand to stop his uncle.

Timms swallowed, glanced both directions as if expecting a French agent to be lurking in Westminster, and leaned forward. "Lady Honoria," he whispered. "She's come."

Brandon's gut tightened. Had something happened to Celia on the way home? He hadn't waited for Arlington to return.

"Where is she?" Edmund asked, glancing past the footman for the street. Following his gaze, Brandon saw his aunt's carriage behind his own. He started back.

"Good luck, m'lord," the footman called after him.

Brandon slowed. He hadn't even considered there might be another reason for his aunt's sudden arrival. If she had heard about his behavior last night, she could have come to test him. Between accosting Arlington and nearly seducing Celia, he had a number of misbehaviors to explain.

He squared his shoulders, vowing that she would detect no change in him. He strolled up to the coach, his manner nothing short of perfection. As her groom threw open the door, he bowed to Lady Honoria, then climbed inside. Edmund followed him.

"Honoria," his uncle said, inclining his head in greeting before perching on the auburn velvet seat.

She nodded coolly. "Sorry to intrude on your time, Brother. I have distressing news about Celia, and I thought you should hear it."

The statement was nearly Brandon's undoing. It took all the discipline of years and every ounce of his will to merely raise a brow and say with equal calm, "Oh?"

His aunt spared him a glance. "I know all about your involvement in that little adventure last night."

Brandon refused to rise to the bait, although he swore the temperature in the coach was heating.

"It was entirely Patrice's fault," she went on to Edmund. "At times I wonder if that girl is my own flesh and blood."

"Nothing of concern occurred," Brandon offered.

Her smile was calculating. "According to my information, any number of concerning things happened."

She would not be toying with him like this if Celia were in imminent danger. Brandon relaxed against the seat. "Do tell."

"To begin with, your friend Arlington fixed his interest on Patrice."

Edmund raised a brow. "You failed to mention that," he said to Brandon.

"I thought it an announcement he should make," Brandon replied.

"The pair of fribbles heartily deserve each other, if you ask me," his aunt said with a sniff. "Unfortunately, giving Mr. Arlington to Patrice will not help the damage to Celia's reputation. She was seen. How could she be so stupid?"

Brandon frowned. "It was a masquerade. I imagine she thought herself anonymous."

"Apparently she stood on a chair and shouted Mr. Arlington's name." Lady Honoria shook her head. "What was the girl thinking? Such vulgar behavior would not have been tolerated in my generation."

Brandon grit his teeth. "I assure you any minor infraction from Miss Rider is nothing against the rest of the event."

"Granted," Edmund said. "However, I take it everyone else remained safely anonymous."

"Precisely," Lady Honoria replied. "She will have to marry Arlington to stave off the gossip."

Brandon leaned forward. "Marry Arlington? Did he not cry off?"

"He tried." Lady Honoria's tone did not hide her disgust. "But truly, she has no choice." She sighed heavily. "What a shame. I shall have to send her regrets to Lord Wilton."

The heat was rising again. Brandon tugged at his cravat. "Wilton offered?"

"He is the third. I rejected the others out of hand as fortune hunters. But Wilton is a distinct possibility."

"A title, even if a mere viscount," Edmund enumerated, "a decided fortune in his own right, some power in the Lords." He glanced at Brandon. "Miss Rider would be fortunate indeed with such a catch. Small wonder she wished to accept."

He could not catch his breath. "Miss Rider is willing?"

Lady Honoria waved a hand. "She would have been, particularly now that the perfidious Mr. Arlington has shown his true colors. Besides, as her great-grandmother, I would be the one to accept or reject the offer."

"Miss Rider is of age, I believe," Edmund pointed out. "And she seems to have some definite ideas as to the type of gentleman she prefers."

Brandon ignored the edged remark. Sweat trickled down his back under his shirt.

Lady Honoria rolled her eyes. "Arlington. I should never have allowed Patrice to keep her in the country. If only I had been given charge of her sooner. Even now, I am persuaded she will be guided by me. She is an obedient girl. And Wilton is such an excellent match!"

Brandon felt a laugh bubbling up and sucked it down. Somehow he doubted that Celia would appreciate the compliment of being obedient. But he couldn't very well burst into laughter in front of Lady Honoria. Besides, she was no doubt right about Wilton. Alexander Devonshaw, Lord Wilton, was one of the most eligible bachelors on the ton. Handsome, affable, honorable—Wilton was everything any woman would want for her daughter.

And he had no family curse to contend with.

"You see why I had to come, Edmund," Lady Honoria was saying. "I must have your help."

"I can see reason for your concern," Edmund replied, "but I fail to see how I can help. Miss Rider seems to have a propensity for getting herself into trouble, as I have pointed out to Hartley."

His aunt flashed him a glance. The calculation in it made the temperature in the coach increase a few more degrees. "You talk of her impersonation of her brother's governess," she said to Edmund. "That was odd, I will allow you. It appears she did not trust us. I find that sad, and I have forgiven the girl."

"And the situation with her fortune?" Edmund pressed. "Hartley was forced to intervene there as well. And I am told she still has not put her hands on the money."

His uncle made Celia sound a true adventuress. He felt sick.

Lady Honoria waved away the concern. "A matter of protocol only. She is the heiress. There is simply no need for her to access the money until she marries."

Edmund crossed his arms over his chest. "Then you will have her live off the Pellidore estate while she waits? That hardly seems appropriate."

Lady Honoria eyed him. "You are particularly defensive. Has the girl offended you in some way?"

"My uncle," Brandon explained with a look to Edmund, "fears that Miss Rider is making fools of us all."

"Well!" Lady Honoria stiffened, dark eyes glinting. "You, Edmund, have been a guardian far too long to see danger in a snip of a girl. I had in mind for you to assist her now, but I see that is impossible. I will make the arrangements for her to marry Arlington immediately."

"Pray do so," Edmund snapped.

Sweat dripped into Brandon's eyes. He blinked it away. "Is this agreeable to Mr. Arlington and Miss Rider?"

Lady Honoria glared at him. "As I said, does she have a choice?"

He met his aunt's gaze. "Yes."

"Oh?" Lady Honoria asked, and Edmund turned to face him fully, brows raised. It was now or never.

"I suggest," Brandon said, "that Celia Rider marry me."

Nineteen

Celia intended to confront Lady Honoria when the woman returned. First she forced herself to calm. This was one time she was glad she could not immediately respond as her heart dictated. Lady Honoria was not one to cross. Look at the cavalier way she treated Patrice. Celia's stepmother was still sobbing in her room over Stanley's supposed defection.

Celia had to go carefully if she was to stop Lady Honoria's interference. Unfortunately, she soon found the lady wasn't the only one bent on making trouble. She was walking in the garden to compose herself when one of the footmen came for her. She almost pitied the suitor who was most likely her caller. She marched into the forward salon to tell the fellow she was in no mood for poetry, only to stop when she saw Lord Pellidore.

"Did I startle you, Miss Rider?" he asked, inclining his head. "No need for concern. I merely wish a word with you."

Celia was no more in the mood for a discussion with Brandon's uncle than she was for praises from a suitor. However, she crossed to the chair nearest him and sat. After a moment's hesitation, he took the chair opposite her.

"What will it take," he said, dark eyes intent on her face, "for you to release your hold on my nephew?"

Celia blinked. "What kind of hold do you think I have?"

"I wish I knew. However, be warned that I am on to your games."

"The only games I play," Celia replied, feeling her temper rising, "are with Martin. I think we should stop this conversation now."

He shook his head, and light glinted off the gray in his hair. "I care too much about my nephew to see him go so easily. Did you think I would ignore how you dealt with Miss Turner?"

Celia frowned. "What are you talking about? I barely know Miss Turner."

"You may pretend high dudgeon, but I know otherwise."

"You apparently think you know a great deal more than I do, I assure you."

"Oh, very good. I can see why Hartley, who is usually so careful, was taken in by your lies."

Celia rose. "I fear I am not up to another scold today, Lord Pellidore, particularly one made up of nothing but innuendos and threats."

He rose as well, glaring at her from a height approaching Brandon's. She stood taller and returned his look.

"If you must have it said precisely," he said, "Miss Turner and her entire family fell suddenly ill and were forced to retire to the country for the Season to recuperate. How very sad for them, and how very convenient for you."

"You think that was my doing? How could I have engineered such a feat?"

"My sister was once an accomplished herbalist. I

have no doubt you made sinister use of her recipe books."

That sounded more like something Sally would try. Yet surely she wouldn't cross town to poison another family when she had so many enemies waiting for her underfoot. Celia shook her head. "As your mind is made up, I will not bother to protest my innocence. If you are so sure of my guilt, I suggest you speak to your nephew. I believe he cares for me."

He stiffened as if she'd struck him. "Has he come to you already, then? Am I too late?"

His face had gone so pale that she almost pitied him. He must truly believe the bile he was spouting. However, since not a word of it was true, she refused to let his feelings do more than temper her words. "We have agreed to wait until he is ready to propose," she told him.

"When he proposes, refuse him," he ordered. "I will see you well paid."

When would he run out of ways to insult her? "You forget, Lord Pellidore, I do not need your money. I am an heiress."

"Oh, yes, the so-called fortune." He stepped closer as if to emphasize his point, and she was suddenly aware that he was nearly as broad-shouldered as Brandon as well. He could easily crush her. She held herself still.

"I do not know what you promised James Carstairs to assist you in this charade," he said, "but if you truly had a fortune, he would have paid you by now."

She felt as if a trap was closing about her. "You are mistaken. I do not need money, and if I choose to marry your nephew, it will be because I love him and he loves me."

"Which is exactly as it should be," Lady Honoria announced from the doorway.

Celia stepped back from him, and Lord Pellidore jerked around. The older man raised his head as if to defend himself. "Honoria, this is none of your affair," he blustered.

She hobbled into the room. "Every bit my affair if you choose to bully my great-granddaughter under my own roof. And I thought you were a gentleman."

They glared at each other for a moment. It was as if Celia could see the animosity, like heat rising from a barren field in the summer sun. Then Edmund snapped a bow and strode from the room. Lady Honoria shook her head.

"Do not listen to him, Celia," she ordered. "I expect you to accept my nephew."

"Your nephew," Celia replied, chin up, "has no plans to offer for me."

Lady Honoria raised a brow as she settled onto the sofa. "I seem to have lost my touch. Everyone to whom I speak is so defensive. Sit down, girl."

Her tone was commanding, which only made Celia smart the more. However, it seemed a petty thing to stand petulantly. She deigned to perch upon the chair she had recently vacated and arranged the skirts of her green sprigged muslin gown. "I apologize if my attitude is lacking," she said to Lady Honoria in what she hoped was a polite tone. "I am merely concerned that you have taken it upon yourself to see me wed."

For a moment, Lady Honoria simply blinked. Before Celia could even frown, she recovered. "Of course I wish to see you wed. What woman would not wish that for her great-granddaughter?"

Something was wrong. Lady Honoria's dark eyes

held secret thoughts. Celia could feel the machinations swirling about her. Yet like phantoms, none could she pin down. "Your kindness is misplaced," she replied. "I can manage my own life. I have done so for several years."

Lady Honoria leaned forward, eyes narrowing. "Have you? Rusticating in Somerset? What could you know of the requirements of Society? Look how easily you let Patrice lead you into a situation where your reputation was damaged."

"I will be wiser next time," Celia assured her.

"A 'next time' may see you dead, child."

Celia chilled. As if sensing her weakness, Lady Honoria leaned back and smiled. The smile only made Celia feel colder.

"I do not think you appreciate the fact," she continued, "that you are a very popular young lady."

She wasn't sure how to answer and decided, "Thank you," would have to suffice.

"You are also a very fortunate young lady. Did you know Viscount Wilton is interested in your hand?"

"Wilton?" Celia grabbed at the name as an anchor in the uncertain waters of the conversation. "But I thought you insisted that I marry Stanley?"

Lady Honoria clucked her tongue. "He is such a poor catch, a country boy with no connections and an estate, though large, of no strategic importance. Wilton, however, is a gem."

"It matters little, as I shall have neither of them."

"That picky, are you? Then are you intent on refusing my nephew as well?"

Celia crossed her arms over her chest. "Lord Hartley will not offer. And I am not interested in marriage at this time."

"Pity you did not consider that before going to Lady Brompton's party."

Celia sighed. "We have been over this to no avail. I care nothing for the gossip."

"Do you not? Even if it affects those around you?"

Celia frowned. "Who else might it affect?"

"Patrice, for one. Someone is sure to remember that she has been escorting you, and questions will be raised. Either she was there, in which case her reputation is as shredded as yours, or she was not diligent in her duties as your stepmother, in which case she merely looks the fool."

"Those are the consequences of her actions. If I must pay for mine, I see no reason she should be spared."

"And you could not move yourself to spare her."

Her conscience tweaked her, and she dropped her arms to her sides. "I would not see her suffer unduly. However, with her upcoming marriage to Stanley, that should not be the case."

"And my suffering is immaterial as well, I suppose."

Celia smiled. "You will not suffer. Everyone I meet is far too afraid of you to utter a twitter against you."

Lady Honoria shared her smile. "Very wise of you to notice, my dear. However, you are wrong about my nephew offering. He will be here at eight. He told me so."

Brandon sat in a corner of White's, fingering the ring he had purchased that afternoon. He had promised Lady Honoria he would come by at eight to ask for Celia's hand in marriage. He should be in alt. For once, fate had conspired to grant his wish, instead of forcing him to go along with the dictates of the inheritance. Why, then, did he feel so blue-devilled?

"There you are!" Stanley proclaimed. He glanced about as if looking for a chair near Brandon to plop onto. As Brandon had chosen the most isolated chair in which to ponder, Arlington had little luck. Ever resourceful, he set about dragging one over from farther away. The wood floor protested with a loud squeak. Brandon could hear the murmured complaints from the rest of the club members.

"There," Stanley said, seating himself at last and clapping hands to the knees of his dark trousers. "Don't know why they put these chairs so far apart, by your leave. Deuced hard to have a conversation, don't you know."

"Mayhap some wish more solitary activities," Brandon replied pointedly.

Stanley frowned. "Why? It is a club, don't you know. I'd expect people to be sociable. And speaking of which, you must talk with the doorman. He very nearly didn't let me in, don't you know. Claimed I either had to be a member or be with a member. I told him I was with you, but I'm not too sure he believed me."

Brandon made a mental note to tip the doorman, heavily. "Did you need me for some reason, Arlington?"

Stanley had been fussing with his cravat. Now his hands stilled and dropped back to his sides. He sighed deeply. "I'm in a deuced fix, Hart. Celia's in the soup, and I seem to be the only one who can get her out."

Now what? He nearly pounced on the man to demand an explanation. Instead, he closed the ring in his fist and straightened in the chair. "What do you mean?" he asked coolly.

Stanley launched into the same tale Lady Honoria had given Brandon earlier. "So you see," he concluded, "her ladyship is certain the only way to quell the gossip is for Celia to marry."

Brandon opened his hand to display the ring. "I agree. She will marry me."

To his surprise, Stanley's pale green eyes filled with tears. "By your leave, Hart, that is the most noble deed I have ever known. You are truly amazing. First you find Celia's fortune, then you take me in, and then you rescue Patrice and Celia from deflowering. I don't care what others say. You are a great gun."

"Arlington," Brandon began, watching in dismay as the tears flowed down the man's cheeks.

Stanley held up a hand. "No, no, I mean it. You inspire me, don't you know." He sniffed and wiped his nose on his sleeve. "But I cannot let you sacrifice yourself for me. It is my duty to marry Celia."

"I thought you loved my cousin."

As he colored, Brandon relaxed. For a moment, he had feared the fellow felt something for Celia after all.

"By your leave, my devotion to Patrice is complete. I have never felt for another woman what I feel for her."

"Even Celia?" Brandon pressed.

Stanley shook his head. "Even Celia. She is a great gun. Not like the other girls, don't you know. It isn't in her to simper or confuse a fellow with mawkish talk. If Celia is mad at you, she tells you straightaway."

"So I have seen," Brandon replied with a smile.

Stanley smiled as well. "I expect it was her back-bone that drew me to her. I figured she could stand up to Father, even if I couldn't."

"If that is what you seek in a wife, know that I cannot see my cousin in that role."

Stanley's smile widened. "Nor can I. But she doesn't need to be in that role, don't you know. When I am with Patrice, I am the strong one. She makes me feel like one of the knights of old in the stories Celia tells. I would dare anything for my lady fair." Brandon thought for a moment Stanley would leap to his feet to prove his point, but he suddenly sobered. "I would even tell my father how I feel."

Now, there was a change in him. From the moment Brandon had met Stanley, his father had been a figure looming in the background, a seemingly omnipotent force capable of ruling his son's future. That Stanley was willing to gainsay him spoke volumes for his devotion to Patrice. Brandon nodded. "You are indeed fortunate, Arlington. Why wish such a gift away? Let me offer for Celia."

Stanley frowned again. "But are you certain, Hart? By your leave, can you be happy with her?"

"I wish to think so." Brandon leaned forward, resolution kindling. "Tell me something. My uncle is certain Celia is an adventuress. You claim to know her well. What do you think?"

Stanley opened his mouth as if to protest, then seemed to think better of it. "My father said the same thing, by your leave," he admitted sheepishly. "That's why he insisted on seeing proof of the fortune before we could wed."

Brandon's fist tightened on the ring, as if even his muscles protested the idea. "Yet you had faith in her."

Stanley smiled. "I liked her. You cannot say she isn't a fine figure of a woman, by your leave. There are few like her in the wilds of Somerset, I can tell you. And there was the fortune."

"So for her fortune, figure, and force of character, you could overlook the chance that she was out for your lands."

Stanley stuck out his lower lip thoughtfully. "I suppose I could. And I had known her since before she left for school, don't you know. Besides, Hart, faith is believing something even when you see the evidence against it before you."

Brandon raised a brow. "That sounds more like idiocy to me."

"No, it's faith, to be sure. Take Celia, for example. There are several things about her that might make one think she is an adventuress. She has that determination. Once she sets her sights on something, she perseveres until she gets it."

"I have seen that as well."

Stanley leaned forward, grinning. "You should have seen her back home. There is a hedge and ditch between our two estates. She was determined to jump it, don't you know. I remember she tried it from this angle and that. She changed horses. She even borrowed my father's prize hunter." He rubbed the back of his neck. "Father scolded me unmercifully."

Brandon could almost picture Celia sailing over the wall of green. "I take it she finally succeeded."

Stanley nodded. "She fell off more than once. But she got over, don't you know." He met Brandon's gaze with a solemn look. "A bit scary when a woman is so dead set on something she'll overlook her personal safety, and yours, to get it."

He could not disagree. However, the thought was as exhilarating as it was frightening. What could such a woman do, given the right circumstances and encouragement?

"It was the same with the fortune," Stanley went on. "She was so determined to get it she came all the way to London alone, with that odd plan about playing Martin's governess. And it looks as if she will succeed there as well." He brightened. "There you have it, Hart. She cannot be a true adventuress. She has blunt of her own, don't you know."

"Money is only one of the things an adventuress covets," Brandon told him. "They might also look for land or family connections."

"Or a title," Stanley mused.

"Or a title," Brandon agreed. Was that what Celia was striving for now? Yet surely if that were the case, she would have accepted Wilton. Of course, he was only a viscount. If Celia married Brandon, and survived him, she would be a titled lady with a considerable fortune, and beholden to no one for anything.

He felt his jaw tighten and glanced up to find Stanley regarding him with a worried frown. Brandon inclined his head. "Have no fears, Arlington. Your story has not deterred me. This evening, I offer for Celia. We shall see how she answers."

Twenty

Celia pressed her back against the chair as the world tilted around her. Lady Honoria cocked her head. "I am surprised. I thought you would be pleased by the fact that my nephew wishes to offer."

So many thoughts spun through her mind that she could not remain still. "Rather say that I am confused," she replied as she popped to her feet to pace. "No, shocked would be a better word. When did he confide in you, under what circumstances?"

Lady Honoria waved a hand. "What possible difference does that make? The boy will offer. If you are as intelligent as I think you are, you will accept."

Only last night she would have been delighted to accept. Now she couldn't help wondering what had changed his mind. He had been so passionate about waiting. He had been so cool this morning. To turn around and offer marriage by evening made no sense. Unless, of course, he simply did not know his own mind.

Or his mind was slipping.

She shuddered. Lady Honoria must have seen the movement as a further sign of weakness, for she pounced.

"Think, girl! He has a fortune to match yours. His title is older than Wilton's and of a greater degree. By this connection, you remove all taint of the merchant class from your children. He is even considered kind on the eyes. You will be the envy of every woman in London!"

Celia shook her head. "I cannot understand you. This morning you urged engagement to Stanley, and now you as easily counsel marriage to Lord Hartley."

"This morning," Lady Honoria said sternly, "you did not have an offer from Hartley. Now you do. Take it. You cannot be certain he will repeat it at a more convenient time."

No, she could not. Yet she also could not agree to marriage in this cold, calculating manner. "If Lord Hartley is intent on proposing, I will listen when he calls." She straightened under the flash of fire from Lady Honoria's eyes.

Lady Honoria clipped out the words in her displeasure. "Perhaps you should retire to your room to consider the matter."

"A moment," Celia said, and watched the lightning arc across the darkness of the lady's eyes again. "I want to be certain we understand each other. While I live under your roof, I will honor your rules. However, in no case will I accept decisions you make for me. Patrice may be content to live that way. I am not."

"I would be careful," Lady Honoria said quietly. "You do not have your fortune yet. Until then, you are beholden to me."

A threat lurked behind those words, but at least this was plain speaking. "I am aware that you pay my bills. However, I stand by my statement. I will respect your wishes, so long as they do not run counter to mine. Good afternoon, Lady Honoria."

She dropped a curtsey, inclining her head to make the movement more respectful. When she glanced up, Lady Honoria's eyes had narrowed, and two spots of color stood high on her cheeks. Feeling the room chill again, Celia turned and left.

Brandon arrived precisely at eight as promised. He had waited for his uncle at White's, expecting Edmund to wish to join him. To his surprise, his uncle insisted he had a previous engagement and would wait for Brandon to return to the club later. Brandon had taken Stanley and decamped.

"Wasn't that the solicitor fellow joining your uncle?" Stanley asked as they settled into the coach. "They let almost anyone in that club, don't you know."

"So I have noticed," Brandon replied as the coach set off. He could only hope Edmund sought the solicitor about the Pellidore fortune and that his uncle was not interfering.

At his aunt's establishment, Patrice was playing hostess. It was easy for Brandon to encourage a private moment between her and Stanley. As soon as she and Arlington had their heads together on the sofa, Brandon drew Celia to the opposite corner.

She did not seem pleased to see him. Her clear skin was pale, and her changeable eyes looked a deep gray, as if the color had been washed from them with her joy. The urge to touch her was almost overpowering. "Are you all right?" he asked.

She managed a wan smile. "A little weary. It seems I have had nothing but difficult conversations today. Did you know your uncle was here?"

Anger poked at his tongue. He tamped the emotion down. "No. Did he offend you?"

"A great deal. Why is he so unkind?"

He gave in to temptation and ran a hand down her arm in comfort. "He fears what you can do to me."

She frowned. "What could I possibly do to threaten the mighty Marquess of Hartley?"

"You made off with my heart."

He watched as she raised her eyes to his. Was it hope he saw? He refused to see calculation. He took hold of her hand. "We must talk, Celia."

She colored as if his touch warmed her and nodded. "Yes. Lady Honoria tells me you intend to offer for me."

He should have known his aunt could not resist crowing. She'd jumped on his suggestion too quickly, making him wonder if forcing him to that position had not been her intention all along. Yet Celia did not look nearly as delighted.

"Does the thought of my offer disturb you?" he murmured, bending closer.

She flashed him a quick glance. "Disturb may be too strong a word. You know my feelings from last night. I do wonder, however, how much we really know about each other."

It was not like her to be coy, so he decided to take the concern at face value. "What would you like to know?"

Her eyes narrowed thoughtfully. He waited, expecting her to probe the story of his father again. Though he had told her most of it, he could not help wondering what others had said. How much horror could the gossips build in to madness? Was that what held her back?

"What do you do for enjoyment?" she asked suddenly.

He blinked. "Enjoyment?"

She chuckled. "Yes, enjoyment. It is a three-syllable

word describing the feeling you gain when you undertake activities for pleasure. I believe you know something of pleasure, do you not?"

"Only since meeting you."

He watched the color build in her cheeks. Would they be hot to the touch of his lips? Ah, what a pleasure that would be to find out.

"Thank you for the compliment, but have you never done anything for the pure joy of it?"

Besides pursuing her? He quirked his lips as he thought. He had run off to the village nearest the estate in Scotland when he was a child. They let him pretend he was a normal boy. But that had been years ago. Gambling was something expected of him, though he did take a certain satisfaction when the turn of the cards favored him. Exercise with the punching bag let out necessary frustrations, and he always felt cleaner afterward. Both were pleasures of a sort, yet he thought she expected something more, some secret passion he hid from her. Unfortunately, she was the only secret passion he possessed.

He shrugged. "Joy would not seem a requirement in my life. Mayhap the closest activity was studying music."

"You studied music? Which instrument?"

Now he was in a fix. It was no doubt a sign of his emotional state that he had painted himself into this corner. He hadn't failed to think ahead like that in years. "The same one my cousin studied."

"The pianoforte? Really? What is your favorite piece?"

"Mozart's Sonata in C Major."

"Why?"

He could not imagine what difference that would

make, but thought for a moment and answered, "It requires dedication and careful thought to execute."

"Dedication and careful thought are very important to you, I have noticed. Yet surely there is more than that. Some gentlemen ride, others race or box. Surely you passed your time somehow before Martin arrived and taught you how to fly a kite."

He smiled. "My earlier life seems dull after that."

When she continued to eye him expectantly, he shrugged. "Very well. My days are no mystery. I rise early, ride, exercise with a weighted leather device designed for me, and clean and dress for the day. I usually take the morning with my steward and the afternoon in the House of Lords, when it is in session. In the evenings, I attend such events as move me. I am fond of drama at the theater. My favorite color is green."

She seized the opening immediately. "What shade of green?"

He felt a smile forming. "I start to think the exact shade of your eyes."

She dimpled. "You like to discompose me."

"I like to flirt with you. I like the way your feelings show in your face and in your eyes. You hide nothing."

"Why should I? I am what I am."

"And that, my dear Celia, is one of your greatest charms."

She glanced up at him from under thick lashes. "So, you think you know everything about me, then, do you?"

Not nearly enough, something inside him urged. The voice sounded suspiciously like Edmund's. "Not everything," he admitted. "Yet if you wish me to know more, tell me what you do for enjoyment other than torment me."

She laughed again, chipping away at his resolve to keep himself at a distance from her. "My life until I reached London was uncomplicated. In the country, I managed the household, rode, read, and entertained Martin."

Nothing devious there. "And your friends?"

She shrugged. "I made some friends at school, but they went on to marry and move away. We correspond."

"And when you returned home?"

"I found Society near our home consisted of married older ladies. They had little use for me, except to plot alliances."

Her life had been nearly as solitary as his. She did not seem to have suffered for it. He liked that. "No watercolors? No musical instrument?"

She shook her head. "I learned to paint in school, but even Miss Alexander, our art mistress, could not give me a proper appreciation of it. And I am all thumbs at the pianoforte."

"I seem to recall a certain telling item of stitchery."

"I picked out those stitches," she said primly. "Though I learned to embroider in school, it struck me as unoriginal."

"And you are an Original?"

She tossed her head. "I like to think so. I may never match the notoriety and spirit of Lady Thomas DeGuis or the witty conversation of Madam DeStael, but I hope I shall never allow Society's rules to dictate my choices."

He caught himself wanting to stroke the candlelight's reflection in her hair and pressed his arms to his sides. "Easier said than done. Society has a way of ensuring its strictures are followed."

"Now you sound like Lady Honoria." She sighed. "Which brings us back to where we started. This morning she insisted that I marry Stanley to stave off gossip. Then she brought up Viscount Wilton of all people." Her shudder gladdened his heart. "Now she seems fixed on you. You must know, Brandon, that I care nothing for what others say. You wished to wait. Please do not jeopardize yourself for me."

He could not help but be warmed by her willingness to put his needs first. "Thank you for that. However, you cannot understand the vicious nature of gossip, or Lady Honoria's determination to enforce her will."

"Oh," she replied, "I begin to learn the latter quite well, but you underestimate me if you think I cannot match her."

He quirked a smile. "In your determination, certainly. However, I would not see you forced against her."

"I do not relish the idea either. However, I like less that you have been put in a position like this. Do you truly intend to offer?"

Before he could answer, Patrice's voice rose from across the room. "No! I do not understand. All I know is that you are leaving, now when I need you most."

Celia's head turned as her stepmother ran from the room. Stanley stood forlornly behind.

"A minor disagreement," he said, but Brandon thought even he doubted the truth of those words. "I shall await you in the corridor, Hart. Good evening, Celia."

She sighed as he ambled out. "Oh, for a moment's peace!"

Disappointment bit sharply. "You wish me to wait to offer?"

She narrowed her eyes as if in thought. "We must talk of more personal things than I am willing to say here. I may have a solution, but its success depends on how many risks you are willing to take."

He cocked his head. "Risks?"

She trilled a laugh. "You make it sound as if I shall require you to dance naked across Parliament. It is nothing so shocking, I promise. Are you willing to wait a day or so for me to arrange a more conducive setting to our discussion?"

"Mayhap," he said, then nearly laughed himself at the caution in his tone. If he loved her enough to marry her, he must love her enough to trust her. Yet he found he could not take such a chance. "You understand the constraints I face?"

"I think I do. I will endeavor to do nothing that might raise a question in anyone's mind about your ability to reason. However, I may require you to do something out of the ordinary."

"Such as?"

She smiled. "I do not know as yet. Simply be prepared to be entertained, my lord."

Celia saw Brandon and Stanley out, then went in search of Patrice. Her stepmother was in her bedchamber, curled up on her bedstead, clutching a satin pillow to her chest.

"What did he say to you?" Celia asked, sitting gingerly beside her.

She sucked in a sob. "He said he cannot marry me

without his father's blessing. He will leave London shortly."

Celia sighed, adjusting herself on the slippery rose-colored coverlet. "Poor Stanley. I suppose he will never learn."

"I thought he loved me!" Patrice wailed.

"He does," Celia assured her. "But not, apparently, more than his father's good opinion."

Patrice scooted herself upright and stuck out her lower lip. "I am being petulant. Stanley does what he must. His father sounds like a tyrant. He could cut Stanley off without a cent. With me having no income of my own, where would we be?"

Celia sighed again, but this time in frustration. "What do you mean, no income of your own? You have a jointure from my father. I saw it on the accounting sheets."

Patrice's gaze dropped. "I seem to have spent it."

"What?" Celia stared at her. "But, Patrice, that was a considerable sum! Even with a dozen new dresses a month, you would not have depleted it."

She plucked at the lace edging the pillow. "I do not think purchasing new gowns was the problem."

"Then what, pray tell, was?"

Patrice glanced up and away again. "The wagers."

"You *do* gamble!"

"Shh!" Patrice grabbed her hands as if she thought Celia would somehow signal all of Society. "Yes and I shall thank you to keep it to yourself. Grandmother does not know."

"Patrice," Celia said with a shake of her head, "Lady Honoria knows everything that goes on in this house and most of Society as well. You can be sure she is aware of your wagers." Nevertheless, she dropped her voice. "Is it terribly bad?"

Patrice nodded, releasing her. "Yes. I do not know how my debts grew so large, but Madam Zala says I owe her several thousand pounds."

The amount was staggering. "Madam Zala?" she probed.

"She manages a *very* select gambling house. James Carstairs took me there, and Brandon and Stanley patronize it as well, so you know that it is fashionable."

"And do they take your money in a more fashionable way as well?" Celia quipped.

Patrice hugged the pillow to her chest again, and two more tears fell. Poor thing! Very likely she simply hadn't known what she was doing. It horrified Celia, though, to think of so much money so easily gone. Was that why Carstairs and Son dallied with awarding her fortune? Did they know of Patrice's problem and seek to keep her from gambling away the rest of the estate? But surely she could not touch Martin's portion. And Celia wasn't about to let Patrice manage hers.

At the thought of her brother, she touched Patrice's shoulder and rose. "I will do what I can about the debts. And do not worry about Stanley either. I am certain he loves you. Now, excuse me, for I must wish Martin good night."

Patrice uncurled herself and hopped off the bed. "Oh, wait for me! I have not seen the darling boy tonight either."

Celia sighed, but she waited while Patrice splashed water on her face and dried away the last of her tears. Then they went together to the schoolroom.

John must have seen Martin to bed, for her brother was already nestled beneath the covers and breathing peacefully. His dark hair curled around his face, which was relaxed in slumber. One hand clutched at the pillow as if even in his dream he held the reins of his precious horse.

Patrice blew out a breath. "Is he not beautiful?"

Celia smiled. "Yes." The dark hair reminded her of Brandon. If she accepted his proposal, would she tip-toe in to kiss another dark-haired child to sleep? Would he have a blond-haired sister nearby? Would their father join her in gazing wistfully at them, his strong arm wrapped around her waist?

Or would they all wonder at the cold stranger who was the lord of the manor?

She put aside the thought and went to kiss her brother lightly on the forehead. Patrice followed suit. Celia started out, then noticed her stepmother had not followed.

Patrice must have seen her look, for she smiled. "I will stay a while longer. I like watching him."

"Then why did you leave him behind?" The words came out on impulse, but she did not want to call them back. She had wondered at the answer for too long.

Patrice's smile grew sad. "A wife's place is with her husband. My David's work was in London. When he passed on, Lady Honoria insisted I stay with her. It was my duty to comply. I was so pleased when she said Martin might come at last."

So it was Lady Honoria who had kept Martin in Somerset all those years. Having seen the lady's hold on her house, Celia could understand why Patrice had been unable to fight her edict. Apparently Lady Honoria thought children useful only when they reached the age to be properly educated.

Still, Celia thought as she tiptoed out, those phantoms of worry were beginning to circle again. If only she could understand what they meant, before someone got hurt.

Twenty-one

Celia made sure she was up in time to breakfast with her brother the next morning. He had questions about where she had been and what she had been doing. He also told her about the horse Lady Honoria was going to purchase for him. That Lady Honoria was so generous reminded her of her concerns of the night before. She was afraid to trust her brother to the lady's not-so-tender mercies if she left.

If she married Brandon, however, would he take on guardianship for Martin? Would that ensure her brother's safety? And what about her own concerns about Brandon's abilities to love? She was so deep in thought that she did not hear her brother address her until he grabbed her hand and gave it a tug.

"Celia!"

She blinked and gazed down at his upturned face. He grinned at her.

"You do not attend," he said with a teasing grin. "If the real Miss Prim were here, she would take away your skittle time this evening."

Celia chuckled. "I doubt I shall have much time for skittles regardless. I told you what happened. I must decide what to do about Lord Hartley."

His grin faded. "Is the answer so hard?"

"Yes. I care for him, Martin, but I am not sure what

he feels for me. He was raised differently. Father, my mother, even Miss Prim encouraged us to say how we feel and act on our beliefs. He was never allowed to do so."

Her brother nodded sagely. "He said he had never flown a kite. I thought he was teasing."

Celia glanced down at him thoughtfully. "I doubt that. I wager he never played at all."

At her brother's look of horror, she felt her own grin forming. "And that is what I shall do, Martin. I shall get Lord Hartley to play."

John, who was attending them, snorted. "Good luck to you there. Lord Heartless they call him." He snapped his mouth shut suddenly and colored. "Sorry, Miss Rider," he muttered. "I keep forgetting who you are and all."

She reached up to pat him on the arm. "Quite all right, John. I have been known to forget myself from time to time. However, if I can get help from you and Martin, I may be able to get Lord Hartley to forget himself as well."

Lady Honoria motioned James Carstairs impatiently into the chair before her, then grimaced as the movement disturbed her foot. Sally hurried forward to adjust the velvet cushion on which the foot reposed. Lady Honoria waved her away with even less charity.

"If you are here to report anything less than success," she told the young solicitor, "our conversation will be unpleasant."

His smile was cool. "The funds have been managed as you specified. However, I thought you should know that Lord Pellidore insisted I dine with him last night."

She felt Sally cringe. Could nothing go right? First that upstart girl was so impudent as to question her decisions and now this! Such news should come through Sally—the woman was paid enough for it. Sally kept the Pellidore coachman supplied with a potent blend of tobacco to ensure his cooperation. Since Edmund had returned to England, she had always known of his activities within the day. How else keep ahead of him?

"Indeed," she said aloud. "Why would he wish your company?"

"He pretended to befriend me. He confided that Lord Hartley is to marry Miss Rider."

He sounded far less annoyed by the fact than she had been. However, there was compensation for the inconvenience. "Can you think of a better way to hide the disappearance of her fortune? Her funds are merely swallowed in his, and no one is the wiser. And we have a few more weeks to finish our work."

He inclined his head, but she could see that he was not satisfied. "The gossip was only a way for Lord Pellidore to test me," he said with a sniff. "It soon became apparent that he wanted to learn more about the Rider fortune."

They could not have been this transparent that Edmund had guessed. "Why?"

"He appears to think the girl is a title hunter."

She chuckled. "Perfect. Then why do you look displeased? Did you not satisfy him in that regard?"

"I told him the same story we told the girl—that we were awaiting information from Somerset and would award the sum shortly."

"Did he accept that?"

His mouth tightened. "No. He seemed bent on proving that Miss Rider is penniless. He also mentioned that Mrs. Rider is engaged."

And that had, no doubt, put James even more out of countenance. Lady Honoria tapped the desk with a finger. "She fancies that bumpkin from Somerset. It is a passing whim."

"You are certain? She does not love him?"

Oh, but the man could get maudlin. As if he knew anything of real passion. "It is only a minor interest, I tell you. She needs someone more stable, more urbane."

James brushed back his pale hair with an elegant hand. "I could not agree more."

Another upstart. Must she endure them on all sides? She inhaled deeply and let it out slowly. Soon. It would be soon. Only for a while longer must she suffer the ministrations of fools. Shortly she would put the last strokes in place for her masterpiece. And her revenge on her father would be complete.

"Thank you for letting me know about Edmund, James," she said. "You may leave my brother to me."

He rose and bowed. "And never could I hope for more capable hands. Do you still wish me to speak to the girl?"

"I suppose you must. She has a stubborn streak and clings to her purpose more tightly than a miser to his purse."

His lip curled in obvious distaste. "She has none of your refinement or understanding."

"Few do. However, if I must deal with Edmund, you can surely deal with Celia. Be patient, James. Everything you deserve shall shortly be yours."

He bowed again, but she thought it was more to hide his eager smile than to thank her.

* * *

Celia began planning her campaign to unleash Brandon's heart immediately. It soon became apparent that, to succeed, she would need access to some funds. Accordingly, she waited in the corridor to waylay James Carstairs when he finished that morning's meeting with Lady Honoria.

She ushered him into the forward salon and perched on one of the chairs with her back to the light. While he sat opposite, she thought about how to open the conversation. Though she needed money to pay Patrice's gambling debts and to go forward with her plan for Brandon, she dared not confide in him either reason. She decided to start by asking the status of her fortune. His answer surprised her.

"We are nearly done with the formalities," he replied with his usual coolness, leaning back in the chair to cross his legs. "I understand, however, that I should wish you happy. I believe you are to marry Lord Hartley."

Celia set her mouth. "That has not been decided."

He paled. "Has it not? Surely after your contretemps in the maze at Lady Brompton's . . . ."

"I do not allow gossip to rule my life. Now, I have an urgent need for a considerable sum. How would you like to arrange its transfer?"

He shook his head. "You mistake me. I said we were *nearly* done. No money may change hands as yet. In fact, I just began the agreements necessary to transfer control to Lord Hartley."

"What!" Celia jumped to her feet. "Why would Lord Hartley control my fortune?"

Carstairs rose as well and reached out a hand as if

to calm her. She jerked away from him. He lowered his hand and inclined his head. "I have upset you again. Please forgive me, Miss Rider. I only meant that by law, when a woman marries, the control of her finances transfers to her husband. It would have happened whomever you married."

"Surely there are ways to protect the money."

"There may be. Would you like me to look into the matter?"

"No," Celia snapped. "Right now I would settle on a draft in the amount of five thousand pounds."

She could see him swallow. "I will see what I can do. Perhaps in a few days, a fortnight at most . . . ."

"Today, Mr. Carstairs," she said. "This afternoon at the latest. If you cannot do this, I shall be forced to tell Lady Honoria of my displeasure."

It was a humbug. She had no interest in letting Lady Honoria know what she was up to. But James Carstairs could not know that, and she was certain he was too devoted to the lady to chance making her his enemy. However, she was surprised to see him smile.

"Please pass along my regards when you see her," he said, and beneath the words she was certain she heard sarcasm. He picked up the portfolio he had brought with him. "Now, if you will excuse me."

She was quite tempted to tell him he must stay, but she had no reason to keep him. She nodded. He moved to the door without so much as bowing to her.

He nearly bumped into Patrice. Celia watched as her stepmother retreated to allow him to leave. By the height of his raised brows, James could see the change in her. Her lower lip trembled, and her hands hung limply at her sides.

"Mrs. Rider," he said, bowing deeply. "Might I be of service to you?"

Celia blinked at the conciliatory tone. Apparently she was the only one he felt comfortable slighting.

Patrice smiled wanly. "No, thank you, Mr. Carstairs. Though you can wish me happy. I am to be wed shortly, I hope."

He stiffened, color heightening. "You deserve every happiness, my dear. More, you deserve a man with the power and resources to do you justice."

Did he dare to malign Stanley? Patrice apparently thought so, for her smile faded to a frown. "Mr. Arlington will make a good husband."

She started past him, but he caught her shoulder. Insolence indeed, Celia thought. Temper rising, she strode to her stepmother's side.

"Mr. Arlington is a gentleman," Celia said, head high.

Carstairs released Patrice to turn an icy gaze on Celia. "You would know, of course, as he was previously engaged to you. Obviously a gentleman of discriminating taste."

Celia sucked in a breath. Was he mad to treat them with such disrespect? Even Patrice heard the sarcasm in his tone, for her hands set to fluttering before her.

"No more difficult conversations, please! I cannot bear it!"

He bowed again. "Of course. Forgive me. Only promise me you will think on what I said. You must marry a man worthy of you."

A tear rolled down Patrice's cheek. "But I love Stanley."

He jerked upright. His face could not have looked more frozen than if she had slapped him.

"I wish you every happiness," he said, then turned and strode for the stairs.

Celia wrapped her arms around her and rubbed them. His actions said that he believed she and Patrice held no power over him. Had the gossip made him think them less than ladies, or did he simply not care to continue managing the fortune? More likely he thought it no longer her fortune to manage. If she married Brandon, the fortune would pass into the Pellidore estate, and James would deal directly with Brandon. No more demands for explanations, no more threats of displeasure.

Celia shook her head. He was a fool if he thought Brandon would let him manage the money with no input. She heard the yearning in Brandon's voice when he talked of taking control of his life. He had plans for that money, and she wouldn't have been surprised if James Carstairs played little part.

Did Brandon also have plans for her money?

She shook her head again. She would trust him; she must. Still, it would be easier if she knew he could share all of himself with her. Surely if she could get him to be at ease, to play, to laugh, she would know that he could love. And if she knew he could love, she could trust him with her future.

"Everyone is unpleasant today," Patrice said with a sigh, going to sit on the sofa.

"Not everyone," Celia replied, joining her. "Before Mr. Carstairs was so rude, I asked him to advance me some funds. I intend to pay off your gambling debts."

Patrice patted her hands. "That is sweet, but you needn't worry. Stanley paid them off. He sent me a note."

Celia frowned. "But you said you owed thousands of pounds. Stanley couldn't lay his hands on that amount of money without going to his father."

Patrice puckered. "Perhaps that is why he must go home. Oh, my poor dear! It is all my fault. I will never so much as look at a gaming table again!"

Celia could only hope it would be as easy as that. Perhaps her stepmother's single-mindedness would see her in good stead in this instance. A shame the rest of Celia's problems weren't so simple. If James Carstairs didn't come through, she wasn't sure how she could enact her plan for Brandon. She hated to enlist too many of the servants, for she wasn't sure whom to trust among Lady Honoria's staff. Because of Lady Honoria's influence over her stepmother, she was also afraid to trust Patrice, which meant she wasn't sure she could trust Stanley either. He would most likely tell Patrice everything.

She could find no answers to any of her difficulties. However, James Carstairs's attitude troubled her the most. The more she thought about their conversation, the more concerned she grew. She had always thought him too patronizing when it came to talking with her about her fortune, but it now seemed he thought to advise Patrice on her choice of husbands as well. It was almost as if he believed he could direct their lives. Yet surely his insolence was no indication that something sinister was afoot. She was once again seeing phantoms in the noonday sun.

Then why did she feel so certain that something horrid was about to happen?

Twenty-two

Brandon intended to wait for word from Celia. However, Stanley announced his intentions to ride with him and Edmund into town the next day so that Stanley could see Patrice. Brandon knew he could not stay away. Edmund's lips tightened as if he realized Brandon would miss one of the last sessions of Parliament, but he said nothing as they climbed down in front of Westminster.

"I shall meet you at your aunt's this evening," his uncle told them as they moved away.

Brandon glanced back in time to see a figure in a dark cloak hurry past the coach to be quickly lost among the people passing the House of Lords. Brandon's frown was matched by the look on his uncle's face.

"What is it?" Edmund asked.

It was a feeling, a sensation, nothing tangible, certainly nothing he could explain to his uncle. Something in the figure's movement triggered a memory. Could that be his old friend Death?

"Nothing," Brandon said. "We will see you tonight. Arlington?"

Stanley fell into step with him willingly, but when Brandon started off in the direction the figure had taken, Stanley pulled him up short.

"I say, Hart, we're more likely to hail a hack in the other direction. I haven't been in London that long and *I* know that."

"Humor me," Brandon replied. Knowing he was likely too late, he led Stanley down the street. What would Edmund think if he knew Brandon was chasing shadows, going on nothing more than a feeling? Brandon could certainly guess what Lady Honoria would think. He pressed on.

Stanley seemed to sense Brandon's intensity, for he began to move cautiously as well. After a few yards, however, he called in a low voice, "I say, Hart, what are we doing?"

Others passing seemed to look at him with the same question. Brandon stopped and stood tall, swallowing his sudden feeling of foolishness. "Never mind, Arlington. We are no doubt too late."

"Too late for what?"

Brandon turned to face him. "To locate the fellow who was waiting for us."

Stanley frowned. "I saw no one."

Brandon grimaced. "No, you would not. Let us go."

Stanley immediately brightened, and they went to hail a hack. While he chattered away, Brandon thought. He had been so intent on offering for Celia to save her reputation, he had nearly forgotten her greater danger. Yet if Death had been stalking her, why would he now be near Westminster as if waiting for Brandon and Edmund? Or was he truly seeing shadows at noon?

As always, any doubt of his reasoning abilities chilled him, and he was glad Stanley did not mention the incident again.

The visit with Celia eased his tensions. As if she sensed his need, she kept the conversation light.

They took a turn in the garden, where she pointed
out plants she knew from the country. He could tell
she wanted to impress him with this side of her per-
sonality and tried to make suitable comments in
response. Later, they visited Martin, and Brandon
was taken to the stables to view a newly purchased
mount. When he pronounced the spirited gelding a
prime bit of horseflesh, both Celia and Martin colored in pleasure.

He did not know how long he and Celia sat talking
by the garden fountain. The sun warmed him,
though not as much as her smile, and he thought he
could easily sleep and sleep well. With her hand entwined in his, he would be content to stay here
forever. It was only when her smile suddenly vanished that he knew they were not alone.

Turning, he saw Edmund standing in the shade of
one of the larger trees. At Brandon's look, his uncle
moved forward.

"Miss Rider," he greeted, inclining his head. "Forgive the interruption. I finished my business early
and thought to collect your visitors."

And it made no difference whether Brandon was
ready to go or not. He was getting heartily tired of
this. Before he could tell Edmund so, Celia rose.

"Then Stanley will be leaving shortly as well. Excuse me. I must speak to him before he goes."

With a last lingering look at Brandon, she hurried
for the house.

As Brandon climbed to his feet, Edmund moved
forward to perch on the seat Celia had vacated. He
glanced up as if expecting Brandon to take his seat
again, too. Loath to stay, but more loath to leave,
Brandon complied.

"She is good for you," Edmund said.

Brandon started. "What?"

Edmund shrugged. "I did not see it before. But I watched you together just now. I have never seen you this happy since before your father died."

Something caught in his throat, and he had to swallow before answering. "Then can you understand my feelings for her?"

"They are difficult to miss, even for you." He sighed and clasped both hands around one knee. "I wish I could shake off my own feelings. Something is wrong, but I simply cannot put my finger on it."

"I sense it as well. Yet I know it is none of Celia's doing."

"I pray you are right." He let go of his knee to rise. "For now, let us be watchful."

Brandon nodded. Now, if he only knew what he should be watching for.

Whether it was because of her browbeating or God smiling, Celia didn't know, but James Carstairs brought her a draft for funds the following day.

"It is not as much as you wanted," he confessed, "however, the bank is aware of your situation and has tendered a line of credit. You should be able to purchase what you need."

He plainly did not think she needed more than a few fripperies. She decided not to say otherwise. With Patrice's gambling debts paid, she needed less than she had originally asked for. At least his demeanor had returned to the professional, even if he did seem inordinately pleased that he could hand her such a small sum.

Stanley was far less pleased when she told him about his role in her plan.

"But I wish to leave for Somerset the day after tomorrow," he complained.

"Delay your trip a day," Celia said. "I promise to make it worth your while."

She tried to instruct him on how to avoid the diligent Lord Pellidore, but Stanley waved her advice aside.

"I can handle the fellow, don't you know. He puts me in mind of my father. A story once in a while is necessary if one is to survive."

She could only hope he was right. Her entire future depended on it.

Patrice was even less cooperative. Celia had to prod and poke her out of the house the afternoon she put her plan into effect. Then her stepmother balked at going to Gunter's.

"I have no money for confections," she said with a sniff. "Why would I wish to even smell what is denied me?"

"I have money," Celia insisted, and she pulled Patrice through the door of the famous tea shop.

She caught Patrice tapping the toe of her pink kid slipper on the tiled floor while Celia finished placing her order. Two gentlemen at the serving tables raised quizzing glasses for a better look at her stepmother. Patrice paid them no heed. It appeared that her stepmother was truly reformed.

As Celia came up to her, Patrice frowned at the boxes in her gloved hands.

"Are those lunches? Do you intend us to eat somewhere outside?"

"I thought," Celia said, "a picnic would be nice."

Patrice wrinkled her nose. She eyed Celia's practical cotton gown. "Yes, you are dressed for it, but I am not. You should have told me. And we could have brought Martin."

"But that would have been a crowd," Celia said with a smile. She raised her voice. "Mr. Arlington, over here."

Patrice whirled. Celia could not help noticing how handsome Stanley looked in his navy coat and cream trousers. She had always thought he had a nice smile, but he positively beamed as he strode toward Patrice. He caught up her stepmother's hand and brought it to his lips, eyes gazing down into hers. "Mrs. Rider, a delight to see you again."

Celia glanced away from the hunger in their gazes. She could feel her cheeks heating.

"Allow me to escort you," Stanley said quietly. He nodded to Celia, then led Patrice to a quiet table away from the door. If Patrice wondered at her absence, Stanley would explain. She had a feeling, however, all Patrice's worries would melt in the warmth of Stanley's smile.

She let the door close behind her and drew a breath. And there he was. Brandon sat in the passenger side of the simple white gig. He looked completely in command of himself in his black coat and dove gray trousers, but she could not help noticing the stiff set of his shoulders. Was even this risk too much for him? She started toward the carriage, and he turned. A smile broke across his handsome face. The day suddenly looked brighter.

She handed the two packages up to him. "Stow these, if you will, my lord. We will likely need them later."

Brandon glanced pointedly at the only other seat, beside him. "And where do you intend to stow Mr. Arlington?"

"Mr. Arlington is unavoidably detained," she informed him. "Would you be so kind as to escort me instead?"

He jumped down and offered his hand to help her up into the carriage. The touch sent gooseflesh prickling her arm. "And he will not mind that we make off with his carriage?" he asked.

"Why should he?" Celia replied, opening a parasol against the sun to hide the reddening of her cheeks. "The carriage is mine."

Brandon came around and climbed into the driver's seat. Taking up the reins, he cast her another glance. "And are the horses yours as well?"

She eyed the matched set of white geldings. "Not entirely. We borrowed them for the day. Now, if you would be so kind as to direct them out the Kensington Road, I believe we can make our escape."

She caught a quick smile from him as he complied.

She had asked Stanley for a pair of goers, and he had certainly done justice to her expectations. The horses stepped smartly out; the little gig seemed to fly. She settled back against the seat with a satisfied smile.

"How did Stanley manage to evade your uncle?" she asked.

Brandon smiled. "Arlington claimed to need my advice on his own trousseau. I told him that if that were truly the case, I would eat his liver."

Celia laughed. "I should have liked to see your uncle's face."

"It was one of Arlington's finer moments. And may I know our destination?"

She glanced at him from the corner of her eye, smile widening. "You may not. Today, you are completely in my hands, my lord. Trust that I will take good care of you."

He nodded, but her mood faded a little when she saw that his shoulders were once more tensed.

As if to comply with her order, he kept his conversation light as they drove out into the country. She had gotten directions from a guide book and watched for the turn. When it came, she touched his arm and pointed.

"There—Kew Gardens."

He raised a brow, but turned the horses accordingly. "Are you on good terms with His Highness, then? His agent grants requests for admittance to the gardens on any day save Sunday."

"He does?" Her spirits plummeted. "And here I thought I'd actually planned ahead for once." She sighed. "Forgive me, Brandon. I was too impetuous once again. I saw the notice in a guide book and thought it sounded so lovely. It never dawned on me that one might need permission."

"Oh, ye of little faith," he said, and pulled the horses to a stop before a small lodge.

At the sound of the carriage, a gentleman strode out. He was most likely the caretaker, for he was dressed in rugged trousers and a rough coat as if to garden. "Good day to you. May I be of assistance?"

"You may. I am the Marquess of Hartley. I should like to visit the gardens."

He bowed. "At once, my lord. If you would pull the carriage that way, we will stable the horses for you."

"You see," Brandon said as he motioned the horses forward, "a title occasionally comes in handy."

Celia settled back with a twirl of her parasol and a smile.

The day was as lovely as she had hoped. They strolled arm in arm among the flowers, had lunch near what appeared to be the ruins of a Roman arch, and watched petals fall on a small lake. It was as if they were the only two people on earth, Adam and Eve in the garden of Eden.

"You've been here before," she accused when he led her unerringly toward a small Grecian temple.

"Edmund and I came here with items Lady Honoria donated from her hothouse," he replied, steering her up the white marble steps. "It is a lovely area for a walk."

She tilted back her head to catch his eye. "A walk? Martin would want to run." She grinned suddenly. "Or play a rousing game of catch-me-who-can." She broke from him and tapped his arm lightly. "Tag, my lord. Catch me if you can."

Laughing, she darted into the trees. She paused only a moment to see whether he would follow. He hesitated, and she nearly lost heart. Then he glanced quickly in either direction and set off after her.

She dodged around trees, pelted down paths, and squeezed behind bushes. She thought she'd led him a merry chase, only to break from a copse of trees to find herself facing the temple once again. Drat, but she'd gone in a circle. Hearing sounds of pursuit from behind, she lifted her skirts and fled up the steps, putting her back to the stone column of the building. Her breathing seemed to echo against the cold stone. She took a deep breath and held it.

The forest around her was silent. Where was he? She dared a glance around the column and found herself face-to-face with him. Leaves dotted his black coat, and there was a smudge of something purple on his cheek. He was grinning.

"Caught you," he said. "I told you I knew this area."

"Unfair," she said, making a show of stomping her foot. "I demand a rematch."

"And I demand a forfeit." He bent closer as if to kiss her.

"But you shall get a penalty," she declared, and ran her hands up under his coat to tickle his ribs.

Brandon threw back his head and laughed.

The sound was wonderful, warm, joyous, unfettered. She felt her spirit soar just hearing it. She wrapped her arms around his waist, their laughter merging. And when he finished and lowered his head, her lips were there to meet his.

The kiss was gentle, full of promise. She trembled with delight against it and felt his arms wrap around her as well as if to keep her safe forever. As he broke the kiss, she laid her head against his chest in contentment.

"Celia Rider," he murmured, voice husky, "will you do me the great honor of marrying me?"

She smiled against his waistcoat. "Now, that was nicely done. Yes, my lord, I believe I shall."

"My lord?"

"Brandon."

His sigh sounded equally contented to her. She raised her head and was surprised to see moisture in his eyes.

"Thank you," he murmured, and bent his head to hers once more.

It was late in the afternoon before they left the gardens. She kept her arm entwined in his and her hand on the ring he had given her. They set off back down Kensington Road. It seemed to her that there was nothing they could not do now that he was comfortable with her. Surely they would be happy.

He sobered the moment they came within sight of the town house. "Something's wrong. That's my carriage waiting across the street."

"The watchdog comes seeking," Celia said with a sigh. "I should have known it was too good to last."

He patted her hand on his arm. "Edmund is coming around."

As he pulled the gig in behind the carriage, she saw his groom running for the door. Before Brandon had even come around to hand her down, his uncle was down the steps, with Patrice and Stanley close on his heels.

"Where have you been?" Edmund demanded of Brandon. "Do you have any idea how worried we were?"

Brandon's hand on her arm was tight. "We can talk of this in the house."

"I will wait no longer," Edmund informed him, color heightening. "Your behavior is irresponsible in the extreme."

"I take responsibility," Celia said. "I kidnapped him."

Edmund ignored her. "Release her at once and get in the carriage."

"Go home, Uncle," Brandon said quietly. "I will talk to you there."

"By your leave, let me walk you to the coach," Stanley offered.

Edmund glared at both of them and turned to stalk away. Stanley hurried after him. Brandon watched, then dropped Celia's hand. "A moment."

He moved out into the street to intercept his uncle.

With a rattle and thunder of hooves, another carriage rushed down the square. Stanley must have seen it first, for he scrambled aside. The coach did not slow. The driver, swathed in a dark cloak, whipped the reins to urge the horses faster. Edmund glanced up, then laid both hands on Brandon and shoved him away from the oncoming danger. Celia screamed.

The coach did not stop.

Twenty-three

Brandon stumbled back amidst the drumming of hooves. Someone screamed, but all he could see was the carriage careening past him. The back wheel swung toward him, and he put up his hands to ward off the blow. The weight smashed into him, crushing his hands back into his chest and hurling him onto the street. The cobblestones came up to meet his back, and his breath left him in a rush. He used the momentum to let himself roll farther from the coach.

Gasping in a breath, he choked on the dust and debris thrown up in the coach's wake. He climbed to his hands and knees, trying for air as the world around him darkened.

"Brandon, dear God, Brandon, are you all right?"

Celia was on her knees beside him, wrapping her arms around him. He sagged against her, sucking in a deep breath. Her hands on his body trembled.

"I'm all right," he said, and slowly straightened until he was sitting upright. His hands ached, and his back stung. He could hear other sounds now, running feet, cries of dismay. Raising his head, he saw Stanley flattened against the Pellidore coach, eyes huge, his arms wrapped around Patrice, whose face was buried in his chest. But he was not looking after the coach that had caused all this. He was staring down into the roadway.

Brandon struggled to his feet. "Edmund!"

Celia rose with him, but he tore away from her to stumble to his uncle's body. Edmund lay in a broken heap in the center of the roadway, like a rag doll tossed away by a careless child. Brandon fell to his knees beside him and reached out, only to pull back his arms in indecision.

Edmund's face was white, and his mouth hung slack. Brandon's breath caught in his throat. As he watched, however, his uncle's eyes opened, and Edmund's gaze met his.

"Hartley."

Brandon bent closer. "Quiet, Uncle. Conserve your strength." Around him he heard people gathering, sobbing, murmuring offers of assistance.

"No time," Edmund murmured. "Watch out for yourself. And watch out for her." His uncle's chest stilled.

"No," Brandon said. The word was so damned inadequate. "No!" He gathered Edmund to him and held him against his chest. So many words he could not say, many he should not say—all he wished he'd had time to say. Did Edmund know that he was father, brother, friend, and confidant? He could not be gone, just like that.

The pain inside him grew to a weight so heavy he thought he might bow under it. It swallowed him whole, leaving him floating in some nether world where he was sure of neither time nor place. Something wet his cheeks, and it was a moment before he realized he was crying.

"My lord." Dimly he recognized Stanley's voice. "By your leave, Hartley, you must release him."

Brandon blinked, gaze still blurred with tears, and focused on Stanley's long face with difficulty. Arlington crouched across from him, both hands on the knees of his dirty trousers. He reached out large hands to touch Brandon's grip on his uncle's shoulders. "Let him go, Hart. We must take him inside."

Brandon's fingers did not obey him to open. It took Stanley's fingers to pry his up. The servants moved in to take Edmund's body. Stanley helped him rise.

"Come into the house, by your leave," he suggested.

Brandon shook his head. "No. I must go home."

"Then I shall go with you. You should not be alone."

"Taking over his job?" Brandon asked, bitterness welling up inside him. "Will you watch me every moment now as well?"

Stanley's face puckered. "You are distraught, don't you know. I thought you might want company."

Brandon shook his head. "Leave me alone." He moved to the coach, feet weighted. It hurt to breathe.

"Brandon." Celia was at his elbow. Tears streamed down her face as well. For a moment, he wanted to push her away, too.

"You did this," he said, and she cringed back, eyes widening. He thumped his chest. "You gave me this, this heart. You made me feel things I never felt, dream of futures I never thought to have. What good is it if all I do is hurt?"

She shook her head, tears falling. "No. I will not apologize. You had a heart already, Brandon, or it would not be breaking now. And these are the risks we take when we love. How could we appreciate the beauty of sunlight if we never see the darkness of the storm?"

And he had seen the beauty of sunlight, in her hair, in the light of her eyes when she looked at him, in the sound of his name on her lips, in the quiet smile she gave him when she thought he wasn't looking. With a groan, he pulled her into his arms and buried his head in her brightness. Her hands stroked his back; her lips pressed a kiss into his hair. He could not have let go if he tried.

She was the one to push him back, gently. She gazed up into his face, brows drawn in obvious concern. "Do you wish me to come home with you?"

With all his heart, but sanity was returning slowly. He felt it in the stiffness of his shoulders and the burden in his heart. And with sanity came the knowledge that he must leave her here. "No," he said, releasing her. "Give me some time. I must make arrangements."

"And you are in no condition to do so."

He shook his head. "I must. There is no one I would want to trust them to, and even with Edmund gone, others will watch me. I must earn the name of Lord Heartless."

She pulled him close again. "I know otherwise," she murmured against his chest. "You are lord of my heart, Brandon. I know you will behave to perfection, because you must. But please do not fear sharing yourself with me. Do not let this accident stop the closeness we felt today."

He held her and hoped she would take it as a promise. At the moment he could not be certain of anything he did.

And it scared him.

Celia thought her own heart might break watching him drive away. Today she had seen his face alive with joy, and now it seemed as if he would never know joy again. She wanted to hold him, to tell him she would always love him, to help him see that there would be a future beyond this. But she had let him leave with only a hug and so very few words. Those and her prayers were all she had to give him.

Patrice and Stanley were equally shaken, but it was Lady Honoria who took command of the situation. In short order, the undertaker's assistants arrived to make arrangements for the funereal décor and clothing. Celia heard her dispatching assistants to the country estate as well and servants to all the Pellidore estates to instruct them to mourning.

They were isolated, and she felt as if she would dry up and crumble to dust if she didn't see Brandon soon. Neither she nor Patrice were allowed to attend the funeral or burial, although Lady Honoria insisted upon going. Only when she returned did her ladyship call them all to her in the forward salon.

Martin settled himself against Celia on the sofa. From his pinched face, she was certain that, like her, he was remembering their father's death. Lady Honoria, already in a black gown used in previous mourning, hobbled into the room leaning on Sally's arm. Patrice hopped up to help, but she waved her away.

"I will stand, thank you. I know you all are as shocked by Edmund's death as I am. At the moment, however, we have a greater duty. Lord Hartley should not be alone at this time, I am convinced. Therefore, I have instructed the servants to begin packing. We shall all repair to Pellidore Place."

Patrice opened her mouth as if to protest, then closed it again. Martin looked up at Celia for guidance. Celia shook her head, then set him aside to rise.

"Lady Honoria," she said as politely as she could, "I know you see this as a kindness, but I fear Lord Hartley needs time to recover. Company surely will not help."

"We are not company, girl," she replied. Her voice was so tight that Celia knew she was furious at her interference. "We are family. And I did not request your opinion on the matter. Be ready to leave the day after tomorrow."

Patrice rose as well and went to put her hand on Celia's arm. "Perhaps it will not be so bad," she said. "After all, we will be near Stanley."

"No, you will not," Lady Honoria said sternly. Patrice blinked in obvious surprise, and Celia frowned.

"Mr. Arlington," Lady Honoria continued, "has decided on my advice to repair to Somerset, immediately."

Patrice puckered. "Immediately?"

Lady Honoria threw up her hands. "Is there no pleasing you? You wish to marry him, Patrice. He requires his father's blessing to do so. Let him go get it. Now go help Mr. Kinders with the packing." She hobbled out again.

Patrice held out her hand to Martin. Celia could tell she was trying to be brave, but tears clouded her eyes. Martin took her hand in one of his and Celia's in the other.

"It will be all right," he said. "Won't it, Celia."

Patrice looked at her askance.

Celia raised her head and gave Martin's hand a squeeze. "Yes, Martin, it will, whether Lady Honoria likes it or not."

* * *

Brandon's head hurt. He wasn't sure when it had started, but the ache did not want to diminish. Like Edmund had, it kept him company through the nights of staying up with his uncle's body; the farewell to Arlington that left another hole in his life; the days of visits by friends, family and servants; and the short funeral procession from the house to the nearby churchyard. It had only worsened as he had ridden back to Pellidore Place with Lady Honoria.

"You look tired," she had commented, dark eyes brighter than the jet beads on her mourning gown.

"I am fine," Brandon had replied from long habit. If he could not tell Edmund when he felt troubled, he certainly couldn't tell this woman.

Of course she would not let him off so easily. "Are you eating?" she demanded.

"When it is offered me."

"Sleeping?"

"Occasionally."

"Taking the medication I had Sally prepare for you?"

"Rarely."

She clucked her tongue. "Do you want me to refuse you, boy? You are a Pellidore. Shake this off."

"I am in mourning," he replied. "Even Lord Heartless is allowed to mourn."

She had left him alone, but he had tried to heed her warning. Yet her medication tasted acidic and only seemed to worsen his headache. Even with Cook doing her utmost, the food tasted like paste, and when he lay down, sleep was a long time coming. He kept thinking about the accident and his uncle.

The driver of the carriage that had struck them both had to know he left carnage in his wake, yet no one had returned to confess. Perhaps the coachman feared repercussions. After all, a man's death had been reported in the papers. Yet Brandon could not help thinking that it was more than an accident.

He also could not help wondering if Edmund had sensed it as well. Too often he pictured his uncle's face there in the street, begging him to take care of himself and Celia. At least, that was what he thought Edmund had said.

When his head protested, it was too easy to think darker thoughts. What if Edmund had meant to watch out for Celia because she was in danger? Had his uncle learned something about the threats to her and her fortune? Did he know the identity of the person behind those threats? What if the driver of the carriage had intended to run Celia down, only to have Edmund get in the way?

But there was an even darker thought yet. Edmund had been so sure Celia was a cunning title hunter. Brandon could not imagine how such a person would have gone about getting rid of Miss Turner and her family, but if she had, surely bribing a hack driver to run a man down was no challenge. Like Miss Turner, Edmund threatened to disrupt Brandon's intentions to marry Celia. In fact, Celia was the only person he could think of who would benefit from his uncle's death, if only because Edmund would no longer threaten her.

The thoughts plagued him so much that he knew he had to take action. While he had felt comfortable questioning Lady Brompton and the shopkeepers, he felt certain that a titled lord would get little information about his uncle's death from the right people. It was time to call in a professional.

Two days after the funeral, he rode into town to hire a Bow Street Runner to investigate.

The man the magistrate directed him to was not the least formidable, even in his brown coat and robin's breast red waistcoat that was his badge of office. Considerably shorter than Brandon, he was also slightly built and balding. His blue eyes, however, were sharp. They remained narrowed the entire time Brandon spoke to him, as if he took everything he heard with hearty skepticism.

"Any likely suspects?" he asked after Brandon explained the accident with his uncle.

And what could he say to that? He refused to implicate Celia, and he could think of no one else who might want Edmund dead. Of course, there was the distinct possibility that it had not been Edmund they wanted. Unfortunately, he could neither decide whether they wanted Celia, or himself, nor determine why.

"Death?" he finally offered.

When the man looked at him askance, Brandon went on to explain about the character in Lady Brompton's maze and the possible sighting in Westminster. The thief-taker raised a brow as if he questioned Brandon's reasoning, but he took the gold and promised a report in a week or less.

Brandon returned home with his spirits rising, only to have them fall when he saw the collection of coaches before his door.

Striding into the entry, he found servants rushing in all directions and the marble floor all but obscured with baggage. He caught one of the footmen hurrying past.

"Timms, what's all this?"

The footman's eyes were wide. "Lady Honoria, my lord. She's moving in!"

"The hell she is," Brandon muttered, releasing him. "Where is she?"

"Last I saw, on the second floor, my lord, choosing a bedchamber."

Brandon climbed the stairs two at a time. Stalking down the corridor, he listened for sounds of voices, only to realize they were everywhere. He stopped in the center of the hall and cast about himself. One of the doors stood open, and he saw a figure cross the space. He stomped into the room.

"What do you think you're doing?"

Celia whirled to face him, putting a hand to her heart. "Brandon, you startled me."

He collected himself with difficulty and moved forward more slowly. She stood in a pool of sunlight from the windows behind her, turning her honey hair to gold and outlining the curves of her mourning-draped figure. So bright did she look that he wondered how he could for a moment suspect that she might be involved in murder.

"Forgive me for startling you," he said. "Where is Lady Honoria?"

"Along this hall somewhere. She thought this room too small for her. I was considering it for myself."

He shook his head, trying to ease the vise that was gripping it. "You are moving in as well?"

Her brows gathered together. "Were you not warned? Oh, this is the outside of enough!" She started past him, and he caught her arm.

"Wait! Do you mean to tell me that everyone is here?"

She nodded. "Lady Honoria and her maid, Patrice and hers, Martin and John, and me. I daresay her ladyship brought a few other servants as well."

Brandon rolled his eyes. "I should have known."

He released his hold on Celia and stepped back. "Forgive me for taking my frustrations out on you. Are you all right?"

Her smile turned tender. "I should be asking you that question. I am sorry I could not attend the funeral. Was it horrid?"

"It was a funeral, which is to say it was intended to remind one of the darker side of life."

She touched his cheek. "I am so very sorry. That has been my one consolation in this move. I might be closer to you if you need me."

If he needed her? She could not know how much, or how much more difficult it would be to show her with Lady Honoria in residence. Edmund had been a watchdog, it was true, but until recently a sympathetic one. He would have no such mercy from Lady Honoria.

Yet he could hardly throw his aunt out. For one, she would question his reasoning, and for another, the ton would consider that her blood ties and age gave her a right to residence.

And if he did manage to convince her to return to London, Celia would be that much farther away. Either way, he was sunk.

Twenty-four

Brandon must have decided not to confront Lady Honoria, or her ladyship must have been convincing in her arguments, for no one came to tell Celia that they were returning to London. She made sure Martin and John were nicely settled in the schoolroom near the top of the house, then set about helping a maid named Bess set the room she had chosen to rights.

Normally she would have been pleased with the room. It had large windows facing the west, walls of a soft blue, and upholstery and bed hangings of a deeper shade. The bed was not too soft, and the carpet was soft indeed.

Now, however, she could not help thinking that she was an interloper. Brandon was not ready to be sociable. The shock from his uncle's death was still too fresh. She could see it in his eyes when he passed her in the corridor, hear it in his deep voice when he spoke to her. She ached to touch him, to hold him, to feel him hold her, but she was afraid he would refuse. He had locked his heart safely away. Lady Honoria should never have insisted on coming.

Her ladyship, however, seemed determined that they act as if everything were normal. Other than the black mourning dress they were all forced to wear, from the least pot boy to the dowager herself, they were to behave as they had always done.

Celia could see that this perfection was impossible. Patrice, for one, moped about as if in deep mourning, when in truth Celia knew she pined for Stanley. Sally Lawton was more spiteful than usual. According to John, Brandon's dapper valet, Mr. Gregory, saw himself as more powerful and took great pains to let the ladies' maid know it. Besides, the other servants were already complaining that the potions she insisted on brewing for Lady Honoria were smelling up the kitchen.

Brandon's other servants were equally affected. Given other circumstances, she thought she might like Mr. Openshaw, the butler, with his powdered wig and military manner. Now he marched about the house tight-lipped and tense. Timms, with his warm brown hair and eyes, should have been as helpful as John, but he more often looked as if he would burst into tears.

Brandon was worst of all. To the world he showed the face they had come to expect—calm, measured, dignified. Yet Celia could see the darkness behind his eyes.

It was Martin who first pierced his reserve. Celia had gone up to the schoolroom to visit, only to find it empty. From down the hall, however, came the sound of voices. Following the noise, she found herself in a large, open chamber, devoid of furnishings except a stand for towels and a dumb valet.

Martin, John, and Brandon stood around a large, lumpy leather bag suspended from the ceiling by chains. Brandon had his coat off and his sleeves rolled up. She could see the muscles flexing on his well-developed arms as he fisted his hands and jabbed at the bag. Martin, watching him, looked no less fascinated.

"What are you doing?" she asked, moving into the room.

They immediately faced her, and Brandon colored. Martin pointed to the bag.

"Look at this, Celia!.John says they should think about getting one at Gentleman Jackson's boxing emporium."

Celia smiled at his enthusiasm, but she could feel Brandon's tension rising as he reached for his coat.

"Please do not stop on my account," she said.

He started to shake his head, but Martin hopped on one foot enthusiastically.

"Please, my lord!.Show her how it works."

"Mayhap you should demonstrate," Brandon demurred.

She could not let him retreat back into the silence of the last few days. She stepped forward and smiled brightly. "I am sure Martin would be delighted, but how much better to learn from the master than the apprentice."

Brandon frowned at her, and Martin's gaze darted between the two of them. He reached up suddenly to tug at Brandon's hand. "Please, my lord?"

Brandon gazed down at him a moment; then his look lightened, tugging at Celia's heart as easily as Martin had tugged on his hand. He returned his gaze to her with a gentle smile.

"Very well. Stand aside, Martin."

Martin and John stepped eagerly back, but not, she noticed, so far that they could not watch him closely. He tapped the bag to set it swaying and brought both fists up before him.

"The idea," he said, "is to exercise your arms and

torso. The device should never cease moving while you do so."

He began to move his arms to drive his fists into the bag. Celia watched, fascinated. At first, she thought he struck randomly, but soon she saw a pattern emerge. It was almost a dance. His movements were strong, sure, balanced. His focus was centered on the bag. The thud of his fists sounded like the beat of an ancient song, his breath the melody. As if he heard it, too, the tension drained from his face, leaving him clean, pure, every inch the man she loved.

She caught her breath in wonder.

He stopped then and put out his hands to still the bag. Martin broke into applause. Brandon inclined his head at the praise, but she could see his polished veneer sliding into place. She laid a hand on his bare arm and felt something hot tighten inside her.

He met her gaze, and she saw he felt, it too. He covered her hand with his own, holding her skin to his as he held her gaze.

"Thank you," she murmured, and saw his gaze move to her lips, and linger.

"Come along, Master Martin," John urged beside them.

Brandon shook himself and released her. He offered them all a bow. "Thank you all for your attention. That concludes our demonstration for today."

It did indeed, but she could not be dissatisfied. Martin had opened a crack in his armor, and she thought, with time, she could widen it.

Lady Honoria, however, thought otherwise. She called for Celia that afternoon.

Celia met her in her suite. She could not help noticing that while Lady Honoria expected them all to be accommodating of the changes, she had chosen to change very little. Her dark, ornate furniture had been brought from London and installed in a similar arrangement in her new suite. The desk sat against one wall, with windows on either side of a tall fireplace in the center of the adjacent wall, and a group of armchairs and a sofa opposite. If it had not been for the gold-toned lower walls, Celia might have thought she had never left Mayfair.

"Come in, girl," her ladyship greeted from the armchair nearest the fire where her foot lay propped on a cushioned stool. She motioned to the chair opposite her. "I wish to know how you get on."

Celia took the seat and spread the skirts of the black silk mourning gown Lady Honoria had insisted she have made. It was in its own way prettier than the ones she remembered from her father's day. Knowing why she wore it, however, she could wish it to perdition.

"I am well," she told her ladyship. "Martin and Patrice are well also."

Lady Honoria nodded. "Excellent. We are all settling in, I believe, except my nephew. I am quite concerned about him."

Celia kept her smile polite. "Indeed. I daresay he misses his uncle."

"Certainly he misses Edmund. Unfortunately, we do not have the luxury of maudlin sentimentality. I believe you two are to be married, are you not?"

"I accepted Lord Hartley's offer. However, I would not presume to pressure him to set a date after what has happened."

"Perhaps that is wise. We could not have a marriage for at least three months in any event, if the mourning period is to be observed properly." She cocked her head. "You are certain he intends to marry you?"

Celia frowned. "Quite certain. He proposed, and I accepted. Lord Hartley is a man of his word."

"Under normal circumstances, yes. Yet I cannot help noticing the change in him since Edmund's death. Have you noticed anything unusual?"

If she had, she certainly would not have said a word to her ladyship about it. Now she merely shook her head. "Nothing."

Lady Honoria shook her head as well. "I have, yet it is nothing I could put my finger on. Before Edmund's death he was happy, dare I say, nearly euphoric."

Remembering his laughter at the gardens, Celia smiled. "Yes, I would say he was happy."

"Now he seems almost sullen, angry."

Celia's smile faded. "That, I think, is to be expected, given the nature of the accident."

"Perhaps," Lady Honoria said. The calculation in the word made Celia raise her head and regard the woman more intently. Her ladyship's smile spoke of something between satisfaction and triumph. Celia shivered.

Lady Honoria reached out and patted her hand. "I have not had an opportunity to wish you happy, child. Congratulations on your upcoming marriage."

Celia nodded, but she was not convinced that her happiness was much on the lady's mind. The woman saw changes in Brandon, changes for the worse in fact, yet she was pleased by them. It did not bode well for any of them.

Brandon returned to his chambers that night and dismissed his valet. He had to have a moment to himself. Everywhere he went there were people. He had thought the house empty with only himself and Edmund in it; now it was entirely too full.

He sank onto the bed and massaged his temples. This damnable headache didn't help matters. He felt as if he walked on eggshells around his aunt as it was. Trying to be civil when his head screamed with every breath was proving nearly impossible. He had snapped at Timms earlier in the day, sending the footman scurrying away with downcast eyes, and he'd been short with the groom when his mount was not immediately ready for him when he unexpectedly called for it in hopes of escaping.

Worst of all, he did not trust himself alone with Celia. All he wanted to do was lose himself in her, but doing so could play into his aunt's hands. He could not give Lady Honoria such power over him. Another time, he was certain, he would be able to think of some way for him and Celia to meet in secret. Lord knew, the house had enough rooms, even with his new tenants. Now it was all he could do to think of anything besides his head.

Rising, he stalked to the fireplace and poked up the coals. The evenings were chilling now as they approached autumn. Parliament had recessed shortly after Edmund's death. Many of the families would have left London for the country. His birthday was only six weeks away. All he had to do was make it for six weeks.

He would not survive another day with this headache.

As if on cue, there was a tap at his door. Resigned, he called for Gregory to enter. However, it was not his valet but the small, dark-haired maid called Bess who opened the door.

"Begging your pardon, me lord," she said, head bowed and round face coloring, "but Miss Rider asked for this to be delivered to you."

She held out a silver tray with a bottle and goblet, as if she expected him to snatch it from her. He moved closer, and she tensed. Good God, had he been so short-tempered lately that even this tiny girl feared he'd forget himself?

He took the tray from her trembling hands before she upset the contents. "Thank you. Was there a message?"

She blinked and bit her lip before answering. "Miss Lawton never said nothing about a message. She just said I was to take it straight up to you or there'd be trouble."

She dropped a hurried curtsey.

So, Miss Lawton couldn't be bothered to do Celia's bidding herself. He'd noticed the sour-faced woman was called to serve as Celia's maid. He'd wager neither was pleased with the arrangement. He'd have to speak to Openshaw. Perhaps there was another maid that could be spared to help Celia. He nodded, and Bess breathed out a sigh of obvious relief and fled.

He carried the tray to the table before the fire and set it down. It was thoughtful of Celia to consider his needs. Perhaps she understood his behavior the last few days. He uncorked the bottle and inhaled. Cherry brandy. How had she known it was a family favorite? Smile deepening, he poured some into the glass.

Celia woke from a deep sleep. She frowned, trying to focus on the noise that had waked her. The dying coals left a faint orange glow to her right. She could dimly make out the shapes of furniture in the room. The noise came again, almost a flutter. Was that someone scratching at her door?

"Hello?" she called.

The noise stopped.

Beyond it rose another noise, frightening in its intensity. It was a scream.

Celia scrambled out of bed, her white lawn nightdress clinging to her legs as she fled to the door and snatched it open. Timms stood just outside, transfixed. In the lamp-lit corridor, other doors opened, the sounds as loud as gunshots. Patrice and Lady Honoria appeared, and Celia heard feet running on the stairs.

"No cause for alarm," Timms said, though his voice shook. "Miss Rider just had a nightmare."

Celia stared at him.

"My word," Lady Honoria said, hand covering her heart. "Are you all right, child?"

Timms's gaze on Celia's was tortured, and she could see his Adam's apple bobbing up and down as he swallowed convulsively. She turned to Lady Honoria. "I am fine, your ladyship. Forgive me for troubling you."

Patrice padded forward to lay a hand on her arm. "Would you like me to sit with you for a while?"

"No need," Celia said. "Timms, I seem to have overturned one of the chairs as well. Will you help me, please?"

"Right away, miss," he replied, hurrying into the room. Celia stayed only long enough to watch Lady Honoria and Patrice head back toward their own rooms before following him and shutting her door.

"What is going on?" she demanded.

He bobbed his head in deference. "Begging your pardon, miss, but you were the only one we thought might help. It's his lordship. He's in a bad way."

"That was Brandon?" Her stomach fell to the soles of her feet. "Take me to him."

"God bless you, miss," he said, hurrying back to the door. He poked his head out as if to make certain the corridor was empty, then motioned her to follow. Not even bothering to find her wrapper, Celia obeyed.

He led her down the hall and up the stairs to the next floor, where Edmund and Brandon's apartments lay. Her heartbeat sounded louder than her footfalls. What could have happened? Had he fallen? Been set upon? Yet surely in either case would they come for Lady Honoria and not her.

Timms paused at one of the doors. "I warn you, miss, he's not a pretty picture. But Master Edmund, he used to calm the previous Lord Hartley by talking and such. We thought maybe you could do it now. Only you mustn't tell Lady Honoria. Do you understand?"

She was afraid she did, and her blood ran cold. "He's gone mad?"

His face puckered, and he nodded. "Yes, miss. Please, won't you help him?"

"Let me in," Celia said.

Twenty-five

Timms opened the door cautiously. Whatever he saw inside must have satisfied him, for he stepped in and held out a hand to pull Celia in after him. She heard the door snap behind her as she took in the scene.

Mr. Gregory and Mr. Openshaw stood on either side of the great bed. Half the bed hangings were torn from their fastenings, and others showed violent rents. Her heartbeat quickened as she moved closer.

The valet looked as if he wanted to cry. His usual cheerful face was gray with dread, and he could not seem to keep his gaze from his hands where they clamped one of Brandon's arms to the bed. The butler looked as if he would be ill, his narrow face puckered.

But Brandon, oh Brandon, was so much worse. The covers lay bunched about his waist, and the fastenings had been torn from his lawn nightshirt. Through the jagged opening, his skin gleamed with sweat. The air was sour with the smell of vomit. She could hear the rough sound of his breathing.

Swallowing her own rising bile, she stepped up to the valet and gazed down at Brandon. His hair was plastered to his head. His face was florid, as if he were either drunk or livid. His eyes were screwed shut, and Mr. Openshaw's free hand was clamped over his mouth.

"We had to keep him quiet, miss," the butler said, and his tone begged her to understand. She nodded, biting her lip to keep from crying out herself.

"Is he awake?" she asked quietly.

At the sound of her voice, Brandon's eyes snapped open. She gasped. There was no reason in them. Indeed, it was as if she looked into an obsidian mirror, so wide were his pupils.

"Watch out!" the valet warned.

Brandon's entire body convulsed. Celia's hand flew to her mouth, and she stepped involuntarily away. The bed shook under his twitching, and the butler and valet doubled to keep him steady. She forced herself to step closer, only to gasp again when she realized he was foaming at the mouth.

"Dear God," she murmured.

Timms hurried over to help the other men. "Do something, Miss Rider, please! Talk to him, pray to God, anything! If Lady Honoria comes upon him like this, we're all lost!"

Celia nodded. Gathering her wits, she lowered her hand and moved up to the bed. "Brandon. Brandon. Can you hear me?"

His back arched off the bed, and one of his arms came free. It whipped about like a beheaded snake. Timms leapt to catch it before it struck Celia. She sucked in a sob.

"Brandon, come back to us. We need you. I need you."

The twitching slowed. Breathing heavily, Timms relaxed his grip. Brandon's eyes drifted shut again.

"How long," Celia managed, "has he been like this?"

"Never seen him this way before, miss, I swear," the valet said. "He dismissed me early tonight, and I thought I should check on him before going to bed myself. I found him in the middle of the room, dancing."

Celia swallowed. "Dancing?"

The valet's eyes were huge. "Yes, miss. Like he held a woman in his arms in the waltz. Only there was no one with him. I thought at first he was thinking of you."

"Oh, right," the butler quipped. "His lordship is in the habit of remembering his betrothed by dancing about half naked."

"Well, he could have," the valet protested. "Only then he started singing as well, and I knew something was wrong. I went straight for Mr. Openshaw."

"And I brought Timms with me."

"And I thought perhaps he was drunk," the footman said, face reddening. "The bottle was half empty."

"Bottle?" Celia asked.

Timms nodded toward the hearth. "Over there."

Celia went to retrieve it. An unlabeled bottle lay open before the dying coals. She picked it up gingerly and sniffed. The smell of cherries was unmistakable. She set it upright and moved to the washstand instead. Pouring some of the tepid water onto a washcloth, she returned to the bed.

"I cannot be certain, but this doesn't look like the effect of drink to me," she told the men, bending to wipe the foam from Brandon's face. Touching him nearly made her cry again. She blinked and laid the washcloth aside.

"No, miss," the butler replied. "It's the madness sure. Lady Honoria will have to be told."

"Begging your pardon, Mr. Openshaw," Timms put in before she could protest. "But maybe it ain't so bad. His lordship's made of strong stuff. Maybe he can throw it off."

The butler looked dubious. He tightened his grip on Brandon's arm.

Celia bent closer. The twitching had all but stopped now, and his face was slack as if he slept. His breath came shallow and quick, however, as if he could not get enough air to fill his lungs. "What happens now?" she asked the butler.

Mr. Openshaw shrugged. "Now we wait. Lord Pellidore didn't allow us to tie his brother to the bed. I have too much respect for his lordship to allow that either. Timms, you and Gregory stay with Miss Rider. I'll spell you later tonight."

"And do you expect morning to be better?" Celia asked with a frown.

"If this is anything like what happened with his father," the butler replied, "he won't see the morning."

Celia felt as if he had struck her a blow. She must have staggered, for the valet dropped his hold on Brandon to catch her shoulder instead. She shook her head and took a deep breath. He released her with a sad smile. She turned and walked back to the fire.

It could not be true! She wouldn't let it be true. He had fought against this threat of madness all his life. She would not allow it to claim him! As Edmund had once stood watch, so would she. Brandon would not want her to give up on him. She heard the door close behind the butler and squared her shoulders. She stalked back to the bed and affixed Timms and Gregory with her gaze.

"We will not wait until morning," she said. "We are going to help him now."

"How do you help a madman?" Timms asked, then cringed as if wishing to call back his own words.

"I have no idea how to treat his mind," Celia replied, "but we can start with his body." She bent and lay a hand on his brow. Beneath the sweat, he was cold. She shivered as the fear sliced through her, but straightened with determination. "He's chilly. Timms, stoke up the coals. Mr. Gregory, close that window."

"But if we release him, miss . . . ," the footman started.

"We will take that chance," Celia said. "I want him comfortable. It is the very least we can do."

They set about the tasks, and Celia bent to tuck the covers more closely about him. He stirred, and for a moment, she nearly called the men back to her. But Brandon merely sighed and settled back against the pillow.

"What next, miss?" Timms asked, returning to her side.

Celia cocked her head in thought. "Do you read?"

Timms colored. "Sorry, miss. I can sign my own name and that's good enough for me."

"I can read," the valet offered.

"Go to his lordship's library and fetch me two books you will likely find there. One will be by a William Shakespeare and should contain a number of plays and sonnets."

"Sonnets, miss?"

"Poetry. Rhymes."

He nodded. "And the other?"

"The Bible, Mr. Gregory. We need all the help we can get."

Brandon knew he was dreaming. That was odd enough. He rarely remembered his dreams, and when he did, they seemed real at the time. This was decidedly unreal, which made it all the more unsettling.

He was lying on his bed, and Openshaw and Gregory were holding him in place. He asked them to release him, he ordered them to release him, and he struggled against their grip, to no avail. In fact, they didn't even seem to hear him! Their faces were as cold as stones and as unfeeling.

What was worse was that Celia was there, and though he begged for her help, she ignored him as well. She insisted upon putting hot compresses on his skull. The heat burned into his head, turning his skin to ashes. He screamed at the pain. She calmly removed the compress and put another in its place.

He wrenched his arm free from Gregory and grabbed hers with it, pushing the cloth away from his face. Her face paled, and her eyes widened. He could see the pupils dilating in her horror. She was afraid of him! That thought was more painful than anything she could have inflicted. He released her and closed his eyes, submitting to the compress for her sake.

The world went dark for a time.

Gradually, he became aware of sound. It started low and built slowly. He strained to catch the sense of it. Were those words? Was it English? Could it be Celia's voice?

"Yea, though I walk through the valley of the shadow of death, I will fear no evil; for thou art with me; thy rod and thy staff they comfort me. Thou preparest a table before me in the sight of mine foes."

"Thou anointest my head with oil," Brandon continued. "My cup overflows."

She sucked in a breath. He blinked, and light came back. It was centered around Celia, seated beside him in a pale gown. The Bible shook in her hands.

"Surely goodness and mercy shall follow me all the days of my life," she finished breathlessly, "and I will dwell in the house of the Lord forever."

"Am I dead, then?" Brandon asked.

She choked back what sounded like a sob. "No, thank God. Do you know me?"

"You are Celia Rider, the woman I love."

She closed her eyes as if offering a prayer, then opened them and rose to bend over him. "And you are Brandon Pellidore, Marquess of Hartley, the man I love."

She pressed a kiss against his mouth. As she parted, he sighed. "How did I come here?"

"What do you remember?" she asked, reseating herself and moving the Bible to his nightstand.

"Sitting near the fire, drinking the cordial you sent me."

She shook her head. "I sent you no bottle."

"A maid said Miss Lawton asked her to deliver it for you."

"She must have been mistaken. You remember nothing else?"

"Only an odd dream in which you tried to scald my skull."

She cringed. "How horrid."

"So, why do I find you at my side reading aloud?"

Her face was sad. "Gregory found you dancing

half naked in your room. When he returned with help, you were screaming."

It couldn't be. Something inside him tightened, as if his body rejected the notion as strongly as his mind. "They are lying."

A tear rolled down one cheek. "No. They sent for me, and I saw you. You were . . . You were not yourself, Brandon."

He struggled to sit, and she leapt to her feet as if in alarm. He froze. "Do you think I shall attack you?"

She shook her head and sat back down. He could see the caution in her slow movements. "Not now," she said.

"Not ever," he protested. Mutely she held up her arm. Purpling along her wrist were four small ovals, like the print of cruel fingers. It was the exact spot he had grabbed her in his dream.

He closed his eyes to block out the sight. "How long was I in that state?"

"A few hours. You have been sleeping for nearly ten now."

"When do they come for me?"

"They?"

He opened his eyes to find her gazing at him with a frown of obvious confusion.

"The custodians," he said. When she still looked unsure, he said as gently as he could, "The guardians from the mental institute in London."

She scrambled to her feet. "Never! We told no one."

He raised his brows. "We?"

She nodded. "Mr. Openshaw, Gregory, Timms, and I. We are the only ones who know. Mr. Openshaw told Lady Honoria you had gone into town early, and Timms made sure she did not question the coaching staff. I told Patrice I was spending the day in my room, and Gregory is making sure no one attempts to disturb me. So far, no one is the wiser."

Was it really that easy? Could he simply pretend it had never happened? Yet if it had happened, it would happen again. He could not allow Celia to be harmed.

"You should return to Somerset," he said. "I am no longer safe."

She shook her head. "No, do not say that. This was only one episode. You told me the symptoms—stammering, euphoria, fits of anger. Other things can mirror them. Perhaps the drink was stronger than you thought. Perhaps you were merely drunk." She smiled weakly. "At least you have not begun to stammer."

He closed his eyes and felt a laugh bubbling up. He choked it down. Opening his eyes, he saw her watching him with a frown again. "Edmund taught me so well. Never show them the least weakness lest they use it against you. I almost lost you for that reason."

"You did not lose me. There is nothing weak about you."

"You think not? You should know all, Celia, so that you can make the right choice." He cleared his throat. Years of discipline fought the urge. He must do it. He had to do it. She had to know. He swallowed.

"My name," he said, then paused to take a deep breath, "is B-B-B-Brandon P-P-P. . . ." He stopped and closed his eyes, concentrating, willing his tongue not to trip over the cursed letter. "P-P-Pellidore."

Opening his eyes again, he saw she was staring, face gone ashen. "That is not amusing," she said.

That wrung a chuckle from him. "No, it is not. Not in the slightest. Would you like a further demonstration? I am certain I can recall a child's rhyme with those letters in it. I was never allowed to say it, mind you; however, I do recall reading it."

She shook her head. "But you speak so well! I have never heard you stumble before."

"I rarely fall over words for the reason that I avoid the letters. You said once that you admired the way I talk—slow and low. There is a reason for that. It allows me to think ahead, to avoid words where I might fail."

"And that is why you say mayhap," she said, "instead of maybe or perhaps."

He shuddered theatrically. "Ah, horrid words. However, I think you see my reasoning. I have all the indications of the disease, Celia. Like my father, I will not live to see my inheritance. Only this time, the title dies with me."

Celia felt as if she were being crushed under a great weight. Brandon could not be going mad! There must be something that could be done, some way to keep him by her side. "But you said that Edmund taught you how to avoid stammering," she protested. "It could not have started recently, then."

"It started shortly after my father died," he replied.

"Then it cannot be the disease! I heard your father died quickly after showing the first symptom. How is it that you have shown the first for years, and you live after an attack?"

He shrugged, but she thought she saw a light of hope spring to his eyes. "Mayhap the disease is different in me."

"No." She was determined now. "No, the other symptoms came on only after you drank that brandy." She cast about for the bottle and found it on a table by the fire. Retrieving it, she sniffed the contents again. All she could smell was cherries and the tang of alcohol. She shook her head, carrying it to the bedside. "What if this were poison?"

He raised a brow. "That mimics the disease so well?"

"Why not? First the creature in the maze, then the carriage that killed your poor uncle, and now poison. You said it came from me, yet I know I did not send it, Brandon." Certain she was right, she reached for the glass beside the bed.

"What are you doing?" he demanded.

She poured out a thimble full. "Every theory must be tested. If I exhibit the same symptoms you did, we shall know of a certainty that you were poisoned."

She reached for the glass, and he caught her arm. "Don't! If it did such damage to me, it could kill you."

She felt chilled, but her determination did not ebb. "Not if I only take a little. You wish to know the truth, do you not?"

"Not at the risk of your life." He tugged her hand away. "Think of another way to test this theory, Celia. I will not see you harmed."

She shook her head in frustration, yet a part of her was relieved not to try the potion. "I suppose we could try it on an animal, but I do not know whether they react the same way to a poison as a human would."

"You would also have to look for a motive," Brandon reminded her. "The Crown gains my fortune and title if I die. Why else would anyone want me dead?"

She had no answer there either. "I do not know, but I will not leave your side until you are well enough to find out."

He smiled, warming her with the tenderness of it. "I would have you nowhere else. However, you cannot stay here forever. Martin will come looking for you. Surely even my cousin will wonder."

She might at that. "And Lady Honoria cannot be bought off for much longer either. Perhaps we should escape, take you somewhere you would be safe."

"Such as?"

She could hear the teasing in his voice. He was right of course. She had already kidnapped him once, and the result had been Edmund's death. She could not simply dash away this time. She had to think it through. Too much was at stake. For once, she had to consider the risks.

She rose. "You rest. I will think. I promise not to do anything without discussing it with you first. We will come through this, Brandon. I swear it."

The look on his face told her he appreciated her devotion, but he remained the skeptic.

Twenty-six

She stayed with him the rest of the afternoon. Plans tumbled through her mind, but as she considered each with more care, she found them lacking. He slept for the most part. She could only hope that was to the good. Every time he murmured in his sleep, she froze. Every time he twitched, she was at his side. Yet there were no more episodes like the night before, and her spirits began to rise.

Mr. Openshaw, Gregory, and Timms poked their heads in from time to time, and she gave them an update. She told none of them about her theory on the brandy. She was fairly certain they could not be behind it, but she wanted to take no chances. Besides, there was still the chance that she was wrong and Brandon was truly following in his father's footsteps.

She refused to dwell on that.

By late afternoon, she knew she had to make an appearance or risk exposure. Accordingly, she left Brandon in his valet's care and went down to change for dinner. Lady Honoria pounced on her almost as soon as she sat at the table.

"What do I hear about you being ill, girl?" she demanded from her place at the head of the long table.

Celia smiled from her spot farther down. "I was just a little blue-devilled. Thank you for letting me recuperate."

Patrice, across from her, returned her smile. "You are welcome, but next time answer my knock. You worried me."

Celia apologized and returned her gaze to her dinner. Glancing up a moment later, however, she caught Lady Honoria watching her with narrowed eyes. She kept her head down for the rest of the meal.

Patrice insisted on playing the piano after dinner, then escorted Celia to her room for the night. Celia had to wait another full hour before Lady Honoria retired as well. Then she slipped upstairs to check on Brandon.

Timms answered her knock and let her in.

"How is he?" she asked.

He smiled, making his square-jawed face almost handsome. "Back to his old self, he is. Bless you for that, Miss Rider."

"It was nothing I did," Celia told him. Peering around him, she saw that the room was empty. "Where is he?"

"Out," Timms supplied.

"Out!" Celia stared at him. "You let him go out?"

He shrugged, but his color heightened. "He is the master, miss. Said if you was to come calling to tell you to get a good night's sleep and he would see you in the morning."

She thanked him and left.

Her bed was hard that night. Oh, the fine cotton sheets were cool against her bare toes, and the thick mattress was soft under her back. She should drift off to sleep easily in such comfort. Yet her body tossed with the thoughts that chased through her mind.

Where was he?

Was he safe?

What was he doing?

What should she be doing?

At last she climbed out of bed and strode to the wardrobe. Flinging open the doors, she fumbled in the light of the dying fire to find her cloak. She'd go after him, that's what she'd do. There must be some way she could help. She'd take Martin's horse. She knew where the tack was kept. She knew how to set up a saddle. She'd mount and ride. . . .

Where?

With a sob, she sank to her knees and buried her face in her hands. Her mind and her body shouted their frustration at her impotence. Always, when trouble threatened, she acted. She loved Brandon. Surely she should do something to protect him! All she wanted was to hold him close, yet all she could do was trust his word that she would see him in the morning.

Morning had never looked so far away.

Brandon arrived in London just as the lamps were being lit. The magistrates had gone home, but the man on duty at Bow Street gave him his Runner's direction. He found the fellow swirling a tankard at the tavern on the corner. The Runner took one look at him and nodded toward a private booth near the back.

"I would have come for you tomorrow, my lord," he said as Brandon sat across from him. "A very interesting case you handed me, to be sure."

Brandon leaned forward. "Then you found the coachman?"

He shook his balding head. "Not at all. I traced the carriage back to its owner. It was a hired hack. The man paid in gold for it. Said it was for his lady employer."

"A woman?" Brandon could feel himself tense. "Who?"

The Runner eyed him. "A Miss Celia Rider."

Brandon's stomach recoiled. He must have paled, for the Runner shouted for a pint. Brandon shook his head as a bar maid brought a tankard. She set it on the table and left.

"Are you certain?" he asked the Runner, throat tight.

The man nodded. "I am. And so were they. Seems she recently bought a carriage from them, so they knew she could be trusted with this one. I have a nose for mystery, my lord. Why would this woman want Lord Pellidore dead, I ask myself. And do you know what I answer?"

Brandon shook his head, dreading the answer, yet knowing he had to hear it. The Runner rubbed his nose with his finger as if his nose relished the mystery even then. "I says to myself, I says, perhaps this woman doesn't want Lord Pellidore dead. Perhaps it is Lord Hartley himself she's after."

He leaned back and took a swig of his ale. Brandon waited, feeling as tense as an overwound watch spring. The Runner leaned forward again to plant his elbows with authority on the scarred tabletop. "So I looked into that, I did. Have you ever read your father's will, my lord?"

"More times than I should, I wager. I know all the rules for my inheritance."

"Ah, but do you know the rules for the next in line?"

"As far as I know, there is no next in line. If I cannot inherit, the title and fortune goes to the Crown."

"Not precisely. The title, of course, goes to the next male directly descended from the original title holder. But the fortune, now, that was not entailed as they say, was it?"

"No."

"And that is why, my lord, it goes to your father's closest male relative. The magistrates confirmed that for me. Do you know a lad named Martin Rider?"

"Martin?" He stared at the Runner. "He inherits if I die?"

"He does indeed, my lord. I understand he is just a tyke. But I also hear that his half sister, this Miss Rider, has worked hard to make herself presentable to you. Might it be that, instead of marriage, she decided she would rather see her brother awarded the money?"

No, it could not be. Celia had sat by him last night, sworn to fight this madness with him every step of the way. She could not have masterminded Edmund's death.

"Watch out for her," the Runner said.

Brandon blinked. "What did you say?"

"Watch out for her, my lord. She has motive a-plenty to see you dead. A woman married has little control over the money. A guardian for a boy is in a far better place to siphon off the funds. I understand her father's fortune is in question. Your money might be the only blunt she'll ever see. My guess is she'll go after it."

Brandon pulled a handful of coins from his pocket with fingers gone as numb as his mind and paid the Runner. He seemed to remember a suggestion of drinking to his health, but the idea was so ironic that he did no more than take the obligatory sip of the ale.

Watch out for her. First Edmund and now the Runner warned him of Celia's treachery. He had not believed his uncle, and Edmund was dead. If he failed to heed the Runner's warning, would his own death follow? Could she really be the cold-hearted, calculating killer they thought?

His stomach recoiled again, and he rose. Pushing his way through the crowd, he made it out the door. His coach stood waiting just a few yards away, but he leaned against the building, sucking in air until his head cleared and his gut settled. The night had darkened while he was inside. With the smoke rising from household fires, he could not even see the stars. It was as if the light had been sucked from his life.

He could not let it be thus.

His father had died in darkness. Edmund had tried to love him, but the fear of the disease had forced him to keep Brandon at a distance, just as he taught Brandon to keep others at a distance. He had honored that teaching, until he met Celia.

Celia was laughter; Celia was adventure. Celia was spontaneity, and delight, and joy. Celia was curiosity and a dash of audacity. Celia granted him the freedom to laugh, to love. She refused to believe in the disease, even with evidence of its existence set before her. She had faith in him. How could he believe any less in her, even with the evidence set before him? He chose to turn toward the light of her love.

He would believe in Celia until his dying breath.

Which might not be that far away.

* * *

Celia woke to the first sounds of stirring in the great house. Slipping out of bed, she pulled on her wrapper and hurried upstairs. She tapped on Brandon's door and shifted from foot to foot as she waited for an answer. The door snapped open. Bess gasped at the sight of her.

Celia frowned at her. "Where is Lord Hartley?"

"Away, miss," Bess squeaked. "Mr. Openshaw said I should clean his room before he returns."

Celia nodded. All the worries from the night before crowded around her. She started to turn away, then another throught struck. She whirled back as Bess started to close the door again.

"Wait! Is there a bottle beside his lordship's bed?"

Bess nodded. "I was going to take it away."

"Let me have it," Celia ordered. "And while you are at it, were you the one who brought it up?"

Her blue eyes were wide. "Yes, miss, just like you ordered."

"I never ordered you to bring that bottle," Celia declared. "Who did?"

Bess shrank away from her. "Miss Lawton told me to. She said you asked her, only she was too busy working for her ladyship."

"I can bet you she was," Celia muttered. She took the bottle from a trembling Bess and marched down to the kitchen.

Sally was finishing her morning preparations near the sink when Celia strode in. Celia stuck the bottle in front of her.

"Where did this come from?" she demanded.

Sally pushed it away. "How should I know?"

"You claim I ordered you to take it to Lord Hartley."

Her smile was nasty. "Oh, that bottle is it, now? I had another girl do it."

"I never asked you to."

She shrugged. "Then I misunderstood her lady-ship." Her smile deepened. "If you have trouble with that, go see *her* with your orders."

She pushed past Celia to stalk from the room. Mr. Openshaw, who had been across the room, moved up to Celia. "Is there a problem, miss?"

She shook her head. "No, Mr. Openshaw. I was simply trying to learn the origin of this brandy."

He took the bottle from her hand and held it up to the light. "Ah, I thought as much. We have batches of this cordial dating back to the time of his lordship's grandfather."

"Does the current Lord Hartley drink it often?"

He shook his head, lowering the bottle. "No indeed. He rarely imbibes, and then only a sip or two."

Small wonder. Drink had been known to loosen more than one tongue. He would want to avoid that possibility. "How would one go about getting a bottle?"

"You would need keys to the wine cellar. The wine steward has such, as do I, and his lordship."

"And Lady Honoria?"

He cocked his head. "Why, I suppose she does."

Celia thanked him, asked him to safeguard the bottle until she or Brandon asked for it, and left.

She did not like the way her thoughts were tending. She had no doubt Lady Honoria had the character to commit murder if she chose. Celia simply couldn't imagine why she would choose to do so. She had control of the Pellidore fortune it was true, but surely she did not expect Brandon to turn her out penniless when he inherited. Why do him in?

Knowing she'd accomplished little, her feet dragged on the way back to her room. Everyone would be up soon, and she'd have to face them, with no answers and no Brandon. Might as well get on with the dreary task. She was halfway across the room to her wardrobe when she heard his voice.

"Do you always wander around at first light?"

She whirled to find him lounging on her bed, propped up on one elbow. He had taken off his coat, and his skin looked warm against the white of his shirt. He pushed himself up, uncurling with the grace of a jungle cat. She launched herself across the room and into his arms.

He caught her easily, but instead of merely kissing her, he rolled her back upon the mattress. In an instant, she found herself on her back, with Brandon's body on top of hers. Surprise quickly turned to pleasure as his mouth descended on hers.

This kiss was different from any they'd shared. It was as if he held nothing back, as if he would give her his love, his heart, and his soul in one moment. She clung to him, desire and joy building together, as their lips melded, parted, and joined again. If he had asked to make love to her, she would not have refused.

After a time, he broke the kiss and moved to her side. His hand came up to caress her face, as if he, too, hated to break the bond they had formed. "I love you."

She wanted to shout and cry at the same time. "I love you, too. I worried about you last night."

His hand stroked her cheek. "I left word I would return. Did you doubt me?"

"Yes," she admitted. "Last night was the worst night of my life. I have not felt that bad since when my father died."

He took up her hand and kissed her fingers, sending fresh waves of desire through her. "Forgive me for frightening you."

She hugged his hand to her chest. "It was not so much that I was frightened. I felt so lost. When people I love are in trouble, even when I feel *I* am in trouble, I act. Last night, there was nothing I could do."

His sympathetic smile warmed her. "What I did, only I could do."

She nodded. "I can understand that. I realized this morning that one of the reasons I act is because I do not believe anyone else will. But I love you, Brandon, and I must believe that you will act, for both of us, when needed. I have to trust you."

"Ah, trust." His smile deepened. "Not the easiest gift to grant. I learned that, too, last night. I went to town to meet with the authorities over Edmund's death. I was told you hired the carriage that ran him down."

"What!" Amazement jerked her upright; anger propelled her off the bed. "That's a lie! Who told you that? Let them say it to my face."

He rose more slowly and came around the bed to take her shoulders in his hands. His touch was gentle, but firm. "Even the dauntless Runner would quail under that fire in your eyes. I know you didn't do it, Celia." He released her shoulders to take her hand and press it to his chest over his heart. "I feel it, here. I am no longer Lord Heartless, it seems. Yet, once again someone interferes in our lives."

"Only this time, your uncle paid the price."

He nodded, then went on to tell her his conversation with the Runner.

Celia shuddered. "Then it was no accident."

He squeezed her hand. "No. It was murder. The Runner is convinced that I was the target, not Edmund. However, I think someone wants to hurt you, Celia."

She started. "Me?"

"You. Think. All this interference started with your fortune. Someone tried to make you think it was stolen. Someone tried to frighten you at the masquerade."

"Someone tried to make you think I was out to trap you."

He nodded. "And now someone seeks to see you charged with murder."

She shook her head. "But that makes no sense. If this someone is willing to commit murder, why not simply murder me?"

"Mayhap," he said with a smile, "they do not have your will to act."

"And mayhap," she said, returning his smile, "I am not the target either."

He cocked his head. "Interesting. What do you suggest?"

"I'm not sure." She went on to tell him of her conversations with Sally and Mr. Openshaw that morning.

"And now you tell me Martin inherits if you die," she finished. "Your aunt seems to have built her life on managing other people's fortunes. We both know Patrice could not have made those investments James Carstairs mentioned when I first met him. And I begin to wonder whether she really spent all that money gambling. What if it were Lady Honoria all along, working with James Carstairs to rob us?"

"First my cousin's jointure," he mused, "then your fortune, then mine. Yet, murder, Celia? For all Lady Honoria loves to dominate everyone, I cannot see her killing. And she was not on the carriage that killed Edmund."

"I cannot imagine being angry enough to kill. Yet surely greed is reason enough. And as an herbalist, she certainly has the knowledge and skills to poison your favorite brandy."

He pulled her into his embrace and rested his head against hers. "I know you want to trust that theory, love. However, we have no evidence that my attack was not genuine."

She thrust out her chin. "And we have the chance that it was false." Keeping her arms snug about his waist, she leaned back to eye him. "Are you willing to take another risk?"

If she had doubted his love before, his immediate answer would have proved his devotion. "Whatever you wish. I trust you, Celia."

She stood on tiptoe to press a kiss of faith against his lips. "And I trust you. Together, we will make your aunt tip her hand."

Twenty-seven

They found Lady Honoria in her suite. Sally did not dare gainsay Celia entrance with Brandon at her side, though the way she wrinkled her nose told Celia how little she relished it.

As they entered, Celia was not surprised to find James Carstairs dancing attendance. He had been driving out to Pellidore Place at least every other day since they had moved. She was surprised at the change in him. His stylish navy jacket hung limp as if he'd lost weight, and he carried himself hunched as if nursing some inner pain. She saw Brandon eying him just as closely and knew he must have noticed the change as well.

"Celia, Hartley," Lady Honoria greeted from her place at the desk. "To what do I owe this visit?"

Celia glanced at Brandon. He smiled at his aunt.

"We thought we should wish you good morning, Aunt," he replied, going to drop a kiss on her brow. Lady Honoria blinked, and even James Carstairs frowned.

"You look pleased with yourself," Lady Honoria said, making the compliment sound like a complaint. "Where have you been? You were not at dinner last night."

"I was detained in the city and decided to stay the night there. I have only just returned."

"What was so interesting?"

He smiled. "Financial matters. Nothing to concern you."

"You seem to have recovered from your bout with the dismals regardless. And did I hear you were unwell the other night?"

Celia's heart jumped. Who had gone to Lady Honoria bearing tales?

"Indigestion," Brandon assured his aunt. "If Cook continues like this, I shall gain twenty stone by Michaelmas."

Celia held herself still as he strolled back to her side. The slight movement of his dark head indicated he had seen the papers on his aunt's desk. The nod that followed told her he had seen something that confirmed their suspicions.

Lady Honoria seemed to sense something, for she shuffled the papers together and set them aside. "I did not want it to come to this, Hartley. You know I am fond of you."

Celia felt Brandon stiffen. "As I am fond of you, Aunt."

"Not as fond of me as you are of this young lady, I fear. I also fear that she has mislead you."

Now Celia stiffened. "What do you mean by that?"

"I mean," Lady Honoria said, "that you are under the mistaken impression that you can hide the truth from me. You are ill, Hartley. Admit it. You have had an attack."

Brandon took Celia's hand and squeezed it. "Mayhap I have felt out of kilter. That is not the same thing."

"Out of kilter? Screams in the night? Failing to rise

from your bed for hours? Disappearances during the day? And your behavior has been sadly short of its usual perfection. Even your devoted Celia has remarked upon it."

He raised a brow, and she felt her color heightening. "You asked me whether he was acting oddly, your ladyship. I merely said I thought his behavior in keeping with mourning his uncle."

"You make excuses for him, my dear. I did so once as well. However, when the well-being of this family is threatened, I must act." She rose. "James, I ask you to bear witness."

Carstairs stepped smartly forward. "Your servant, ma'am."

"So it would seem," Brandon drawled, and the solicitor colored.

"Hartley," Lady Honoria continued, eyes narrowed to black slits, "you leave me no choice but to confine you to your room for observation. If you truly exhibit no signs of this disease, I will allow you your freedom. Another episode, however, and I will see you taken where you can do yourself and your family no more harm."

Celia's pulse quickened, but she squeezed Brandon's hand. Lady Honoria was too good at picking them off alone. They had to stand together to stop her.

Before Brandon could answer, there was a rap at the door.

"See to it," Lady Honoria snapped to Sally, who scuttled forward.

Brandon inclined his head to his aunt. "Given the circumstances, your action would seem warranted. However, I start to think there is more afoot than madness."

Voices rose behind them, and Celia turned in time to see Mr. Openshaw elbow Sally out of the way so that he and Patrice might enter. Timms followed them with a tray.

Turning to face Lady Honoria again, she saw that James Carstairs had straightened. His gaze followed Patrice as she came to join them, and Celia was shocked by the raw hunger in his look.

Lady Honoria frowned. "What is the meaning of this?"

Mr. Openshaw did not hesitate, waving a hand to indicate that Timms should set his burden on the desk. "His lordship's orders, madam."

Patrice stopped, face puckering. "I was told we were celebrating. Has something happened?"

"It has," Brandon said. "I am getting a license so that Celia and I may marry immediately."

Patrice clapped her hands in delight.

"I am pleased you can think of the future, Hartley," Lady Honoria said. James Carstairs tightened his lips.

Timms lifted the bottle from the tray. Lady Honoria's gaze locked on it. Did she pale? Celia glanced over at Brandon and saw him watching as well. There was enough left in the bottle from Brandon's room that Timms could pour a small amount for each of them. He passed the goblets around. Lady Honoria's eyes narrowed.

"It's lovely stuff," Celia assured Patrice, who had sniffed it and wrinkled her nose. "Brandon had some the other night."

Lady Honoria's hand froze.

Brandon raised his glass high, watching the old woman. "To Celia, my love."

"And to the Marquess of Hartley," Celia countered. "Long may he live."

"To Celia and the Marquess of Hartley," Patrice echoed. She and James Carstairs lifted the glass to their lips. Neither Brandon nor Lady Honoria moved.

"Stop," Celia ordered. "It's poisoned."

"Poisoned!" Patrice dropped the glass. It tumbled to the carpet, scattering drops of brandy across the expanse of gold.

"She is overwrought," Lady Honoria replied. "How could it be poison?"

"You should know," Celia said. "You poisoned it."

Lady Honoria smiled. "And why should I do that? Besides, I heard that you were the one who sent the bottle to his room."

Had the woman planned to implicate her all along? Celia's blood heated. "You planted that tale," she accused.

"Did I now? And who stands to gain if he dies?"

"Her brother," James Carstairs's supplied, stepping to Lady Honoria's side and setting down his own glass. "He inherits the Pellidore estate. As you agreed to settle your inheritance for a paltry sum, you covet his."

"I never settled my inheritance!"

Brandon squeezed her hand, and she did not need to be Lord Oberon to know he warned her against falling into their trap.

James Carstairs's smile was cool. "You accepted a draft in the amount of a few thousand pounds just days before Lord Pellidore died. That is all you have coming."

"You lie." Brandon's voice was quiet, but it held all of its usual power. James Carstairs flinched. "Nothing you say will make me doubt Celia. It is clear to me that my aunt was after murder. Will you go down with her, Carstairs?"

The solicitor licked his lips as if considering the matter. Lady Honoria leaned on the desk.

"Murder?" she said, eyes widening and hand going to her heart. "You think I could murder? Was I on the box that day when Edmund was killed?"

"No," Brandon agreed as Carstairs grew more pale. "Yet I think I know who was."

"You can prove nothing," the solicitor said, stiffening.

"Mayhap not. However, I wonder whether the authorities will find a dark cloak in your wardrobe." The words hit like a hammer to nails, each stroke true. "Is that not what you wore as Death, as the creature who followed us from the House of Lords, as the coachman who killed Edmund?"

Carstairs shook. "Be silent! You know nothing!"

"But I know a great deal," Lady Honoria said with a sneer. She turned to Brandon. "Well done, Hartley. Send for the authorities. He will surely hang."

"No!" Carstairs bolted. Celia had to hold herself not to pelt after him. Brandon merely nodded, and Timms dashed out.

"Wicked, wicked man," Lady Honoria lamented with a shake of her head. She sank down in her chair as if weary. "Very likely he has been stealing from the estates as well. How he had us fooled."

"Almost as much as you fooled us," Brandon said.

She raised a brow. "You cannot believe that nonsense about my involvement."

Celia shared his glance. "I can," he said, "and I do."

Lady Honoria shook her head. "Then you are mad after all." She pointed to Patrice. "Patrice, you are the only one I can trust. Take the carriage to Bow Street and tell them that the Marquess of Hartley has gone mad."

Patrice blinked. "Has he?"

It was as if Celia could see the strings Lady Honoria held in her pale hands. With Brandon, she used fear, dangling the threat of the madness. With Patrice, she used duty, ensuring her stepmother that here at least she was needed. She was not sure what Lady Honoria thought she held over her, unless it was the threat of being blamed for Brandon's death. Now that Brandon believed in her, that was no threat at all.

"No, Patrice," Celia said. "It is Lady Honoria who has gone mad. She tried to kill Brandon, and I wager she killed Brandon's father as well."

Patrice shook her head, blanching. "No, it cannot be!"

"It can," Brandon said, stepping forward. "It is over, Aunt."

"They are lying," Lady Honoria spat. "Do as I say, girl! Do you not want Martin to inherit the fortune?"

Another string pulled. Patrice jerked visibly. Then she shook her head. "Martin has a fortune. My David left it to him. He doesn't need Brandon's."

"That's right!" Celia crowed. Patrice smiled as if pleased she had remembered.

"This is ridiculous," Lady Honoria said, rising. "I shall go myself."

Brandon blocked her path. "I think not. I see it all now. Edmund said you hated him and my father for coming along after you. They took your father's affections."

"Yes!" She raised her head to meet his gaze. "*I* was the future of the house of Pellidore. My father doted on *me*. Until your father came along, and after him Edmund. And then all I was good for was a marriage to ally our family with another as powerful."

Her hateful gaze sickened Celia, though Brandon did not flinch.

"I thought I would have sons, but I had the weakest of daughters. She was good for nothing but marriage as well. Then her husband gambled away everything I had worked for, only to die with his wife and leave me to raise my mewling kitten of a granddaughter." She turned her glare on Patrice, who shrank under it. Celia put her hand on her stepmother's arm in support.

"I went to my father and begged him for help. He could not be bothered. His precious third wife had died, and he could not think of any need but his own. A little foxglove in his tea and he was gone. Heart attack, they said, as if he had a heart."

"You poisoned him as well?" Celia cried.

"And my grandmother?" Brandon demanded. "Was her madness a lie?"

"Oh, yes," she sneered. "It never even happened. No one was left to gainsay me. I made up a horrid tale of her death, and when I poisoned your father, no one thought it was anything but the disease."

Brandon's fists balled at his sides. "Then the madness was false all along. I lived cloistered, forsaking friends, forsaking love, for nothing?"

Celia moved to his side and put her arm about his waist. "You found love despite it, Brandon."

He gazed down at her, and the tension drained from his face.

But Lady Honoria was not about to let him go so easily. "Love? Is that what you cry for, Hartley? Be grateful Edmund cared for you. If he had not taken you to Scotland, I would have gotten the both of you sooner. I would have crowed my triumph in his face if that lust-obsessed James had not bungled his attempt on that ridiculous country bumpkin."

"He was after Stanley!" Celia cried.

"The idiot wanted Patrice for himself," Lady Honoria sneered. "I did not think he had it in him. But ridding me of that creature would have been a blessing."

"Creature?" Patrice glared at her. "You wanted my Stanley dead? You wicked woman!"

"Oh, be silent, Patrice," Lady Honoria snapped, "or you will shortly outlive your usefulness as well."

"Enough," Brandon said. "I cannot understand how love turns to such hatred; however, your reign of terror is over, Aunt. My father and Edmund may have fallen for your tricks. I will not."

"But you did," she replied venomously. "You are pathetically easy to manipulate. Lord Heartless, ha! Lord Wears-His-Heart-On-His-Sleeve more like. All I need do is threaten your precious Celia. What shall it be for her, I wonder? Belladonna in her soup, or fly agaric in the brandy?"

Brandon's arm wrapped protectively around Celia's waist.

"You think you know us," Celia said, emboldened by his touch, "but you know nothing. I love Brandon, and he loves me. We know you for what you are—a spiteful, vindictive witch with a heart bound in envy. Do your worst. We will stand against you."

"You will fail!" Her voice rose with her hands, and she jerked forward, closing the gap between her and Brandon. For a moment, Celia thought she might claw his eyes out then and there. But Brandon's fists came up to protect his face, blocking her hands. With a twist of his wrist, he caught her fingers in his. She yanked on him, but he held tight.

"You cannot stop me!" she railed. "I cannot fail! I must approve your right to inherit. I will never do so."

"Then I shall take my chances in court," Brandon replied. "A shame I shall have to testify as to why you are no longer fit to act as trustee. I imagine the magistrates take an even dimmer view of murder than they do of madness."

Lady Honoria blanched. "You would not dare put this family through such scandal. It would mark you and your children."

Brandon glanced at Celia. "I have lived through such a mark. We will take that chance." Releasing her, he stepped back.

Lady Honoria leaned heavily on the desk, as if her power was spent. She stared at Celia with dark eyes dulling. "You should understand," she said. "Your father served you as mine did me. It is not too late for you to help. Denounce Hartley and help me. Together, we can set your brother up as a power to be reckoned with."

Celia shook her head. "I would never let you touch Martin."

Lady Honoria's head came up, eyes narrowing. Before anyone could stop her, she lunged at the desk, snapped up a glass, and drained it. Only Sally found a voice to cry out.

"I told you you could not win," Lady Honoria said, licking the last drop of the red liquor from her lips. "I shall beat you, if only to the grave."

Twenty-eight

Eight Months Later

"Is that him?"

Celia smiled at Stanley's look of amazement. She glanced across the grass at Hyde Park to where Brandon was accepting the string of a kite from Martin. Pulling back with one arm, Brandon pelted across the grass. His tall figure was lithe, his steps sure. The kite soared upward. Martin jumped up and down and crowed with delight.

"That is my husband, Mr. Arlington," she said proudly. "And where is your delightful wife?"

"Shopping." He rolled his eyes as he threw himself down beside her and the picnic basket. Rummaging in the hamper, he drew out a leg of chicken with a contented sigh. "She says because we will only get to the metropolis on the quarter days, she must make the most of her time. It is her first trip back since she was out of mourning, by your leave."

It was indeed. Patrice had been one of the few to mourn Lady Honoria's passing. Brandon had not even waited the requisite time to mourn his uncle before procuring a special license to marry Celia. Patrice had married Stanley months later in Somerset.

"Are you happy?" Stanley asked suddenly.

Celia blinked. "Deliriously so. And you?"

His grin spoke volumes. "Surprising, isn't it."

She could understand his statement. A few months ago, none of them had seemed likely to be happy. After drinking the brandy, Lady Honoria had not lived the night. Fearing for her own safety, Sally confessed to writing the note supposedly from Celia that was to lure Brandon to the masquerade. Lady Honoria's plan, it seemed, was for Celia to marry Brandon so that she might be blamed if anyone suspected murder instead of madness. Sally claimed innocence in the matter of Miss Turner, although Celia could not help but wonder whether she had a hand in poisoning the family as well. Luckily for Sally, Lady Honoria provided for the maid in her will, which Brandon honored, and Sally left their lives as unlamented as her mistress.

James Carstairs, whom Timms had apprehended, had been remanded to Bow Street and ultimately deported to Australia. While Celia could not regret his punishment, she felt for his father. The older Carstairs could not begin to put all the estates back to rights and resigned his other commissions to work solely for Brandon. He tried to refuse payment, but Brandon insisted that he should not be punished for his son's mistakes and continued to pay his salary.

With Lady Honoria's death, Brandon was forced to go to court to have his fortune awarded. However, the magistrates were impressed by his address and made the award in a unanimous decision.

"Will you miss your brother when we take him home to Somerset?" Stanley asked beside her, bringing her back to the warmth of the sun and the pleasures of the moment.

Celia smiled, hand going to rub her rounding

belly. "Yes, but I think I shall soon be too busy to give him the time he needs. Besides, he should be with boys his own age. Thank you for sending him to school, Stanley."

He inclined his head. "It was the least I could do, don't you know. I am only glad that we could find a school so close to the estate. Patrice is in alt that he can come home Sundays and on holidays."

Celia nodded, watching as Brandon handed the string of the kite to Martin and strode in their direction. The breeze ruffled his dark hair, and she swore she could see the sunlight reflected in those dark eyes before he knelt at her side.

He pressed a kiss against her lips, one hand resting lightly on her belly. "And how are the two I love most in all the world?"

"My word, Hart," Stanley proclaimed before Celia could answer, "I am honored, don't you know."

As Celia chuckled, Brandon grinned at him. "Joining us for dinner, Arlington? The more the merrier."

Stanley grinned as well, climbing to his feet. "I cannot agree. It looks to me as if you and your bride would like a few moments alone. I think I shall see if Martin cannot teach me the hang of the thing."

As Stanley strolled out onto the field, Celia nestled into Brandon's arms. "Enjoying your day, my dear?" she murmured.

She could feel his smile. "Immensely. And you?"

She snuggled closer. "Oh, yes." Her conversation with Stanley tickled the back of her mind. It seemed he still doubted her ability to be happy with Brandon. She marveled at the very idea, but perhaps she should check to make sure her husband did not harbor similar concerns.

"I do not think I have told you how happy I am in

our marriage," she said, touching his hands where they crossed over her chest. "You are everything I could have dreamed of in a husband—loving, open, gentle."

"And you are more than I could have dreamed of in a wife," he replied, taking her hand and bringing it to his lips. "Until you, I did not know what it was to dream, to love."

"Then you are happy in our marriage?"

He kissed the top of her head. "It is truly p-p-perfection," he said.

Warm in his embrace, she could not agree more. They would love each other until death did them part.

A bargain was a bargain after all.

ABOUT THE AUTHOR

Regina Scott started writing novels in the third grade. Thankfully for literature as we know it, she waited until she knew a little about life before submitting her work for publication. *Perfection* is her fifteenth work of Regency-set fiction for Kensington Publishing. Learn more about her on her website at *www.reginascott.com.*

Ms. Scott loves to hear from readers. You can e-mail her at regina@reginascott.com. If you send a letter via Zebra, please enclose a self-addressed stamped envelope if you would like a reply.

More by Best-selling Author
Fern Michaels